MLR PRESS AUTHORS

Featuring a roll call of some of the best writers of gay erotica and mysteries today!

Maura Anderson
Victor J. Banis
Jeanne Barrack
Laura Baumbach
Alex Beecroft
Sarah Black
Ally Blue
J.P. Bowie
P.A. Brown
James Buchanan
Jordan Castillo Price
Kirby Crow
Dick D.
Jason Edding
Angela Fiddler
Dakota Flint
Kimberly Gardner
Storm Grant
Amber Green
LB Gregg
Drewey Wayne Gunn

Samantha Kane
Kiernan Kelly
JL Langley
Josh Lanyon
Clare London
William Maltese
Gary Martine
ZA Maxfield
Jet Mykles
L. Picaro
Neil Plakcy
Luisa Prieto
Rick R. Reed
AM Riley
George Seaton
Jardonn Smith
Caro Soles
Richard Stevenson
Claire Thompson
Kit Zheng

Check out titles, both available and forthcoming, at
www.mlrpress.com

A Donald Strachey Mystery

The 38 Million Dollar Smile

RICHARD STEVENSON

mlrpress

This book is a work of fiction. Names, characters, places, and incidents either are products of the author's imagination or are used fictitiously. Any resemblance to actual events or locales or persons, living or dead, is entirely coincidental.

Published by
MLR Press, LLC
3052 Gaines Waterport Rd.
Albion, NY 14411

Visit ManLoveRomance Press, LLC on the Internet:
www.mlrpress.com

Cover Art by Deana C. Jamroz
Editing by Judith David
Printed in the United States of America.

ISBN# 978-1-60820-013-9

Issued 2009

ACKNOWLEDGEMENTS

Two books have been especially helpful to me as I have worked to understand Thailand. *Thailand Confidential* and *Bangkok Babylon*, both by Jerry Hopkins, are shrewd and insightful guides to Thai life and culture. When I wrote this book, Warren Olson's *Confessions of a Bangkok Private Eye* provided an eye-opening and somewhat alarming picture of the Thai criminal justice system.

Also helpful were numerous Thai and *farang* friends and acquaintances in Bangkok — you know who you are — as well as a forthcoming and mildly conscience-stricken Bangkok police official who prefers not to be named.

Ellen Griswald — 1. ygor   seer
                    Gary — Mango
              2. older
                 Bill ~ Amanda, Mark
                 (Sheila) 6

        Sandy Tessig
Algonquin Steel
    Alan Rainey — treasurer

Hughes Weinstock
    Angie Hogencamp

Lou Horn — Key West   Sandy Tessig
Elise Flanagan — Key West
Geoff Pringle → Thailand , fall)

Rufus Pugh
Kawee
Mango — Donnott

(Sheila) Hubbard + Martz)

CHAPTER ONE

"Mr. Strachey, do you believe in reincarnation?"

"I've never given it much thought."

"So you won't mind my telling you, I think the whole idea is perfectly absurd."

"Go ahead."

It had been Ellen Griswold's idea to meet in the bar at the Albany airport at six thirty. She was picking her husband up from the US Airways flight from Washington that theoretically got in at seven forty but sometimes arrived around nine or ten. So we had plenty of time for going over the mysteries of life.

"I know you've spent time in Southeast Asia," she said. "So I assume you know something about Buddhist philosophy."

She was nicely turned out in a beige linen suit, the sea green silk wrap she had been wearing against the early April chill now slung over the chair next to her. Still on the underside of fifty, I guessed, Mrs. Griswold was raven haired, with clear dark eyes, a handsome beak, and apparently had had some minimal cantilevering and other structural work done on her chin and cheeks, though nothing that would have overtaxed Le Corbusier.

I said, "I was in the war there, so I know a little. But even in Army Intelligence, my thinking was focused and practical. The larger questions relating to the Asian psyche were left to the deep thinkers at the Pentagon. How did you know I was in Vietnam?"

"Bob Chicarelli told me."

A lawyer I knew. "I've done work for Bob."

"And have played squash with him. He also says you're gay. That's good, because so is my ex-husband, who is the problem here, I think."

"Ah, the problem."

I liked that she drank beer. She had a large bottle of Indian Kingfisher she was working on, savoring each sip but without making a spectacle of it, like Timmy's and my lesbian friends who drink beer while they inexplicably watch men play football on television.

Mrs. Griswold said, "My ex-husband, Gary, believes that in a previous life he was Thai. What do you make of that?"

"Thai, as in a person from Thailand?"

She sipped her Kingfisher, and I sipped my Sam Adams.

"Gary not only believes that he was Thai, but that he will be Thai again in his next life. This is a man I was married to for six years."

"It sounds as though he may have been problematical for you on multiple fronts."

This got a little half smile. "Well, yes. We were married on January seventeenth nineteen eighty-one. I should have known. It was three days before Ronald Reagan was inaugurated."

"An auspicious week, as a sometime-Thai like your former husband might say."

A curt nod. "I think he would say that, yes. Not back then necessarily. But now Gary would think of it in exactly those terms. Astrology, numerology, karma, reincarnation, the whole nine yards. All that new age hooey. It's really disappointing. When I married Gary, he had his obsessions, which were generally harmless — bicycle racing, and so on. But he was also one of the most rational people I knew."

I said, "East Asians don't think of karma and reincarnation as new age hooey. They think of them as the way the universe is ordered."

I meant this as a point of information, not a lecture, and she seemed to take it that way, unperturbed. "That's fine if it works for the Asians. I've lived and worked abroad, and cultural relativism is fine with me. But for Gary, Eastern ideas turned into a kind of trap, I think."

"How so?"

"As a way of avoiding responsibility."

"Uh-huh."

"I don't think of myself as an overly materialistic person," she said. "But I do believe in managing the assets you have like a grown-up. Whether you earn it or you inherited much of it, as Gary and Bill did, flushing your money down the toilet I find totally incomprehensible."

"Who is Bill?" I asked.

"My husband, Bill Griswold. Gary's older brother."

This was getting complex. I said, "What did the Reagans make of all this?"

She smiled rather sweetly. "Around the time Gary's and my marriage was unraveling — largely because of his coming to terms with his being gay — Bill's fell apart, too. He had married a Long Island JAP of a certain type when he was nineteen — a looker, a serious shopper, and not much else — and Bill needed somebody more stimulating. We had always liked each other, and we both liked to read and travel. For fun, we took a trip to Budapest together, and that was it. It's been as good a marriage as anybody could hope for, overall."

"And your husband's first wife was not Japanese?"

"Jewish American Princess. You've heard the term, I'm sure."

"It could have been another Asian in the picture."

"I would not have used Jap that way."

Her cell phone played what Timothy Callahan might have identified as the opening strains of Gluck's overture to *Orpheus and Eurydice,* but for all I knew could have been Andrew Lloyd Webber. She flipped it out of her handbag and told me with an apologetic shrug, "It's either one or the other."

Ellen Griswold's end of a brief conversation included the words *please don't* more often than I normally use them on the phone.

"That was Amanda," she said, putting her phone away. I noted a diamond on one finger that, while not quite ostentatious, did not hide its light under a bushel, as well as a demure ruby on a nearby digit.

"Amanda is thirteen," Mrs. Griswold said. "Mark is fifteen. They're both good kids, but they are kids. They pretty much have their feet on the ground, but there are times when I have to try hard not to scream."

"These are Bill's children, not Gary's?"

"That's right. Do the math."

"Gotcha. But we're not here to talk about Amanda and Mark, apparently."

"No."

"On the phone, you said you believed that a family member was in trouble, and you wanted my help in getting him out of it. So we're talking about your former husband and current brother-in-law?"

This was the moment when, in the olden days, Mrs. Griswold would rummage in her handbag for a cigarette, and I would light it for her and then fire up one of my own. Now we both had to make do with a barely perceptible tightening of her facial restructuring and a swig of beer for me.

Watching me with no particular expression, she said, "Gary has vanished in Thailand with thirty-eight million dollars. I'd like you to find him, check to see if he is all right, and help him out if he isn't. And if Gary is alive and hasn't gone completely around the bend, help us talk some sense into him."

I said, "That sounds simple enough."

"Look, don't laugh. I know it's a big job. Bob Chicarelli said you could do it."

"Okay."

"I could hire an international private investigations agency. I know that."

"You could. It's what most people would do."

"Or, Bob told me he could locate some reputable private detective in Bangkok, if such a thing exists."

"I'll bet such a thing does."

She thought for a moment and said, "You could farm out some of the work to people there. That would be up to you. But I'm more comfortable paying someone who is known and trusted by someone Bill and I know and trust. And since you're familiar with that part of the world, it's a huge advantage, no? Plus, of course, you presumably would have easier entrée to the Thai gay scene, a good place to start looking for Gary. He went over there on vacation two years ago, and in addition to reincarnation, apparently discovered some gay Shangri-La. He never really came home, except to sell his condo in Key West and then fly straight back to Bangkok. But Thailand has not turned out to be a paradise for Gary. At least not from where I'm sitting, it hasn't."

Where she seemed to be sitting was pretty. A second portion of a sizable family fortune remained intact if I was hearing her correctly. I said, "Please tell me (a) about the rather large sum of money Gary took along — can I assume he didn't earn it over there? — and (b) about his vanishing, as you put it."

This got a look of mild surprise. "So you're interested in taking this on?"

"Maybe."

"I was beginning to think you wouldn't. You seem so skeptical about everything."

"Not everything. My, no."

"But," she said, "I think you're skeptical about me."

"A little."

"Why would you be?"

I noticed that the flat-screen television set over the bar was tuned to CNBC, where a reporter who looked something like Mrs. Griswold was mouthing words that I supposed concerned the day's main news topic, the crashing dollar. If I had been able to read lips I might have phoned my bank immediately and converted everything into Burmese kyat.

I said, "Mrs. Griswold —"

"Please call me Ellen. I think we're more or less contemporaries."

"Yeah, more or less. Ellen, this thirty-eight million dollars — which, by the way, might now be worth somewhat less than it was worth ten minutes ago — this thirty-eight million your ex-husband has or had in his possession — to whom does it belong?"

"To Gary, of course. But the point is, there are indications — and I'll get to those — that Gary is throwing his money away. *That's* the issue."

"Well, it is and it isn't. That's where a lot of my skepticism — you're right about that — comes in. Your gay ex-husband-brother-in-law may well be over in the Land of Smiles, as the brochures call it, spending thirty-eight million dollars on things *you* would not necessarily spend thirty-eight million dollars on. Beach houses, money boys, dried squid on a stick, who knows what. But spending money foolishly is what some people do. And while the spectacle can be upsetting to others, nauseating even, especially to the spendthrift's loved ones, there's rarely anything anybody can do about it. Or needs to. Hiring a private investigator is seldom called for — even when it's a family member who appears to have gone off the rails, fiscally speaking."

She was looking increasingly unhappy. "So Bill and I should just — sit back?"

I said, "When you say your ex-husband has vanished, what do you mean by that?"

"It means what it sounds like. No one has heard from Gary for nearly six months. He doesn't respond to e-mails. His snail mail letters don't get answered. His home phone and Thai cell phone accounts have both been shut down. He just seems to have — you know."

"I know." *Fallen off the face of the earth.* She heard herself thinking the cliché and decided she was not someone who would use it.

"Gary was never much for staying in touch," she said. "Even during his Key West years, he rarely e-mailed or phoned. Business matters with Bill, but little else. And after his and Bill's parents died, we saw very little of Gary. Even though I think he was basically happy that Bill and I had gotten together — at some level, relieved even — he seemed to feel awkward around us. He had a couple of boyfriends in Key West — one of them fairly long-term — but we never met them or knew exactly who they were. Whether it was internalized homophobia or something else, I don't know. What I do know is, Gary didn't seem to fully come out and grow up as a gay person until he went to Thailand."

She blinked a couple of times, realizing she may have blundered.

"So your ex-husband is not a grown-up, and at the same time he is a grown-up?"

"What I meant," she said, recovering handily, "was that on the one hand Gary seems finally to have found a way of being comfortably gay. While on the other hand, his long-term happiness and well-being have been seriously jeopardized by his fiscal irresponsibility, his susceptibility to Eastern religions — there was at least one sizable investment decision Bill and I learned was suggested by his astrologer — and by his choice of boyfriends over there. The last one he mentioned to me — in a short note about some estate business before we stopped hearing from him — was a Thai man named Mango."

"That's vivid."

"You've been there, and you may know better. But I would find it very difficult to take seriously a man named Mango."

I said, "On some Bangkok R and R from Saigon, I once spent a pleasant weekend with a Thai man named Bank. He had a brother named Book. Thais sometimes give their children English nicknames of objects they value. So I wouldn't make too much of that."

Mrs. Griswold took a good swallow of beer and said, "Well, then, Don, let me run a very different name by you, and let's see if this gets your attention." She waited.

"Ready when you are."

She said, "Algonquin Steel."

"Uh-huh."

"Max J. Griswold."

"Oh, so you all are *those* Griswolds. If you were Thai, you might have named your son Blast Furnace. Or your daughter."

"The company Gary and Bill's grandfather founded is publicly traded now," she went on. "But Gary and Bill both retained substantial holdings. Last August, Gary sold his shares for thirty million dollars and change. Bill learned this from Alan Rainey, the company treasurer. Alan also told Bill that when Alan questioned him, Gary said he had been offered an investment opportunity that was too good to pass up and would lead to his recouping his investment many times over in a short period of time. It was easy enough, also, for Bill to learn from Angie Hogencamp at Hughes-Weinstock, our brokerage, that Gary had liquidated all of his remaining eight million in assets and had all of it — thirty-eight million in toto — wired to a bank in Bangkok." She eyed me coolly and waited for my reaction.

I said, "Remind me never to do business with Hughes-Weinstock if I want my portfolio activity kept confidential."

She ignored this and added, "All of this bizarre and potentially disastrous financial activity coincided with the arrival of Mango on the scene and came a little less than a month before Gary..."

She waited and I said it. "Seemed to fall off the face of the earth."

"And by the way," Mrs. Griswold said. "Blast Furnace would not be an appropriate Griswold name. The company has steel wholesale and fabricating facilities in eleven states — plus, of course, the nationwide Econo-Build home and building supply chain of stores — but no actual steel mills. Anyway, most of the steel sold and used in the United States these days comes from Japan, Korea, Russia and Brazil. I think it's safe to say few Griswolds have ever laid eyes on a blast furnace."

I did not reply that Bill and Ellen Griswold might then have considered naming their only son Middleman. I thought about it quickly and said, "I guess I have to agree, Ellen, that the situation you have described to me does sound worrisome."

CHAPTER TWO

"Thirty-eight mil?" Timothy Callahan was impressed. "That's getting close to being real money these days. Not for some major CEO, who might find thirty-eight million stuffed into his Dick Cheney's-birthday-bonus envelope. But for the family screwup, it sounds like a perfectly respectable sum to fritter away in the tropics."

We were dining late at a Thai place on Wolf Road after my meeting with Ellen Griswold and were enjoying some decent tom yam kung and steamed rice. I was eating around the flavorsome but inedible debris in my soup bowl — the lemongrass, galangal root and kaffir lime leaves — and Timmy was picking his out of the bowl, bit by bit, and arranging them on a separate small plate he had requested.

I said, "Gary Griswold wasn't always a screwup, and that's partly why his family is concerned. He did the marketing for their Econo-Build stores in Florida for six years and turned them into serious competitors with Home Depot. Then he ran an art gallery in Key West that wasn't a big moneymaker, Ellen Griswold said, but apparently succeeded well enough. It wasn't until he discovered the quirky charms of Bangkok that he apparently flipped out money-managementwise. If, in fact, he did. Griswold claimed he was investing the thirty-eight million in a sure bet with a quick payoff."

Timmy transferred another reed of tough lemongrass out of his soup bowl and said, "My Aunt Moira once lost five thousand dollars in a Ponzi scheme."

"I'll bet a priest told her it was okay."

"He was probably running it."

"Another reason to worry," I said, "is this business of the astrologer Griswold once accepted investment advice from."

"Griswold bought Enron?"

"No, Ellen said it actually worked out. Some land deal in Bangkok. But all the Griswolds were fit to be tied at the time."

"There you go. You're always so skeptical about the relative positions of the planets and stars on erroneous charts drawn up centuries ago affecting people's personalities and events in their present-day lives. Let this be a lesson."

"Anyway, in the go-go Southeast Asian economy, most land deals probably work out these days. Also, that investment was about three hundred K, and now we're talking thirty-eight million, Griswold's entire net worth. And the fact that he seems to have broken off all contact with his family sounds bad. He never said a word to them about moving or dropping out of sight or that anything had gone wrong. All he said in his last e-mail was that something had come up that would keep him busy for a while and he might be out of touch, but not to worry. Then, for six months, nothing. He just seemed to...you know."

"Fall off the face of the earth?"

"Exactly."

Timmy said, "And then there's Mango, the refreshing tropical fruit drink."

"The Griswolds know nothing about him, just that apparently Gary Griswold was seriously smitten. Mango may have nothing to do with either the investment, so-called, or the seeming disappearance. It is true, of course, that Thailand harbors more than its share of sexually alluring flimflam artists. Somebody once rudely called the country a brothel with temples."

"So," Timmy said, "are you flying over? You've talked for years about going back to the region for a visit."

"Ellen Griswold's retainer is ample and her expense limit high. So, sure, it makes sense. Once I'm there, it shouldn't take long. Griswold probably cut a swath."

"A guy with thirty-eight mil is bound to stand out among the rice paddies."

"Why don't you come along?" I said. "You've got some leave time built up. You could do legwork for me. Brain work, too, as is your habit. It would be a legitimate expense. And it's a fascinating part of the world, as I have gone on and on and on about on countless occasions."

"What on earth could you possibly be referring to?" he said and transferred another kaffir lime leaf onto his mulch pile.

"Also, the war's over. I'd like to see Bangkok without it being overrun by drunken, drug-addled, horny American GIs such as myself. I'm sure the place is very different now, and we could check it out together."

"But what if," Timmy wondered, "we got over there and Griswold's situation turned out to be something really complicated and dangerous and ugly? That certainly seems possible with somebody vanishing with that amount of money."

"It's true," I said, "that the Bangkok I knew in the seventies had a harsh underside. You could, for instance, have somebody bumped off for a few hundred dollars. That would be for killing a Thai. A *farang* might be double that. It's also a fact — I suppose I should mention — that the Land of Smiles, home to some of the sweetest people in the world, has one of the most corrupt police forces in Asia — which is saying a lot — and some of the most nightmarish prisons anywhere. Few people emerge from Thai prisons sane, or even alive. It's also a sad reality that in legal disputes between Thais and foreigners, the foreigner is always wrong and may have to lay out big bucks — backhanders, they call them — just to save his own neck. There is a lot about the Thai paradise that's not so heavenly, I know. And it's entirely possible that Gary Griswold has fallen victim to some aspect of that not-so-delectable Thailand."

Now Timmy had set down his soupspoon and was giving me one of his looks. "You're not making any of that up, are you?"

"No. But otherwise it's a lovely country. The Thais have their rice, their Buddha, their beloved king, and their well-developed sense of fun. That's the Thailand I'll bet Griswold fell in love with — until something somehow went awry."

"Oh, awry," Timmy said.

"Look, if it turns out that Griswold has fallen into something grisly and there's real danger, then you'll get back on the plane and fly home. That would be simple enough."

"I understand. And you?"

"Well, we'd have to see. It would depend on if I could be helpful or not, or what I might have to do to earn my fee."

Timmy looked down at his tom yam kung and said to it, "Here we go again," and my heart went out.

§ § § § §

Back at the house on Crow Street, it took me under ten minutes to come up with the name of Gary Griswold's most recent boyfriend in Key West. Ellen Griswold thought the man's name might be Horn, and she was right. When I called an old friend of Timmy's living in Key West — one of the former Peace Corps mafia whose humanistic tentacles are everywhere — she confirmed that Griswold had been a well-known presence in Key West over a period of about a decade and had had a boyfriend named Lou Horn. Horn now owned and managed the art gallery the two had founded together, which now was named Toot Toot.

I got Horn on the phone with no trouble. He not only didn't mind being called at ten forty at night, but said he was very worried about Griswold and fearful about what might have happened to him. Horn was relieved, he said, that I would be searching for Griswold. He said he and two other Key West friends had been in occasional contact with Griswold until about six months earlier, when all communication from Griswold's end had inexplicably ceased.

I asked Horn if, before his disappearance, Griswold had said anything to anybody in Key West that seemed out of character or otherwise odd or set off alarm bells. Horn said, "Well, maybe." When he assured me that he and other of Griswold's Key West friends would willingly tell me what little they knew, I thanked him, called Delta, and booked a flight for the next day.

I also phoned a PI friend in New York City who I'd done work for and obtained a list of reputable investigative firms and individuals operating in Bangkok. I had just begun checking these agencies out online when I became aware of an eerie silence above me. Normally, at this time of night, Timmy was upstairs in the bedroom guffawing at *The Daily Show*, and frequently so was I. Instead, when I went up, I found the television off and Timmy with his wireless laptop open on the bed.

"Working late for the people of New York State?" I said. "If so, we thank you."

His look was grave. "I Googled Bangkok crime statistics. Holy Mother!"

"Timothy, this is not going to help."

"Oh yes, it is. I'm not going, and I'm not sure you should, either."

This was my fault. I should only have told him about the golden reclining Buddhas. I said, "You're getting a distorted picture. New York City looks sinister and forbidding on a police blotter, too. I sometimes do work there. So do you. We like New York."

"It's true," he said, "that there's very little street crime in Bangkok. It's peaceful in that respect. But if you're doing business there — as Griswold may have been doing — look out. A favorite way of settling money disputes is for one party to hire a guy on a motorcycle to drive by and shoot the other party in the head. Extrajudicial killings by the police are routine. Get this: in July two thousand one, a Bangkok newspaper ran a front-page story with the headline, 'Police Death Squads Run Riot.' In one region, the police general dealt with drug dealers by sending cops out to shoot them. 'Our target,' this police official said, 'is to send one thousand traffickers to hell this year, to join some three hundred fifty before them.' Could Griswold have gotten enmeshed in some gigantic drug deal? That could explain the so-called quick return on investment. If so, he could be six feet under in the backyard of a police station. Land of Smiles, my ass, Donald. The Thailand I am seeing in front of me here is bloody treacherous."

I leaned over his shoulder. "Timothy, this is great stuff. Really helpful. Would you mind printing this for me? I'll read it on the plane to Key West tomorrow. I'm going down to talk to Griswold's friends there. It turns out they're quite worried about him, too."

"And then" — Timmy went right on — "I came across a book I think you should read. I'm ordering it tomorrow from Stuyvesant Books. It's *My Eight Years of Hell in a Bangkok Prison*. It's by some American bozo who got on the wrong side of somebody over there, and he landed in some nightmare *Midnight Express* situation he didn't have enough ready cash to buy his way out of, the way the rich Thais do."

"Well," I said. "All this stuff is frightening, sure. It makes me apprehensive too. But it's also all the more reason to worry about Gary Griswold. He sounds like a basically good guy — adventurous in a harmless way, a spiritual searcher. Maybe too naive and susceptible, but that's hardly a moral crime. And he may have been victimized by the Thai subculture displayed so garishly on your screen there. Griswold may be in trouble, and he needs help. I've been hired to help him, but of course, you don't need to be involved."

"I intend not to be."

"That's up to you."

He said, "It's not that I don't get it. I agree that Griswold could well be up to his ears in some hideous mire — a swamp of his own making or not — and he needs somebody to come along and drag him out. All I'm saying is, Bangkok sounds as if it can be a very dangerous place, and I'm frightened for myself and for you."

"I know."

"And the other thing is, how objective are you being about this? Wouldn't it make more sense for the Griswolds to hire somebody on the scene there instead of somebody who hasn't set foot in Bangkok for years? Maybe," he said, "your judgment is a bit off because you mainly want to get back to this part of the world you once found so compelling and do it at somebody else's expense. And maybe reconnect with Bank or Book or Mango or Dragonfruit or like that. Is what I have just described a distinct possibility, or isn't it?"

A relentlessly keen-minded piece of work was my beloved. I said, "Yes, all that is a distinct possibility. And I want you to know that I am resolving at this moment — thanks to you — to turn into a perfectly rational human being and to behave accordingly."

"Uh-huh."

I added, "In my next life."

He seemed unamused by me, gave up and tried Jon Stewart.

CHAPTER THREE

The photograph of her ex-husband that Ellen Griswold had given me was about a year old, she said. In it, a lithe, well-tanned, curly-haired man in his midforties stood in front of a frangipani tree in splendid full bloom. Griswold wore khaki shorts and a lime green polo shirt. While not striking in appearance, he seemed a leaner, looser version of his older brother Bill, a tense and weary business traveler with a five o'clock shadow whom I met briefly at the Albany airport when his flight from Washington unexpectedly arrived only twenty minutes late.

In the picture, Griswold's dark eyes shone brightly as he peered confidently into the camera lens. His full-lipped smile, while not beatific, looked natural and relaxed. Buddhists say we inhabit our bodies only temporarily, but in this picture, at least, Griswold's soul appeared comfortable in its then-abode.

I looked at the picture and the other material on Griswold on the first leg of my Key West flight, a two-hour ride down to Atlanta. Ellen Griswold had provided regular-mail notes from Gary and hard copies of e-mails sent from Thailand. Nearly all were addressed to Ellen, not to Ellen and Bill. In his messages, Griswold spoke glowingly of his new home — he wrote, "the Thais are a truly free people" — and of the contentment he had found in Buddhist ethical systems and through daily meditation. He also mentioned being pleased with a condo he had purchased in Bangkok. This was about eighteen months earlier, and Ellen had included the street address in her packet.

There were several references to what Griswold termed "the romance department." All the romances seemed to be with Thai men. Early in his life in Bangkok, there was Keng, "a sweetheart of a man," and later "delightful" Sambul, and then "quiet" Poom. No mention was made of any of these relationships ending. It seemed as if when one halted or dwindled out, Griswold just moved on to another. This left me wondering what the exact nature of these liaisons might have been.

The last boyfriend mentioned, in an e-mail dated the previous July 17, was Mango. Griswold called him "a beautiful man and a fantastic human being." He also said, "This one's a keeper, I hope." This was a month before Griswold sold all his holdings in the US for thirty-eight million dollars and two months before he disappeared.

The other material Ellen provided me, at Bob Chicarelli's direction, was biographical and statistical data. I noted that Griswold had been a business major at Cornell with an art history minor. His résumé consisted mainly of marketing positions with Algonquin Steel, the family company. He started low at Albany headquarters then climbed steadily, with his company career culminating in his becoming head of marketing in the US Southern region when he was in his early thirties. Then Griswold left the company and ran his Key West art gallery before departing for Thailand.

On the smaller plane from Atlanta to Key West, I looked through the Lonely Planet guide to Thailand I had picked up that morning at Stuyvesant Books. In the "Dangers and Annoyances" section that Lonely Planet quaintly and helpfully includes in all its guidebooks, unscrupulous tuk-tuk drivers were listed, as well as fake-gem scams. No mention was made of drive-by shootings or police-run massacres. The emphasis in Lonely Planet's Thailand was on the green landscape, the golden temples, and the smiles.

§ § § §

"I have to admit," Lou Horn said, "that in retrospect we should have seen it coming — Gary mentally and physically sailing off into the blue. There were signs."

Marcie Weems added, "Thailand, swell — nice people, nice place. And Buddhism, that's fine, too — the ethics of tolerance and acceptance and nonviolence. And, of course, all those cute monks with their shaved heads and gorgeous orange robes. But astrology? Numerology? I don't think so."

"And before his transformation Gary was so even-keeled most of the time," Janice Romeo said. "And smart and fun to be around. The four of us took trips together, and Gary was always a delight. He was focused, yes, even obsessive about some things, like his bike racing and his good causes. But he was never really muddleheaded. And after he got out of the Algonquin Steel power job *sturm* and *drang* and opened the gallery, he was pretty relaxed too. Of course, it was also around that time that he started getting into the weirdness."

"He was weird, but still not weird," Weems put in. "Gary was Mister Moderate-and-Conventional with most things — food, alcohol, dress. Key West is famous for its eccentrics, but Gary was hardly one of the seventeen thousand four hundred and twelve local characters."

"And men," Romeo said. "Don't forget men — another area where Gary was Mister Middle-of-the-Road. No Mangos or Pomegranates or Pomolos for the Gary we knew. He went for Lou, to cite a nearby example. An excellent, levelheaded choice. Lou, are you hurt that we all think of you as a merely reasonable object of desire?"

They all laughed as Horn digested the ambiguous compliment. We were seated at a table at Saluté, an open-air mainly Italian place along the Atlantic Avenue beach on the no-cruise-ships quiet side of Key West. A half-moon hung in the evening sky behind palm fronds rustling in a warm breeze. I had my Sam Adams and the others their Ketel One vodka with a side of ice, apparently the national beverage of the Conch Republic.

Horn was a broad-faced man in his late forties with a salt-and-pepper beard, a few skin-cancer scars scattered about, a one-time middleweight wrestler's build now starting to respond to the tug of gravity, and a twinkle in both his eyes and his step. He had brought along Griswold's two other closest friends in the keys. Both Weems and Romeo had moved to Key West twelve years earlier when the New York publishing house where Weems had been a senior editor was bought by Argentinean beef producers and most of the house's functions were moved to Buenos Aires. Now they ran a small B and B, Romeo said, and only served pork products for breakfast.

Easy to look at in their pale cottons and silks, the two women seated across from me, one olive-skinned and ample, one creamy and svelte, were also merrily festooned with skin cancer Band-Aids, apparently a small price to pay for life in what was still a pretty good place for getting away from it all. Key West still had allure, despite cruise ships the size of the Pentagon lumbering in daily, and the influx of millionaires who had left the island unaffordable for lesser new arrivals. Gary Griswold had seemed more or less at home there, and his three friends said they were stunned when Griswold suddenly announced, after a vacation trip to Thailand, that he was abandoning them and his life there for a country on the other side of the world.

Horn said, "Gary and I were no longer partners in the personal sense by the time he left. So, emotionally it was more or less okay. That part of our relationship had petered out more than a year earlier, and we both had been seeing other people."

"*Seeing*," Weems said. "Such a darling way of putting it."

"Anyway, I had always been the one to play around," Horn said. "Gary, being more serious and focused about everything he undertook, was more of a serial monogamist."

"This is true," Romeo said. "Marcie and I once certified Gary as an honorary lesbian."

"I sometimes wonder," Horn said, "what would have happened if Geoffrey Pringle had never invited Gary over to Bangkok. Though, of course, Gary had begun to change almost a year before that. At the time, we thought maybe it had something to do with Gary falling off his bike, screwy as that might sound. Another biker ran into him in a race up near Ocala, and Gary wiped out and landed on his head. He was wearing a helmet, but he had a bad concussion, and the whole thing seemed to throw him for a loop like nothing else we'd ever seen. He went around in a daze for a week after he got out of the hospital. And it was not too long after that that he got the astrology bug, and he started seeing a woman on Stock

Island who claims to help people get in touch with their past lives. I've read that head injuries can sometimes cause personality changes, temporary or even permanent, and we all wondered at the time if Gary hitting his head had somehow jarred loose his bullshit detector."

I asked, "Who is Geoffrey Pringle?"

"A longtime Key West full-timer who moved to Thailand four or five years ago," Horn said. "It was Geoff who invited Gary over for a two-week visit."

"What does Geoff do in Thailand?"

"He's retired," Romeo said. "His family in Chicago made a fortune in grain futures years ago. A while back, Geoff inherited forty or fifty mil, and bingo, off he flew."

I asked if anybody had checked with Pringle about Griswold's current situation. Wasn't this guy likely to know something?

"We tried," Horn said. "But Geoffrey won't really talk to us. Apparently he and Gary had some kind of falling-out. I got Geoff on the phone in Bangkok about a month ago. He said he didn't know where Gary was, and he 'couldn't care less,' his words. Geoff also told me in no uncertain terms that the day I phoned him was not an auspicious date for him to be taking a transoceanic telephone call, and he just hoped that I had not fucked up his entire month."

Romeo laughed and said, "And Geoff didn't even land on his head, as far as we know."

Some food arrived, an aromatic bounteous antipasti for the table.

"Don't be dainty," Romeo said. "Shovel it down. There's more where that came from. Plus, the pasta dishes."

As we dug in, Horn said, "The numerology thing with Gary was especially uncomfortable for all of us whenever nine-eleven came up. Gary had bought into a theory bouncing around the Internet about the date, eleven, and the shape of the two New York towers, and some supposed prediction by Nostradamus made in the fourteenth century that historians say was fake.

There was even more to it — something about the flight numbers of the crashed planes adding up to something significant — and Gary took it all very seriously."

"After a while, of course, Gary didn't really talk to us about any of that," Romeo said. "When we were casually dismissive, or just unresponsive, he tended to drop the subject for a while. We didn't want to insult him or hurt him. But we weren't about to indulge this looniness, either. What do you do? What do you say? We loved Gary, but we were just flabbergasted. Some people are susceptible to these notions and some aren't, and we happen to fall into the latter category. It just got terribly awkward."

"He obviously cared what you thought of him," I said. "And after he moved to Thailand, he stayed in touch. But you said, Lou, that Gary gave indications that things were starting to go wrong. What were those indications?"

They looked at each other. Horn said, "You know about Mango, right? From Ellen Griswold."

"I do. Apparently Gary was head over heels for the guy."

"He was," Janice said, "and then later he wasn't. In one e-mail he sent me late last summer — I've got a hard copy for you to take with you — Gary said Mango might not be who he said he was. This was extremely distressing for Gary. He had trusted this guy, he said. Gary had also been to a seer — that's the word he used. And what the seer predicted was 'bloodshed' in Gary's life, and 'great sorrow for people close to him.' Again, the seer's words."

That's all? No specifics?"

"No."

"Did Gary tell anybody the seer's name?"

"No."

"Not death, just bloodshed? That was the word? And sorrow?"

"It is tantalizingly and unhelpfully vague," Horn said.

I asked Janice how she had replied to Griswold's unnerving e-mail, and she looked sheepish. "I never really responded, really. What I thought was, this is supermarket tabloid stuff. Gary didn't have to go all the way to Thailand for this. He could have picked up forecasts like that for a couple of bucks at the Winn-Dixie checkout. He said the seer was some kind of renowned figure in Thailand, but it sounded like a racket to me. I wasn't about to say that, though, so I just let it go. About a week later, I sent him some chirpy message about nothing at all. I stupidly just ignored this thing that obviously was terribly important to Gary."

"Well, if it was a scam," Weems said, "Gary could afford it. He had more money than God and Buddha put together. Anyway, what could you possibly have said? Sometimes when people are acting screwy, silence from friends is the only kind and useful response."

I asked if Griswold had informed any of the three that he had transferred his entire fortune to a Bangkok bank and that he planned on a large investment with an early big payoff. No, they said, they had not known about this until I had told Horn on the phone. "You scared the bejesus out us of with that one," Weems said.

"We're just hoping that something really horrible hasn't happened," Horn said. "Gary has all that money over there in a part of the world that I assume can be dangerous. And then there's the Griswold family history of violent death. It almost makes you believe in fate or karma or people being doomed by forces beyond their control or understanding. Notice I said 'almost.'"

I said, "What Griswold family history of violent death? I don't know about that."

"I suppose there's no reason Ellen would have mentioned it," Horn said. "But Gary's parents died in a small-plane crash fifteen or so years ago. This was just a year or two before Bill's ex-wife, Sheila, sailed off on a Caribbean cruise and disappeared at sea. Presumably, she fell overboard, though nobody knows for sure."

So the JAP was actually the late JAP. "This is news."

"It does help show," Horn said, "why Gary might take predictions of bloodshed by a fortune-teller more seriously than a lot of us would."

"It seems," I said, "as though Gary was closer to his former wife than to his brother Bill. Why might that be true? Or am I wrong?"

"There was never any love lost between Gary and Bill," Horn said. "They were just two different types of animal. It was partly the gay thing. The Griswolds only accepted that grudgingly, and it just wasn't discussed. But there were other big differences. The steel and building supply businesses never really interested Gary. He was in it for fifteen years to prove something to his family and to himself, I guess. And then he walked away from the company without giving it a second thought."

"Plus," Romeo said, "Gary's brother was some kind of big Bushophile. That was certainly an issue. It was another topic that could never be mentioned among the Griswolds."

"Gary hated the militarism of the Bush people," Horn said. "He was constantly giving money to peace groups and to human rights organizations like Amnesty International and Human Rights Watch. A big part of Thailand's draw for him was the Buddhism and the philosophy of nonviolence."

I told them I wasn't surprised that the reality of Thailand for Griswold may have turned out to be something other than a travel-poster Buddhist paradise. "I am also fond of the place," I said. "But if you don't like militarism, it's hardly the place to go. Thailand has had a dozen or more military coups since it started electing governments in the nineteen thirties. The generals, of course, always go to the country's beloved King Bhumibol to ask his permission to overthrow the elected government. If he ever said, 'No, sorry, you can't do that,' I'm not aware of it. The place also has a thoroughly corrupt police force that's been known to simply execute suspected drug dealers, as I recall. And drive-by shootings are sometimes used to resolve business disputes, I've heard."

The three were now looking at me queasily. I guessed I should have told them, as with Timothy, only about the reclining Buddhas. I said, "But the Thai people generally are gentle and humor-filled. And deeply spiritual. And they have a highly developed sense of fun — *sanuk*, they call it. Sanuk infects just about everything the Thais do."

"Like their drive-by shootings?" Romeo asked.

The waitress arrived to clear away the antipasti platter, which we had picked clean. Griswold's three friends, subdued now and a bit shaken, decided this would be a good time to order another round of drinks.

"Look," I said, "I think you're right to worry about Griswold. It's reasonable to think that anybody vanishing in Southeast Asia with thirty-eight million dollars at his disposal has either met foul play or is in hiding in order to avoid foul play. Or — and I know you'd much rather not think about this — Griswold has himself done something illegal, and he is in hiding not from criminal bad guys but from Thai-cop bad guys. Which are sometimes one and the same thing, I'm sorry to say."

They all set down their glasses of Ketel One and looked at me soberly.

After a moment, Horn said, "I guess we were hoping you would tell us things about Thailand that were more reassuring."

"I wish I could."

"Well, then," Weems said. "It's good you're going over. When do you leave?"

"In a couple of days, I think. I've booked space on both Thursday and Friday."

"Are you going alone? Or do you have a staff?"

"I may have help. That's unclear."

"Poor Gary," Horn said. "I can't believe, really, that he's done anything wrong himself. The guy is just so *decent*. So, something really bad must have happened to him. Oh, God."

Our pasta dishes arrived, and we talked quietly about what Horn, Weems and Romeo all saw as the good life in Key West.

There were rising costs and overpopulation and the threat of catastrophic hurricanes. But low-pressure island life was still the best, they all agreed and wished that Gary Griswold had not lost his capacity to be happy in this place that his friends all loved.

We were well into our lasagna and fettuccine when an acquaintance the three hadn't seen for a while stopped by the table to greet them. Nadine Bisbee, an angular, middle-aged woman in a sarong and fourteen pounds of turquoise and silver jewelry, was introduced to me as another friend of Griswold who was quite concerned about him. Horn told her I was a private investigator preparing to fly to Thailand to search for Griswold.

"Oh," Bisbee said, "I don't think we need to worry about Gary anymore. Elise Flanagan saw him two weeks ago in Cambodia."

Horn and Romeo said it at the same time. "She did?"

"It was at a border crossing. Elise was on a tour bus on her way from Bangkok to Angkor Wat with her Antioch-alum architecture history group, and there was Gary at Thai passport control heading back into Thailand from Cambodia. She yelled at him, she said, but he either didn't hear Elise or for some reason he didn't want to run into anybody he knew. Elise said she thought maybe he had some underage youth in tow and was embarrassed by it."

I said, "Does Gary have a history of underage youths as a sexual interest?"

Romeo said, "Just Lou."

"Thank you, dear."

"No," Weems said. "It had to be something else. Was Elise sure it was Gary she saw?"

"Elise said it was definitely Gary. Elise has been getting forgetful in recent years, but she certainly knows Gary as well as any of us. I mean, she bought art from Gary and Lou for years and was in the gallery at least once a month, wasn't she, Lou?"

"Elise would certainly know Gary," Horn said somberly. "Maybe this means he's been in Cambodia for six months, and that's why nobody has heard from him."

Romeo said, "For chrissakes, Cambodia surely has telephones and post offices. Even the Internet, I'll bet. Am I right, Don?"

"In the Khmer Rouge era, it didn't. But now Cambodia is not so cut off, no."

"So, what's going on with Gary?" Weems said, and they all looked at me.

CHAPTER FOUR

Despite creeping gentrification, Stock Island, just east of Key West, had one of the few remaining low-rent districts in the lower keys. It had dockage for fishing and pleasure boats, some warehouses, and a few good seafood restaurants. But it wasn't yet, Horn told me, one of the fashionable, high-cost addresses for habitation.

Sandy Tessig lived in one of the island's two-story plain-concrete multiunit townhouses built on stilts to be safe from storm surges. So far, the design had worked; the place had not been swept away by rampaging seas. Tessig had no big sign up, just a discreet notice next to her door buzzer that read *Sandy — Past, Present, and Future Knowledge — The Freedom to Know and to Be.*

Tessig had agreed on the phone to talk to me, and Lou Horn dropped me off at ten in the morning, planning to pick me up in an hour. Tessig had said she was worried about Griswold too, and was willing to help if she could. And, she said, maybe while I was there I would like a reading.

Sandy's apartment didn't give me the kind of willies I was expecting, and neither did she. There were a couple of astrological charts on the living room wall over the couch, but no rooms painted black and no sinister aromatherapy. I could see Disney-character decals on the side of the refrigerator in the kitchen and the only smell was of the orange Doritos in a dish on the coffee table. The CD box on the player next to the goldfish bowl was an early Barbra Streisand collection.

I relaxed on the couch and Sandy brought me a cup of Nescafé. She was pleasantly beefy in tight jeans and a Conch Nation T-shirt. She had clear skin, a big expressive face, and streaked hair cut short.

She perched on a hassock across the coffee table from me and told me she was excited to have me in the same room with her.

"Why?" I asked.

"You've been everywhere. You've done everything. Oh, my God!"

I knew what was coming, but I said, "I was in the army, and I've always enjoyed travel."

"Wait. Don't tell me. Lithuania?"

"Nope. Never Lithuania."

"No, no. Fifteenth century. The royal court."

"I'm not aware of this."

"No, but I am. I have the gift. That's why Gary came to me. It's why you're here, Donnie."

"Nobody has called me Donnie for a number of years. You must have me mixed up with someone else," I said in a kidding way, trying to get her off this track.

"Are you saying you are not that person anymore? You will *always* be little Donnie. Always were, always will be. And many other little Donnies in time and space too."

"You're sounding a little too much like my mother, Sandy," I said, trying again for a jocularity that did not come across as too disrespectful. "Can we talk about Gary Griswold? You said you were as worried about him as so many of his other friends have been." I told her that a Key West woman apparently had seen Griswold alive at the Thai–Cambodian border two weeks earlier, but that his noncommunicativeness and apparent secretiveness were still a serious cause for concern.

"Gary is home where he belongs. Home is where the heart is."

"True enough."

"He told me after he got back from his first trip to Thailand that I had been right to urge him to go there, and that he had found his spiritual and ancestral true home. Here he suffered from dislocation. I'm not knocking Key West; don't get me wrong. I grew up a quarter of a mile from where we're sitting, and it's fine that I'm here now, because I've been in Monroe

County for most of my past lives. This place has been good to me, except for once in the thirteen forties."

"That's pre-Columbian," I said.

"What? You think there were no people in Monroe County before Columbus got here?"

"No, in fact I'm impressed. And who can argue with firsthand experience?"

She gave me a smile that appeared genuine. "You're a doubter, I can see. But that's okay. Your skepticism in no way alters reality."

"That's been my experience."

"But you're missing out on something fantastic, Donnie. Full self-knowledge. It's liberating. Knowing not just who you are but who you were enables you to see yourself in your natural place in the cosmos. Once you grasp this, you'll never feel dislocated again. Or alone."

I said, "How come people in your line of endeavor, Sandy, tend to locate clients in a cozy royal court? Couldn't I have been a rural Lithuanian Jew getting speared in the neck by marauding Cossacks?"

"Of course," she said. "That's what happened to me in 1343, until forty-six. Not in Lithuania but here in Florida. It wasn't Cossacks, it was Seminoles. It accounts for a good deal of my present back pain. But I sense strongly that you were either royalty or were close to royalty. You have also lived many other lives, of course, some of them perhaps replete with rage and physical agony. But rediscovering those lives would require time and effort."

"I'm afraid my immediate concern has to be Gary Griswold."

"I couldn't agree more. It would be so, so sad if Gary's bliss had gone by."

I said, "So it was you who suggested that Gary vacation in Thailand? I was under the impression that former Key West resident Geoff Pringle had invited him for a visit."

She adjusted her back — were the Seminoles the problem, or the hassock? — and let loose a grin of pure satisfaction. "I knew Geoff was over there. He, too, is a client of mine. But it was Gary's journey back to his young life at the nineteenth-century court of King Mongkut that made him realize his bliss awaited him in Siam."

"So, Gary was royalty too?"

"Gary himself was not of the Chakra dynasty. He was the child of a minor court official. But one of his classmates in the court school run by the incredible Anna Leonowens was the future King Chulalongkorn, and Gary later became King Chulalongkorn's palace art curator. So, you see? Running an art gallery in Key West was really nothing new for Gary."

"You know," I said, "most of that *Anna and the King of Siam* and *The King and I* saga was hooey. Leonowens made nearly all of it up, and later Rodgers and Hammerstein ran with it. Tunefully, to be sure. But I know that the Thais think it's a crock."

Tessig was unruffled by this additional evidence that I was just another doubter. She said, "Gary remembers Anna as being a wonderful woman. If she embellished, that's only natural. After all, she loved a king and was loved in return by His Majesty."

"Thai scholars say the woman was demented. There was no romance. And Mongkut never hopped around blurting 'Is a puzzlement!'"

She smiled even more serenely, impervious. "Talk to Gary. He can tell you."

"I'd like to. I'm flying to Thailand later this week." I reiterated the fears Griswold's family in Albany and friends in Key West had for him, not having heard from Griswold for six months.

"Yes, Gary stopped e-mailing me too," Tessig said. "It was perplexing, and then I began to worry. His last few messages had been replete with foreboding. A Thai soothsayer had given him a bad reading, and his sign of Jupiter had entered the seventh house. Gary was also disappointed in a man he had been involved with named Mango. Apparently the guy had turned out to be dishonest, and a flaming A-hole to boot."

"Did he mention what Mango had done to upset him?"

"No, just that Mango apparently had misrepresented himself in some serious way. So, who saw Gary in Cambodia? At least that's promising news."

"Elise Flanagan," I said. "She's here in Key West. Do you know her?"

Now Tessig really lit up. "Elise! She's a client of mine! But she didn't speak to Gary?"

"He seemed not to want to interact with her or even to be recognized. So, does Elise Flanagan also have past-life connections with Southeast Asia? Or was she just a tourist?"

"I don't know, but I sure plan on finding out. Elise will be here Friday morning. I know she was Mongolian. Sometimes it's hard to tell with Elise, though. She sometimes gets confused, since her diagnosis."

"Diagnosis for what?" I asked, wary.

"Early Alzheimer's. She does sometimes confuse people she knows with other people she knows. So it's probably best not to make too much of her spotting Gary, supposedly. Oh, that's really too bad it was Elise and not somebody more reliable. Her long-term memory is still sharp, though. She's especially clearheaded on the great migration across the Bering Straits from East Asia to the Americas."

I glanced out Tessig's living room window to see if perhaps Lou Horn had parked outside and was waiting to drive me back into Key West. I recognized his old red Camry, and as soon as I politely could, made a beeline.

CHAPTER FIVE

I phoned Timmy from Atlanta and told him my connecting flight to Albany would be over an hour late, getting in close to midnight, and I would not leave for Thailand until Friday. I said I had some things I needed to check with the Griswolds — and about the Griswolds.

I gave Timmy a quick summary of my Key West visit with Horn, Weems and Romeo, my informative session with Sandy Tessig, and my brief visit early that afternoon with Elise Flanagan. Lou Horn had driven me over to her house so that we might get a firsthand account of her sighting of Griswold on the Thai–Cambodian border. Wan and sinewy in a gauzy dun-colored sack of some kind, Mrs. Flanagan at first insisted that the man she saw had to have been Gary Griswold. He had been her dear friend for years. But then, she said, the man she saw did look a lot like Raul Castro, and that was confusing. As she went on, I could see Horn's now-faint hopes fade even further.

I told Timmy I had booked just one seat on the JFK–Bangkok flight a day and a half later, but that it probably wasn't too late for him to join me.

"Thanks, but no thanks."

"Timothy," I said, "when did you become such a travel wuss? You're Mister Peace Corps. This isn't India, I know, but you loved India way back when. And, like me with Southeast Asia, you've talked about going back someday. We could wrap up this strange Griswold business in Bangkok and then stop over in your old village in Andhra Pradesh on the way home. Most of it would be on Ellen Griswold's dime. It's the travel opportunity of a lifetime."

He laughed. "Mo Driscoll, one of the guys in my India group, went back to his village in Maharashtra last year. Some people actually remembered him. He said word spread all around that the guy who wiped his ass with paper was back."

"Sargent Shriver would be touched."

"It's actually a telling Peace Corps story. Yes, we made some nice connections while we were there, and may even have done some useful work in India. But we were always convinced that basically the villagers thought of us as Martians."

"Were any of Driscoll's chickens still flapping around when he went back?"

"He wasn't in poultry development," Timmy said. "Mo was in the family-planning program."

"Apparently it didn't work."

"Oh, I'm not so sure."

"Yeah, if it hadn't been for the Peace Corps, India's population today might be one-point-three billion people instead of one-point-two."

He laughed, but not heartily. Timmy and his Peace Corps pals could themselves be cavalier when discussing their youthful development work. But when others cast doubt, they often became stern. I deeply envied him his Asia experience, though. Peace beats war any day.

"Of course, I want to go back to India," he said. "I just don't want to be a nervous wreck when I get there. Or show up with a bloody hole in my head. Or a boyfriend with a hole in his."

"I don't know why you're fixating on the Bangkok drive-by shooting statistics. We don't know that anything remotely like that has happened to Griswold, or is likely to. Sure, there's reason to worry about the guy. But let's not leap to any conclusions. My own plan is to take it one cautious step at a time."

"Is it possible," he said, "that one reason you want so badly for me to come with you is that you don't quite trust yourself over there alone? That you're a little afraid that you'll fall in love with the place the way Gary Griswold did? The place, and of course all those happy-go-lucky, silky-skinned, sanuk-loving Mangos? And if I go along, then you're much more likely to retain some grip on reality and come back to where you belong in a timely manner? Since I don't know Bangkok at all, I wouldn't be all that useful over there. Surely you know that. So I'm just trying to figure out what it is that's actually going on here."

After a long moment, I said, "Well. So you think maybe I want you to come along so that you can be my mother?"

"No, not your mother. Just your boyfriend of many years gone by, as well as many years to come. Anyway, that's certainly what it sounds like to me."

"Okay," I said, "what if I do maybe want to re-fall in love with Thailand — Thailand in peacetime — and maybe I want you to come along so that you can fall in love with Thailand too? We can re-fall in love with the Land of Smiles — yes, drive-by shootings too, but mainly the Land of Smiles — together. Doesn't that sound just as plausible as what you just said? Whatever the hell it was you just said."

Now Timmy was quiet. Then he said, "That I would have to think about."

§ § § §

When I got home just after one in the morning, Timmy was snoring exuberantly — "calling the hogs," as his Aunt Moira called it — and I went online to see if I could get Google to cough up some answers.

The deaths of Max and Bertha Griswold got considerable play in the *Albany Times Union* in early June of 1993. He had been a business leader, and both were benefactors of the arts and numerous Jewish and other charities. So it was shocking to many when the couple, who were in their early sixties, died in the crash of a Piper Comanche piloted by the aircraft's owner, Dave Kane, who was also killed. The plane had gone down in a pasture as it flew from the Albany County Airport to Rochester, where the Griswolds were to have received an award in recognition of Algonquin Steel's in-kind contributions to a concert hall restoration project.

Follow-up stories said FAA investigators had found no mechanical problems with the aircraft, but that an autopsy showed the pilot, sixty-eight years old, had died of a heart attack, probably before the plane went down, causing it to crash.

Somewhat less prominently reported was the disappearance just under a year later, in May 1994, of Sheila Griswold of Clifton Park, former wife of Algonquin Steel president and CEO William Griswold. The initial story made page one below the fold, but follow-ups soon fell into the B section before vanishing altogether.

Mrs. Griswold, who had no children and had not remarried, apparently fell overboard from the Norwegian cruise liner *Oslo Comfort* on the night of May 21, somewhere off St. Kitts. Shipmates had seen Mrs. Griswold in the dining room earlier. She was reported missing the next morning when she failed to meet dining room companions for a book signing with mystery author Deidre McCubbertson and crew members discovered that her bed had not been slept in. Family members speculated, the paper said, that "alcohol could have been a factor in the tragedy," though the speculating family members were not identified.

There were three daily English-language newspapers in Bangkok, the *Post*, the *Nation*, and the *Daily Express*, and I scanned their archives for mention of a Gary Griswold. None turned up.

Ellen Griswold had given me the name of the Bangkok bank Griswold had had his thirty-eight million wired to. It was just after noon Thursday in Thailand, and I got the Commercial Bank of Siam on the phone. I said I was Gary Griswold and needed an account balance. Mrs. Griswold had told me the account number, and I recited it. After some minutes, a man came on the line and told me in English that was a little hard for me to follow that the account had been closed. I said, oh, that's right, I had the money moved to an interest-bearing account but I had forgotten the number, and may I please have it along with the balance? No, the man said, sounding a bit wary now, there was no other account in the name of Griswold at the Commercial Bank of Siam.

It didn't seem as if it would help if I screamed, "Then, where the bloody hell is my thirty-eight million?" So I said, "Oh, God, where did I transfer that cash to? Was it Bangkok Bank?"

This was taking a chance — was there such a thing? — but the man said, yes, I had done exactly that.

"When?"

"You no remember?"

"Please pardon me. I'm so disorganized."

A long silence. It wasn't even staticky. Modern telecommunications are such a marvel.

"I can no help you, sir. You must phone Bangkok Bank. Okay?"

"Oh, jeez, what's my account number there? You must have had it for the transfer."

What he gave me instead, and then quickly rang off, was a telephone number for Bangkok Bank. I called them, but they required an account number in order for our conversation to proceed. All this would have to wait until Saturday, when I would arrive in the Thai capital to work my magic in the flesh.

§ § § §

Lunch on Thursday with Ellen Griswold at her house in Loudonville got off to a bad start when I suggested why her former husband might be susceptible to dire forecasts by fortune-tellers. I said it could have something to do with the Griswold family history of people dying violently.

"Where did you get that information?" she demanded to know. "What exactly are you referring to, and what's that got to do with anything?"

I told her Gary's friends in Key West had brought it up — the plane crash and the Caribbean cruise disappearance — only in the context of Gary's heightened sense of foreboding and karmic doom, nothing more than that.

"Oh God. Well, you know, there were people at the time who thought Bill had something to do with Sheila's death — had her shoved overboard or God knows what. She had been squeezing him really hard financially. This was when Max and Bertha's estate was tied up in probate. When Sheila died — or presumably died — it did take a lot of the pressure off Bill. There were people, I know, who saw that as a little too convenient. In a way it's funny, and yet it's kind of pathetic."

"So Sheila was eventually declared legally dead?"

"It took four or five years. For-bleeping-ever. Bill got nothing back. Sheila's maid and her cats got some, and the state got the rest. But at least she wasn't constantly dragging him into court anymore. Sheila was so aggressive for so many years, though, it wouldn't surprise me if she strolled up through the herb garden right now and rapped on the window and waved a summons in our faces."

We were seated at a nicely designed table with a sculpted aluminum base and a white polypropylene top in the Griswold's sunporch. The bright room overlooked an herb garden and a broad expanse of trees and lawn stretching for some distance beyond. Most of the herbs were still covered, but some daffodils had sprung up and looked about to bloom in their cheerful, ephemeral way.

I had dug right into the crab salad and crusty baguette Ellen had brought out, and so had she. She had her worries, but they hadn't hurt her appetite. She was drinking tap water with lemon, as was I, another healthful choice for midday. I rather liked Mrs. Griswold — her confidence, her direct approach, her draping only mild refinement over peasant appetites — and I wasn't sure why I didn't quite trust her.

I said, "You know, the Thais believe in ghosts. It's good that your husband isn't the Griswold who's over there now, or he might run into his first wife's restless spirit. Has he ever been to Southeast Asia? Have you?"

"No, never had the pleasure."

"You mentioned you had lived and worked abroad. Where was that?"

"I spent a month on a kibbutz when I was in college and lived in Geneva for a year doing marketing for Pepsico's new Buzz Saw line of power drinks. I enjoyed both experiences in their entirely different ways. Though I have to admit my French became somewhat more fluent than my Hebrew."

"It's hard to imagine the Swiss on all that caffeine," I said.

"Oh, they were scarfing it up by the time I was done with them."

I didn't doubt it. I summarized my Key West findings for Mrs. Griswold and told her they basically squared with what she had told me about her ex-husband-slash-current-brother-in-law: his unsettling passionate interest in past lives, numerology, and astrological forecasts; his involvement with the wonderful and then less-than-wonderful Mango; his large-scale financial transfers followed by his apparent disappearance.

"In fact," I said, "Gary did not tell his Key West friends about converting his assets and wiring cash to Thailand, nor about the so-called surefire investment. When I mentioned it, that was news to them."

"If they're sane — which it sounds to me like they could be — I'm sure they would have thought Gary was nuts, and possibly said so. Which Gary no doubt would not wish to hear. Bill and I only know about it because Alan Rainey was involved in selling the company shares, and he asked Gary what was going on. Gary apparently thought he had to tell us all something."

"Perhaps," I said, having a thought, "Gary told Rainey he wanted the money for an investment because he thought Rainey would find that reassuring. And he really wanted the thirty-eight million for some other purpose."

She mulled this over. "Possibly."

"And if the actual reason for the transfer was known to your family, you might have waged an all-out campaign to keep Gary from doing whatever it was he was actually going to do."

"Oh God. Maybe that's it. This could be even worse than we thought."

"Well, worse or not worse. What had Gary spent large sums of money on in the past?"

She screwed up her face to the extent she was able to. "Not much. Art. Art books. Fancy European bicycles. His condo. Gary lived comfortably and liked having money. But he was no serious spender."

"Did he give money away?"

"I'd say he was like his parents. Generous, but responsible. I know he gave to arts groups and to human rights organizations. But I would be very surprised if he ever went into capital for charitable giving. Of course," she said, "I'm talking about before Gary started losing his marbles and babbling about past and future lives and all that garbage. God knows what was going on inside his brain six months ago when all this looniness apparently came to a head."

"Gary's friends in Key West have wondered if his falling off his bike during a race and landing on his head brought about some kind of personality change. Do you know about this?"

"What? No. How bizarre."

"The timing could have been coincidental."

"Gary never mentioned this to Bill or me. Was he hospitalized?"

"Just briefly, with a concussion."

"Wasn't he wearing a helmet?"

"He was. But I guess the brain can still get badly rattled around in a crack-up."

"Well, this is a new one. So, somebody thinks Gary's brain was injured, and he suddenly started hallucinating about past lives in Thailand, and maybe he gave his money away to the poor people of Asia or some weird thing like that?"

"It's far-fetched, I know."

"Anyway," she said, "if Gary was going to drop thirty-eight million in a monk's alms bowl, why would he have to disappear in order to do it? No," she went on, "I don't think so. Weird bump on the head or no weird bump on the head, I think something bad happened to Gary in Thailand that he was not expecting and which he had no control over. Something totally external. And that's what I am paying you a lot of money to uncover and — if it's what's needed — do something about it."

Her summary was a sound one, I thought, and her continuing concerns about Griswold's well-being justified.

Both our fears were only heightened when my cell phone rang and it was Lou Horn with the news that the *Key West Citizen* was reporting the death of Geoffrey Pringle in Bangkok. The newspaper said the man Gary Griswold had visited on his initial trip to Thailand — and later apparently had had some major disagreement with — had died three days earlier in a fall from his twelfth-story condominium in Bangkok's Sathorn district. The death appeared to have been a suicide, the newspaper reported, although Thai officials had said that was uncertain.

CHAPTER SIX

"You said it would be hot here in April," Timmy said. "But this is ridiculous. It's like India."

"This is a good sign," I said. "You're already getting sentimental."

"Anyway, I'm just happy to be off that plane."

"Maybe we'll be lucky and die here, and we won't have to get back on the plane and sit immobilized for another seventeen hours."

"Please don't say that."

We were waiting in the taxi queue outside Suvarnabhumi Airport in Bangkok. The night I got home from Key West, Timmy had left a note on my pillow. At first, I thought he had forgotten to gather up an official document of the New York State Assembly, an uncharacteristic untidiness on his part. Then I saw that it was a message for me, composed following our Atlanta airport–Albany phone conversation of a few hours earlier. The note read: *About you and me falling in love with Asia again — sign me up!*

I had told Ellen Griswold that my aide and I preferred flying business class, and she had replied, "Of course. Are you kidding?" But even with Thai Airways orchid-garnished entrées and comely cabin attendants of both sexes, we were glad to be on the ground after the nonstop slog and standing out-of-doors in the soaking heat.

"This doesn't look like India at all," Timmy said, once we were in the taxi speeding down an eight-lane expressway. "Bangkok looks more like Fort Lauderdale or San Diego."

"What does India look like?"

"Oh, Schenectady."

"Anyway, this is not the Bangkok I remember — all these skyscrapers. This is the shiny all-new Asia. In the seventies,

Bangkok was still mostly quaint, filthy canals and teak houses on stilts."

"Are you disappointed?"

"No," I said, "I'm sure that just below the surface it's still very much Thailand," and noted the Buddha figures on the dashboard and the amulets and garlands of jasmine dangling from the rearview mirror. Getting into the taxi, I had had a back-and-forth with the driver, Korn Panpiemras, over whether he would lawfully employ the meter or we would instead pay an extortionate flat rate — we eventually settled on the meter — and this ritual also was reassuringly Thai.

As we approached the city center, the late-afternoon traffic was nearly as thick as the air, and we didn't reach our hotel until almost seven o'clock. The Topmost-Lumpinee, described on a gay-travel Web site as "gay friendly" and convenient to gay bars and clubs — and not far from Gary Griswold's last known address — was a pleasant tourist hotel with a spacious lobby adorned with gold-leafed Siamese dancers and smiling elephants. In the time it took to fly from JFK to Bangkok, the dollar had declined even further against the Thai baht — and most other currencies — but the Topmost still looked like a bargain at under fifty dollars a night.

When the bellhop checked our room key, he exclaimed happily, "Nine-oh-nine! A lucky number!"

When we got up to 909, however, the key didn't fit. "Oh," the kid lugging our bags said with a dark look. "It is six-oh-six."

Inside the unlucky room, Timmy headed for the shower and I phoned Rufus Pugh. This was one of the Bangkok private investigators my New York PI friend had suggested I try. I had liked the look of Pugh's Web site. It said he spoke fluent Thai and employed Thai investigators. Other Web sites I looked at made no such claims, even though they all seemed to be run by foreigners. Also, most of the others specialized in "cheating husbands" and "cheating girlfriends," and Pugh Investigative Services also listed background checks, surveillance, due diligence and, significantly, missing persons. So I had e-mailed

Pugh, and he replied that I should phone him when I got to Bangkok.

I reached Pugh on his mobile, and wherever he was, the reception was poor. He said he was tied up on a stakeout with a team, and we made a plan to meet for breakfast at eight at the Topmost. Pugh had an accent of some kind that I couldn't place. I figured with a name like his it had to be Arkansas or Louisiana.

Timmy and I had slept on the plane, thanks to Griswold family business-class largesse. So we picked up a Bangkok city map at the hotel front desk and set out to have a look at Griswold's apartment building on the way to dinner. It looked like a twenty-minute walk. And I soon saw on the map that Geoff Pringle had lived less than half a mile away from Griswold before he died in the fall from his balcony a week earlier.

Moving through the premonsoon Bangkok night heat felt more like swimming in swamp water than walking through air, and our polo shirts were soon drenched. The part of Sathorn we passed through was a mix of city office towers and apartment buildings on the main streets, and smaller shops, restaurants, and food stalls on the *sois* that ran off them. The street food was as aromatic as I remembered it, and we paused for some noodles in a pork broth with herbs. We sat on tiny stools at a tiny table on a sliver of sidewalk and were served from a tiny cart with a full kitchen inside it that was operated by a small nuclear family. Timmy said it was the best food he ever ate. It cost a dollar, not that Ellen Griswold wouldn't have sprung for two.

Among the vehicles zooming by in the soi a few feet from us as we ate were motorcycles, some with single male riders. Timmy glanced up at these apprehensively from time to time, as well as at the motorcycles upon which entire families were lined up one behind the other, the small children in front as if they were air bags.

Lou Horn had obtained Geoff Pringle's address from a mutual friend and passed it on to me, and Timmy and I paused in front of the building. It stood along narrow but heavily traveled Sathorn Soi 1. Cars, taxis and motorcycle taxis cruised quietly up and down the street — with an occasional three-wheeled tuk-tuk as a reminder of old Bangkok — with pedestrians treading carefully along the narrow walkways on either side.

Bougainvillea and yellow and scarlet flamboyant tree branches spilled over white stucco walls along the route, including one in front of Pringle's building. An enormous portrait in an elaborate gold frame of a gravely contemplative King Bhumibol stood among the decorative plantings, along with brushed stainless steel lettering identifying Pringle's building as the Royal Palm Personal Deluxe Executive Suites. Many of the building's balconies had potted trees and flowering plants on them as well, talismanic reminders of the Thais' origins as agricultural villagers, or in the case of most of the farangs, probably, pretty tropical ornaments.

A uniformed security guard in an orange vest stood under a streetlight at the entrance to the building's small driveway. I said *sa-wa-dee-cap*. He sa-wa-deed me back, and I said I was sorry to hear about Mr. Geoff.

"Oh, very bad. Mr. Geoff. Oh, Mr. Geoff. Bad. He your friend?"

"He was my friend's friend," I said quickly. "Did he live up there?" I pointed.

"Yes, fall down," the guard said, indicating an area of low foliage where some branches looked newly broken.

"Bad," I said.

"Oh, bad."

"Did you see?"

"No, no. No see. I hear."

"You heard Mr. Geoff fall?"

"Yes, yes. Very bad for me. I hear him say."

"He said something? After he fell?"

"No after. Before. I hear 'oh-oh-no!' He just say like that. 'Oh-oh-no!' I am in hut," he said, indicating the small sentry box a few feet from us. "I hear big sound. He fall down."

"I'm sorry."

"Very bad for me."

"What time was it? Late?"

"Very late. People sleeping."

"Did anyone else see or hear it happen?"

"El-suh?"

"Was it only you who heard him fall?"

"Only me. Bad luck for me."

"Did you phone the police?"

"Later. Police come later."

"You phoned the police. But they came later?"

"Police? Ha!" He made some gesture with his head, but I wasn't sure what it meant. It seemed to be a negative opinion.

I said, "Do you think Mr. Geoff fell accidentally or jumped from his balcony?"

The guard may not have known all the English words, but he seemed to understand the question. It was a question he must have given a good deal of thought to over the previous week.

The guard said, "Maybe fall. No jump, I don't think. Maybe — *bee-ah*," he said, making a guzzle-with-a-bottle motion. "Maybe he fall. Maybe bee-ah. Maybe" — he got a hard look now — "maybe I don't know."

I tried to learn from the guard whether any of Pringle's friends had visited him that night, or in recent days, but I had reached the limits of the guard's English and didn't make any headway. I thought maybe Rufus Pugh could learn more. I wished the guard good luck, and Timmy and I walked on.

"It doesn't sound as if there was any serious police...anything," Timmy said.

"No. I'll try to find out."

We turned up a quieter, less-traveled soi toward Griswold's condo. Bangkok's Miami-like skyline glowed in the near distance, but the prettily walled-off places along this tranquil lane were individual homes of the well-off — a lighted swimming pool was visible behind one low wall hung with flowers — and the back entrances to a couple of the smaller European embassies.

When we passed the discreetly appointed entrance to Paradisio, Bangkok's best-known gay bathhouse, Timmy said, "Oh, I've heard of this."

"We may have to check it out in our search for Mango. Or I may have to."

"Me get left out? I don't think so."

"Bangkok is full of ghosts, the Thais believe. Maybe Cardinal Spellman's is over here keeping an eye on you."

"An eye and a roving hand. His spirit is probably in there right now frolicking. The Holy See is way over on the other side of the world."

"What with such things being unheard-of in Rome."

A taxi cruised down the soi and turned into Paradisio's palm-adorned driveway. Two farangs got out, paid the driver and went inside. Timmy said, "This could be where Griswold met some of his multiple Thai boyfriends."

"This or any one of hundreds of other gay bars, clubs, bathhouses, and massage parlors. But since Griswold lived nearby, Paradisio is a good place for us to sniff around when we get the chance."

Griswold's apartment building was about a hundred yards beyond Paradisio. It was one of the tonier in a tony neighborhood, with meticulously tended gardens below and balconies above, and an easy-on-the-eye white-with-silver-trim art deco design.

The security guard standing in the driveway — apparently building guards in Bangkok were not allowed to sit and risk dozing off — returned my sa-wa-dee and smiled politely. I told him I was Gary Griswold's brother and was looking for Gary, not having heard from him for some time. Did Griswold still live at the same address?

"Yes, but he not here now."

"When was he last here?"

"Mr. Gary come two weeks before. Then go. No stay."

So Griswold was alive, at least. Or had been two weeks earlier. "Are you sure it was two weeks? Not three?"

"Two weeks. Today Saturday. I no work last Saturday. Mr. Gary too much no here. He go 'way."

By establishing that I was Griswold's brother, a term that in Thailand can mean sibling, cousin, second or third cousin, or close friend, I was able to engage the guard long enough to learn that Griswold had visited his home only a few times in the past half year. And those visits had been brief and late at night. Griswold had arrived and departed by taxi and had been unaccompanied. If he had carried anything in or out of the apartment, the guard was unaware of it.

I asked if I might look inside Griswold's apartment to see if he had received mail from me, but now I was pushing it. The guard was a slight, dark-skinned Thai, probably from impoverished Isaan in the Northeast, supplier of cheap labor for greater Bangkok. *Kreng jai*, the Thai highly refined attunement to social status and its rituals of deference to be shown or received, meant that as an older white foreigner I had to be catered to. But only up to a point. The security company had its own kreng jai, and this man no doubt needed his job. So he played it safe and passed me off to the building manager, Mr. Thomsatai, who soon appeared from around the back of the building.

In black slacks and a blue polo shirt similar to mine, minus the sweat stains, the super was an older Thai who didn't smile so readily. Here the kreng jai was also complex. Out of earshot of the guard, I told Mr. Thomsatai the truth, that I was a PI working for Griswold's family and needed to get into his apartment to check on his welfare. I thought honesty might pay off, and also it couldn't hurt if word got back to Griswold that somebody unthreatening was searching for him. The manager sized me up, and something in his coolly noncommittal manner suggested that another Thai custom might be brought into play.

I thanked Mr. Thomsatai for the time he spent talking with me and said I wished to give him a present. I palmed him a thousand-baht note, thirty bucks, and he quickly led Timmy and me into the building and up to Griswold's condo on the ninth floor. The man opened the door with his master key, showed us the light switches, then went out and left us.

Timmy said, "That was sleazy. Jeez."

"Yes and no. People need to get by."

"Oh. Okay." For such a Peace Corps old boy, he was not big on cultural relativism.

The view from Griswold's capacious living room was splendid, with an oasis of red tile roofs and green foliage below, along with a few turquoise-lighted swimming pools, and the office- and hotel-tower skyline beyond. The furnishings were a nice mixture of Scandinavian modernity and traditional Siamese wood and stone carvings of dancers, guardian spirits, and Buddha images. One wall was all shelves full of art and art history books. The graphic art on the wall was astrology related, signs of the zodiac and various astral and planetary configurations. One entire interior wall was covered with numbers in interlocking circular patterns. The numerical sequences seemed random, but this was not my area of expertise.

"What do you make of that?" I asked Timmy about the wall of numbers.

"I don't know. I think there might be more nines than anything else."

"Maybe they're upside-down sixes."

"Why would the sixes be upside down and not the other numbers?"

"You tell me."

I took a picture of the wall with my cell phone. Griswold's landline phone was dead when I lifted the receiver. He — or someone — was paying the condo fees and the electric bill, but not for a telephone. A desk in an alcove looked as if it had been where Griswold had set up a computer; a space that was now empty was just right for a laptop. There were no personal papers on the desk or in any of the drawers, just some art exhibition announcements and catalogs, none dated during the previous six months. Nothing in, on, or around the desk looked like an "investment" guide. I looked for a calendar, date book, or address book and found none. Nor was there any reference anywhere to Griswold's bloodshed-forecasting seer.

I unlatched the sliding glass door to the terrace, and we stepped out of the fiercely air-conditioned room into the Bangkok night oven. Next to the rattan porch chairs was an array of elegantly glazed ceramic pots, some holding feathery young bamboo plants and some white azaleas. One pot overflowed with purple and white orchids. Only a few dead leaves lay around the plants — apparently sweeping up dead leaves was still a Thai national pastime — and a watering can sat in a corner.

I said, "Somebody's been looking after the plants."

"Who?"

"We should find out."

Timmy peered down at the shadowy driveway far below. "I'd hate to fall off one of these things. Like Geoff Pringle."

"It's not how anybody wants to die."

Griswold's dining room had a well-crafted teak dining table in the center and eight semicomfortable-looking teak chairs around it. The most interesting object in this room was not the dining table, however, but a carpeted two-foot-high platform off to the side, upon which rested an elaborate shrine. It was a Hindu temple–style spirit house like the ones found outside many Thai buildings, including modern office towers, where offerings were left to appease the natural spirits displaced by the structures. Griswold's building had one near the main entrance, as did Pringle's, and our hotel.

Griswold's personal spirit house had a seated Buddha statuette inside it, about a foot high, in the raised left palm *mudra.* This is the attitude of the Buddha's hand that means *you are in the presence of the Buddha; do not be afraid.* Freshly burned incense lay in a dish in front of the spirit house and its pleasantly scratchy aroma still hung in the air. The garlands of marigolds, jasmine, and rose blossoms that lay in front of the shrine, brownish and wilting, appeared a day or two old.

I said, "Griswold is really into it. He's sincere."

"So is somebody else with a key to this apartment."

"We need to talk to the super again."

In the bedroom, a king-size bed with cream covers was pristinely un-slept-in. In the closet, there were plenty of designer label, warm-weather clothes, but empty spaces too, and no luggage. The bedroom art and decoration continued the astrological motif, with more stars, planets, and numbers flying around. There were no rich-gay-guy paintings or prints with muscular male nudes striking I've-been-waiting-for-YOU poses or clutching a rope.

Timmy and I did not have to seek out Mr. Thomsatai to find out who had been entering Griswold's apartment, for now the manager reappeared. He had quietly let himself in, found us in the bedroom, and asked if we were finished with our visit.

I asked him, "Have other people been in the apartment besides us? Someone has watered the plants. And left offerings. Or do you do that?"

"No, no. Kawee has a key. Kawee comes sometimes."

"Who is Kawee?"

"Kawee is Mr. Gary's friend."

"Thai?"

"Of course."

"When does Kawee come?"

"I don't know. Sometimes I see him. He has a key."

"No one else comes?"

"No, I don't think so."

"Have others such as myself come looking for Mr. Gary?"

"Of course."

"Who?"

"Thai man. I don't know his name. He comes sometimes and asks where is Mr. Gary. He comes on a motorbike. He is unfriendly. I don't like him. He asked me to phone his mobile if Mr. Gary comes."

"How much did he pay you?"

"One thousand baht. Like you."

I produced another note. "Have you got this man's phone number?"

"Of course."

CHAPTER SEVEN

"I'm confused," I said to Rufus Pugh. "I thought you were probably American."

"Yeah, ha-ha. This happens all the time. Some clients get up and walk out."

"I find it reassuring that you're Thai."

"Yes, it helps to be Thai if you're operating in Thailand. You'll see."

Pugh, Timmy, and I were in the Topmost dining room for the breakfast buffet. Timmy had his papaya and yogurt, I my omelet, and Pugh four slices of pineapple and a side of bacon.

"So, is Rufus your real name?" Timmy asked. "It sounds so…I guess American."

"No, the name my parents gave me was Panchalee Siripasaraporn." Pugh spelled it out, letter by letter. "But we Thais are not so rigid about names as you foreigners are. It can be confusing, I know. Sometimes Thais change their names. And we have different nicknames for different situations and relationships. Am I making myself unclear?" He laughed.

Pugh was a wiry little man who looked tough as old lemongrass. I could imagine somebody trying to fish bits of him out of their tom yam kung. He had the dark-faced, flat-nosed look of the North, meaning he was a man who got what he needed in Thai society with his wits and industry and not with his looks or his family history. What he had that was almost universally Thai was his humor.

"But why 'Rufus Pugh'?" Timmy asked. "It doesn't sound anything like your real name."

"I picked the name up when I went to Duke," Pugh said.

"Oh, you went to Duke? I went to Georgetown."

"How long were you there?" Pugh asked.

"How long? Four years."

"Well, I was only at Duke for a week. I was visiting my friend Supoj. He had a roommate named Rufus Pugh. I liked the sound of it. Oh, have I confused you gentlemen again? When I say I went to Duke, I mean I went to Duke on a Greyhound bus." He chuckled.

I said, "Where did you take the bus from, Rufus? Not Bangkok."

"From Monmouth College, in West Long Branch, New Jersey. I was there for one semester. Then I came home and completed university at Chulalongkorn in Bangkok. It was cheaper. That way, my three sisters had to fuck only three thousand seven hundred and twelve overweight Australians to put me through college instead of five thousand two hundred and eleven."

Timmy said, "I'm sorry. God."

"No need. This was twenty years ago. Now two of them are back in Chiang Rai with their lazy husbands, and the other married one of the large mates and lives in Sydney. I help them out — I look forward to getting my hands on some of the Griswold megabucks — and my wife and children are not big spenders. Neither is my girlfriend. But I do need to hustle. That's why we're here, isn't it?"

"How did you turn into a PI?" I asked.

"I was in the police, but eventually I started feeling guilty about being on the wrong side of the law. How about you, Mister Don?"

"Army Intelligence originally. I also had ethical issues."

"I'll bet. That must have been the US Army."

"In the seventies. I was here a few times."

"In Bangkok?"

"Bangkok and Pattaya."

"I was a child at the time. But maybe you fucked one of my sisters. Or me. I picked up some spare change on a few occasions."

"No, no youngsters for me. Anyway, I'd remember you. You make an impression, Rufus."

He smiled again, briefly, then said, "If you were in the American military, then you must know that the Thai military has its corrupt elements."

"I do know that."

"Parts of it are busy ruthlessly stamping out the drug trade, and parts of it are busy buying and selling drugs. Some elements do both. The police are often involved, and also our authoritarian neighbors, the Burmese generals, as well as the Burmese generals' authoritarian friends, the Chinese."

"So I've heard."

"I bring this up," Pugh said, "because you told me that your Mr. Gary Griswold planned on investing thirty-eight million US dollars and making a quick killing."

"That's what he told someone. It may not be true."

"With that kind of money, we may be talking drug deal. Heroin, *yaa-baa*, who knows? If that is the case, his family is correct to fear for his well-being. So let's hope he was up to something else."

"A drug deal," I said, "would be seriously out of character for this guy." I told Pugh about Griswold's discovery of Buddhist philosophy and meditation, his deepening interest in past lives, astrology and numerology, and on top of all that his infatuation and then de-infatuation with the mysterious Mango. "I think," I said, "that Griswold would consider heroin dealing, what with all the social harm involved, unethical if not downright evil. Unless, of course, it's Mr. Mango who's the gangster here, and it was Griswold's discovery of that that led to his disillusionment with Mango. And he actually believed he was investing in something else."

Pugh chewed on a slice of bacon. I had some too, with my omelet. It was the most flavorsome bacon I had ever eaten. I had once seen listed on a Thai menu "deep-fried pig vermiform appendix." Bacon seemed like a classically American food, yet it was plainly the Thais who knew exactly what to do with a pig.

"Yeah," Pugh said, "I think you're right that Mango's involvement means something here. Or nothing. Well, not nothing. A warm smile, a pretty dick, and a shapely butt, it could be. Or maybe more; we'll have to see. As for ethical considerations, it sounds like you know your man. But with your permission, may I please point out that when our own esteemed Prime Minster Samak was asked how Thailand could do so much business with the Burmese generals — who run what might be the nastiest police state in the world — the PM said, oh, the generals are praying Buddhists, after all, so how bad can they be?"

"Point taken," I said. "But Griswold has no history of being a hypocrite."

"The Buddha never specifically listed hypocrisy as a sin," Pugh said. "Though I think we have to consider it within the penumbra of Dharma teachings. See, I'm not at all a spiritual strict constructionist." He grinned at us and chortled.

I told Pugh about Griswold's consulting a Thai fortune-teller — renowned, supposedly — and the seer's dire predictions of "bloodshed" and "great sorrow" in Griswold's life.

"You have no name of this man?"

"No, unfortunately."

"He could be a charlatan. Or perhaps not. It would be good to know which one it is. If Mr. Gary consulted him previously and is now in distress, he will almost certainly consult him again."

I said, "So, some Thai fortune-tellers are frauds and some are not?"

"Are some American corporate CEOs frauds, and some are not?" Pugh asked. I had no clue from his look what he was thinking.

"Then let me ask you this. Do fortune-tellers ever give financial advice?"

"If it's requested. Generally on small matters. When to buy a lottery ticket. What's a lucky number for a lottery ticket. Perhaps on larger financial matters on some occasions. The scale of the question and the scale of the answer could both conceivably flow from the depth of the seer's client's pockets."

Timmy said, "Thailand looks like it's awash in money — all this urban building and development. Couldn't Griswold have been involved in something completely legitimate that then fell apart? And he'd gotten other investors involved, and now they want their money back or something, and Griswold is afraid of them? I read that sometimes in Thailand business disputes turn violent. Business-related drive-by shootings are not unheard of here. Isn't that a possibility?"

"Very good," Pugh said. "You two have done your homework. I've been shot at eleven times and hit twice." He hiked up his polo shirt and then tugged it down again, giving us a quick glimpse of a jagged scar on his mocha-colored rib cage. "This one was in broad daylight right over on Sukhumvit Road, not far from here. Timothy, I'll show you the other scar sometime, if you're interested. You'll get quite an eyeful."

"Oh, I don't have to."

"Aren't you just a little bit curious?" He leered mischievously.

Timmy actually blushed. "Oh, I can't really say."

Pugh laughed and had some more bacon. He said, "We can speculate all we want about what Griswold was, or is, involved in financially. I think, though, that our most fruitful approach will simply be to find the guy, sit him down, and say, 'Hey, Bud, what the heck is going on here?' And then, one way or another, get him to tell us."

I described to Pugh our findings of the night before: The visit to Geoff Pringle's building and the night security guard's apparent suspicion that there was something very odd or even sinister about Pringle's fatal fall from his balcony; the visit to Griswold's apartment and our discovery that he himself had been there briefly as recently as two weeks earlier; the revelation that someone named Kawee was watering Griswold's plants and praying at a shrine in his apartment; then the news that an "unfriendly" man on a motorbike had been trying to locate

Griswold. I told Pugh I had obtained a potentially useful piece of data — the unfriendly man's mobile telephone number.

Pugh said, "You're off to a good start. Very professional."

"Well, yes."

"I think I'd like to work with you on this."

"Great. But I thought it was I who would be interviewing you, in a sense. To make sure you were the real thing. I assumed on the phone and from your Web site that you were. And obviously you are legitimate — despite the confusion that your name inevitably produces."

"Yeah, well, Mr. Don, it works both ways. I needed, also, to see if you were the real deal and not one of the doofus-y, alcohol-besotted farang shmucks we often see doing PI work here in Bangkok. And you certainly are for real, which is excellent. So, let's do it. Understand, though, that you'll need me a whole lot more than I'll need you in finding Mr. Gary and providing a good outcome for his situation, whatever it turns out to be."

This all sounded plausible enough. But I had to ask Pugh, "What is it that you think you'll be able to bring to the investigation that I won't be able to manage?"

"Your survival, my friend," he said. "Your survival."

§ § § §

Pugh and I agreed on the financial terms and carved out a division of labor for the next day or two. He would identify the owner of the phone number I'd gotten from Griswold's building manager. He would use police sources to find out if Gary Griswold's name had appeared in any police report in the past six months. (Pugh said reporters were sometimes bribed to keep the deaths of foreigners from turning up in newspapers and scaring the tourists away.) And he would get hold of the police report on Geoff Pringle's death — which had been reported in the *Key West Citizen* but not in any of the Bangkok papers.

One of my jobs would be to track down plant-watering, shrine-visiting Kawee by purchasing the promise of Griswold's super and his security guard to phone me when Kawee showed up again. I had brought along my international cell phone and had picked up a SIM card and five thousand baht worth of minutes at a 7-Eleven. My other job would be to find Mango. Pugh said it was not a common Thai name or nickname. He would call a number of gay sources — mainly bar and massage-parlor owners — and try to come up with leads among the Bangkok ex-pat gay population that I could follow up on. Pugh guessed that Mango had had other farang admirers.

When Pugh had eaten all his bacon and strolled out of the hotel, Timmy said, "Mr. Rufus might have an easier time finding Mango than we will. Don't you think Rufus might be gay? I'm sure the guy was flirting with me."

"Yeah, he was, a little. But I wouldn't make anything of it. With all his wives and girlfriends, I'd be surprised if it was any kind of invitation. It's just that Thais are a casually sexualized people. They are generally modest about it in public, but they are very comfortable in their own sexual skin. Puritanism, Catholic guilt, all that — it's as if they never heard of any of it. And when it comes to gender, they can be pretty fluid about it. They enjoy the humor of sex, too, and you were getting some of that from Rufus."

"It's a bit startling."

"You'll get used to it."

"I don't know whether I can adapt. All I know of Asian gay sexuality is India, a nation of Larry Craigs."

"You won't have to work hard adjusting. Other than over in the fuck-show district, there's nothing at all insistent about Thai sexuality. This is not Provincetown during carnival week. It's just part of what's in the air. And you need do nothing more than breathe it, if you so choose."

"Oh, so it's only one element in addition to the scent of jasmine and the occasional whiff of raw sewage."

"Ah, there's my observant Georgetown grad."

"What do you think Pugh meant when he said he needed to help you survive? That certainly got my attention."

"He meant survive in the professional sense, would be my guess," I said, apparently unconvincingly, given the look I got back.

CHAPTER EIGHT

The word *voluptuous* when used about a person suggests amplitude, and yet here was maybe the most voluptuous human being I had ever met, and he was quite small. Kawee Thaikhiew was Lolita, he was a Caravaggio boy siren, he was the twenty-year-old Truman Capote draped over that recamier in the 1948 dust jacket photo for *Other Voices, Other Rooms*. And all of the above weighed in at no more than a hundred twenty pounds.

Kawee wore ironed jeans and a pristine white tank top over his delicate brown chest. Around his neck, an amulet dangled on a gold chain with what looked like the image of an aged monk. He had flip-flops on his feet, so all could see and admire his toenails, carefully painted a resplendent fuchsia. His face was finely crafted and his luminous black eyes lightly mascaraed, his lips perceptibly glossier than most Thai lips, male or female. Kawee was the living, breathing embodiment of ambigenderal sensuality, and yet it was impossible to imagine any actual sex with this person who looked as if, during the act, he might easily snap in half.

Timmy and I had gone over to Griswold's condo to make a deal with Mr. Thomsatai on notifying us if Kawee turned up. After pocketing another thousand baht, Mr. Thomsatai said, "This is lucky for you. Kawee is upstairs now."

At first the boy — or boy-girl-man-woman; *katoey* is the nonjudgmental Thai term — tried to make a quick exit. We had badly frightened him. I tried to reassure him by brandishing my New York State PI license — he stared at it as if its script were in ancient Pali — and I also produced a letter from Ellen Griswold attesting that I represented her in a search for her missing brother-in-law.

"I don't know where Mr. Gary go," Kawee told us in a breathy voice, his eyes fixed not on Timmy and me but on the exit. We had found him placing offerings at Griswold's shrine.

He had left one marigold garland, a lotus bud, and an open can of Pepsi with a straw sticking out of it.

I said, "Mr. Gary may be in trouble — we know that — but we are not the trouble. We need to let him know that we can help him with his trouble. You can help him by helping us do that. Don't you want to help Mr. Gary? Isn't he your friend?"

"Yes, he my friend."

"How do you talk to him? By telephone?"

"No, no telephone. He tell me no telephone."

"When did he tell you this? Have you seen him?"

"He just phone me. On my mobile. But he doesn't have phone. He call from Internet shop."

"In Bangkok?"

"I don't know."

"When was the last time?"

"Before two days."

I asked Kawee if Mr. Gary was his boyfriend.

"No, no boyfriend. Friend friend. Mr. Gary help me so much. He is kind man."

"Where did you meet Mr. Gary?"

"At Paradisio. That gay sauna for meet people for sex. Most farang just want to fuck Thai boy. But Mr. Gary, he love the Buddha. He is kind. I help him, and he help me. I take care of flowers and I make offerings until he come back."

"When will he come back? Did he say?"

"No. Maybe long time. He send me money for offerings — and for me. He help me very much."

"But he does come here sometimes, late at night. Do you know why?"

"No. Mr. Gary no say."

I asked Kawee how money from Mr. Gary was sent to him. In an envelope via motorbike messenger, he said. Once a week, to the room he shared with three others in Sukhumvit. Then the messenger picked up Griswold's mail, which Kawee had collected from his friend's mailbox. Here was a direct link to Griswold that looked as if it would be not too difficult to follow.

I said, "Did Mr. Gary tell you why he is not living here at home?"

"No. He not tell me. Maybe Mango know."

At last. "Who is Mango?"

"He was Mr. Gary's boyfriend. But he hiding, I think."

"They are no longer boyfriends?"

"They fight."

"Fight?"

"Big argue. Mango angry Mr. Gary."

"Mango made Mr. Gary angry? What did he do?"

"No, Mango angry. He say Mr. Gary bring bad luck. Mango make merit, he say, but Mr. Gary bad luck. Bad men try hurt Mango. He must hide."

"In Bangkok?"

"I think so. I saw him many time."

"Where did you see him?"

"Paradisio."

"How can he hide in a public place?"

"No, Paradisio safe for him. The bad men he hiding, they no go there. They not gay, he don't think."

"When did you last see Mango at Paradisio?"

"Last Sunday. He like go Sunday. Me also. Sunday busy."

"Today is Sunday. Will you be going today?"

"I think so."

"Would you mind if Timmy and I tagged along?"

"Tagalog?"

"Came with you. Maybe Mango will be there and you can point him out to us."

Kawee thought about this. "Are you gay?"

"Yes, we are. Timothy and I are partners."

He smiled for the first time. "Which one top?"

Timmy said, "Oh, really."

"It depends on the phases of the moon," I said.

"Ahh."

We made a plan to meet at the entrance to Paradisio at two.

"Maybe you meet Mango," Kawee said. "Anyway, you have too much fun!"

Timmy said, "Too much fun is just barely enough for us," and Kawee looked over at him and smiled coyly.

§ § § §

"The motorbike guy is a bad actor," Pugh said. "I don't mean a bad actor like Jean-Claude Van Damme is a bad actor, or Adam Sandler. I mean he's a mean and dangerous man with a criminal history that you want to be very, very careful of."

We were back at the hotel and about to head out for lunch when Pugh phoned me.

"Rufus, you're obviously well connected with the police you think so poorly of."

"The police are still the police. But this man's name I obtained from a friend at AIS, the mobile phone service. A police official, did, however, run the name for me. The information is reliable too. This helpful acquaintance is a captain to whom I send a case of Johnny Walker once a month on his birthday."

"He sounds old."

"And wise. And often informative. As today. I won't recite the motorbike man's full Thai name. You'll never remember it. He goes by the nickname Yai. That means large. Perhaps his name should be Yai Leou, big and bad."

"I'm making a linguistic note."

"Yai served two years on an assault charge. He ran his motorbike over an Austrian man who chastised Yai for driving on the sidewalk. Yai turned the bike around and drove into the man, knocking him to the ground. Then he turned around and drove over the man a second time, causing serious injuries. It was lucky for Yai that the victim was a tourist. If he had done the same thing to a Thai of any consequence, he might have been facing considerable hard time."

"And what are Yai's current pastimes?"

"This is unclear. Some of his associates are people with likely narcotics connections and others have probably been involved with the trafficking of human beings — sex slaves for our pious Muslim brothers in Riyadh and certain C of E chappies in Belgravia. Yai, my sources believe, is at this time freelancing. So we must learn more about Yai, but we must take great care in doing so."

"I'll leave that up to you."

"Yes, for now."

Rufus had made a number of calls to gay bar owners and the bars' habitués to get a bead on Mango. I told him we might not need any of that, for I had found and spoken with Kawee, who not only knew who Mango was but where he sometimes could be found.

"Ah, Paradisio. One of the few revered institutions of Bangkok I have not had the privilege of setting foot in."

"They would let you in even if you're not gay. I'll bet you could fake it."

He laughed. "Could, and after a beer or two, have done. Was Kawee otherwise helpful in our search for Mr. Gary?"

I told Pugh what little I had learned from Kawee. I said that since Griswold phoned Kawee from time to time, I had urged him to tell Griswold that friendly people were looking for him and wanted to help him out of whatever trouble he was in. I dictated Kawee's multi-syllabic full name, which the young katoey had somewhat reluctantly provided me, so that Pugh could check Kawee's mobile phone records and try to ascertain which Internet café Griswold had been phoning from. This could help locate him in a particular Bangkok neighborhood, if he was in the city.

Pugh said he would do this, and he asked me to alert him if I was able to track down Mango. "I'm thinking," Pugh said, "that we should stake out Paradisio and, if Mango appears, tail him. I have staff who can do this, and quite expertly."

I said that sounded good. "If I meet Mango, I'll follow him outside when he leaves and pass him off to your team. But how will your guys recognize me?"

"I have already seen to that."

"You photographed me? I missed that, Rufus."

"No, your photo appeared in the *Albany Times Union* on July twelfth, two years ago. This was after you got into what the newspaper said was a sarcastic back-and-forth with a gay-baiting judge while you were testifying at a client's trial, and you were cited for contempt of court."

"Yes, I did get my picture in the paper that time. That fine cost me, too. It was twice what my fee was with that putz of a client. Anyway, the guy never paid me."

Pugh chuckled. "I wish I had been there to see it. Keep in mind, however, that in Thailand, the fine would have been even higher for causing a man of high office to lose face. You might have had to pay with your profession. Or an organ or two."

"I'll keep that in mind."

"Good. Here we have other ways of getting a job done. We don't ride an elephant to catch a grasshopper."

"As it relates to the current situation, that's a bit cryptic for me," I said. "But maybe it will all come clear a little later."

Pugh said, "You bet it will."

CHAPTER NINE

"Yes, I will talk to you," Mango said, glancing quickly around the pool area. "But not here. Private. We go to cubicle."

Kawee had spotted Mango by the swimming pool soon after we had arrived at Paradisio. Most of the men lying on sun-splashed chaises trying to darken themselves were farangs. Most of the Thais sat on chairs in the palmy shade, trying to keep from getting any darker. Mango was among the Thais.

Kawee had approached Mango first and showed him my letter of introduction from Ellen Griswold and my PI license, which I had tucked into the towel I was wearing. Even as I wielded this paraphernalia of farang kreng jai, Mango looked skeptical, even a bit anxious. But I came over and assured him that I had been sent to help Griswold if he needed any help. Mango should have been further reassured by our meeting under circumstances where he had to know he could maintain masterly control.

I saw why Mango made some gay hearts skip a beat. Lean and fit in a graceful and seemingly effortless way, and taller than most Thais, Mango was luminously caramel colored, like some flavorsome Thai street-stall sweet, with aristocratic Asian cheekbones under big dark peasant eyes and eyelashes the length and elegance of the architectural details on a pagoda. You could imagine how happy a tiny songbird might be perched on one of Mango's overhangs. His black hair was cut short, almost monklike, though the tranquil confidence he projected was outward- instead of inward-looking. When he said "we can go to cubicle," he gave a flash of smile with a hint of humor in it, despite the apprehension he had to be feeling.

We climbed a winding, Busby Berkeley-style staircase from the pool and café area to the second-floor locker and cubicle area, all of it decorated more like a Hyatt or Marriott than like the illegal-immigrant detention-center trappings commonly found in gay saunas in the US. The message seemed to be that clients were here for pleasure, not punishment. The music flowing out of the ceiling and through the mutely lighted spaces was not dance-club-throb but Fats Waller sweet-and-easy.

Along a long corridor, men lingered, conversed quietly with one another, greeted friends and acquaintances, and cruised unhurriedly. There was no rush, for it appeared there was sure to be plenty of sanuk to go around. Most of the men were Thais, their average age 28.3, I guessed. There were some young farangs, too, but the foreigners' average age I estimated at 58.3, a number that also described many of their waist sizes. I heard British and German accents as we passed several dozen men, some of them Americans, and what I guessed were Swedish voices. Here was famed Southeast Asian sexual tourism, that quaint term.

Mango led me into a raised cubicle, slid the door shut, and latched it. Again, it was less like a flophouse cell than like a Thai countryside hut, with dark walls and a floor cushioned with vinyl padding and penlight-sized illumination down low on one end. There was no cot or bed, just as in Thai village houses, where people generally ate, slept and socialized on the floor. The top of the cubicle was open, and the ambient noise included both low voices and the odd moan or happy yelp from nearby cubicles.

Mango and I each flopped down and sat facing each other with our backs against opposite walls, our towels unremoved in a businesslike way. I told Mango how worried Gary Griswold's family and friends were, and I thanked him for agreeing to talk to me, despite the falling-out that he and Griswold apparently had had.

"Gary treat me very bad," Mango said. "But I don't want him get hurt. *I* don't want to get hurt, too," he said, "and some men want me say where Gary. I tell them, I don't *know* where Gary. They think I lying but I not. So I hide at my friend house. But my friend go back to Germany. So I bored. Maybe I find other friend. You have condo in Bangkok?"

"No, I live in Albany, New York."

"America."

"Yes."

"I had American friend. Five. No, six."

"Six years ago?"

"No, six American friend. California. Tennessee. Boston. Harrisburg, P-A. Ohio. And…Mr. Mike come from Alaska."

"You lived with each of these men? They were boyfriends?"

"I like foreign men. Yes. I don't like Thai so much. No money, ha-ha."

"Aren't there Thai gay men with money?"

"Yes. But they just like other Thai gay men with money."

"What about hooking up with a Thai gay man with no money? Just for friendship and for love?"

"Oh, I have Thai boyfriend. Donnutt. I love Donnutt. We build house in Chonburi. Live Chonburi later. Now Donnutt in Oslo with Knute."

I said, "Did your falling out with Gary have anything to do with your many boyfriends, by chance? Donnutt, Mike, Tennessee, and so on? Were any of these fellows in your life during your time with Gary? If so, did he know about them?"

Mango looked down at his lap. I noticed for the first time that a few lines of age were beginning to show around his neck. Was he pushing thirty? Would he accumulate enough of a nest egg for him and Donnutt to finish their house in Chonburi before all the foreign "friends" moved on to fresher pickings?

Mango said quietly, "Gary not understand Thai man."

"He thought your relationship would be monogamous? No sex or relationships with other men?"

"I thought he know. He like Thai, so I thought he know Thai. He don't know. He find out about Werner and ask me if other ones. I tell him. Big argument. I leave."

"Who was Werner?"

"From Cologne. I have sex with him two time. Two! Too sad. Gary make me too sad."

"So you had been living with Gary in his condo?"

"Sometime. I keep my place in Sukhumvit. It good I keep. It okay. It cheap."

I asked Mango if Gary was having any money problems that he knew of.

"No money problems. Gary rich. He good to me. Generous. Kind. I put money in bank in Chonburi for house build with Donnutt."

"Did Gary know about Donnutt?"

"He know Donnutt my friend."

"Some Thai men," I said, "have longtime, sometimes lifelong, relationships with foreign men. It sounds as if you never wanted that."

A wilted smile. "Not without Donnutt."

"How long have you and Donnutt been boyfriends? How old were you when the relationship began?"

"Eleven."

"You were eleven years old?"

"Yes. In our village. Now we both thirty-two."

"Didn't Gary understand that history when you explained it to him?"

"No, he jealous. He want I want him only. I love Gary. He Buddhist. He love the Buddha. I teach him. I teach him pray. I teach him meditate. I teach him make merit. I love Gary, but Gary no understand Thai."

"Thais are not so sexually possessive, I guess, as farangs tend to be."

"Possess? Possess just house, motorbike. No possess for sex. Sex for pleasure. Sex for fun. Like food. Like air."

"Sanuk."

"Yes, sanuk. But I love Gary. I am sad."

"Is it possible," I said, "that Gary was upset about something else, and that affected how he reacted to Werner and your other somewhat-numerous revelations?"

"I don't think so," Mango said.

As he spoke, I was working hard now to concentrate on what he was saying, as the two men in the next cubicle were getting up a nice head of steam. It was plainly a Thai and a farang, because one of them was making little cries of *oh-oh-oh* — the farang — and the other one was uttering little squeals of *oi-oi-oi* — the Thai.

Mango seemed unaware of any of this. It was just another feature of the Bangkok atmosphere, like the aroma of jasmine. He went on. "Gary not angry at other people, just me. Gary happy then. He rich, he say, and he get more rich, and then he make big merit. Gary so happy. But after I go, something happen. He not happy. I hear this from Kawee. Gary leave, he hide."

"He was going to become more rich?"

Mango thought about this. His towel had shifted a bit, and now another of his numerous excellent attributes was dimly visible. That and the *oh-oh-oh-oi-oi-oi* racket next door weren't making my job any easier at what plainly was about to become a critical juncture in the investigation.

Mango said, "Big investment."

"Investment in what?"

"I don't know."

"He didn't talk about it at all?"

"No."

"How do you know it was an investment?"

"He say he go bank, get money for big investment. Make rich, make merit."

"What was the merit he was going to make?"

"No say. But for the Buddha. For the Dharma. For the Sangha."

"The Sangha. That's the monkhood? Was he going to give money to the monks? To a monk?"

"No monk, maybe. Maybe seer. Gary go to seer. Gary like seer. Seer tell Gary many things. He say Gary see blood. Gary people hurt. Then he say Gary make big merit, no blood, no hurt. Make bad luck good luck."

"Do you know who the seer was, Mango? Do you know his name and where he is?"

"Yes, he is soothsayer Khunathip Chantanapim, and he here in Bangkok."

I said, "Now we're getting somewhere," just as one of the chaps in the next cubicle got somewhere too.

§ § § §

Timmy and Sawee were not by the pool when I came downstairs, so Mango and I stepped into the nearby multi-tenanted labyrinthine steam room for a refreshing bout of heatstroke. Both of us had been feeling a certain amount of tension following our conversation about Griswold, though when we emerged from the busy steam room and headed for the cold showers some minutes later, much of that tension had been dissipated.

Mango told me how to reach him if I needed to talk to him again, and he gave a fairly detailed description of the two men who had threatened him two months earlier and roughed him up when he insisted that he had no idea where Griswold was. One of the two goons sounded like Yai, the motorcycle assault artist. Mango said he wished I — or somebody — could do something about these two. He needed some more foreign "friends" to keep his Chonburi house fund going, and keeping such a low profile was crimping his style in that regard.

Timmy reappeared a while later at poolside. "Where's Kawee?" I asked. "Is he okay?"

"Oh sure. He's in the shower, I think."

I told Timmy about my productive talk with Mango and about the news of the soothsayer who apparently talked

Griswold into some major Buddhist merit-making venture, probably involving a large amount of cash.

"Wow, this is the breakthrough you needed."

"I think so."

"Great," Timmy said, looking pleased but a little distracted.

"So. Are you having fun? No drive-by shootings? Plenty of smiles."

"You got it."

"But nothing worth mentioning?"

"Well. I guess I should tell you."

"Uh-huh."

"Well. It's this. I just spent a lovely hour and a half in a cubicle with Kawee." He actually smirked, something I wasn't sure I had ever seen him do.

"*Kawee?*"

More smirk, though faintly cracked this time.

"You and little katoey Kawee?"

"It was his idea. But it didn't take much coaxing, and I'm happy I did it because he's really quite delightful."

"Timothy. Don't your tastes generally run to — how shall I put it? — men a bit more butch?"

"Yes, obviously. But in the semidarkness that sweet lad is plenty butch enough, believe you me. Anyway, he's just so...so *nice.*"

"I'm...I'm be-dazed."

"Anyway, while he's a katoey, he's not transgendered in the full, clinical sense. He plans, for example, on keeping his dick. He's totally happy with it. As well he might be. Anyway, we didn't do much. Basically we just cuddled and chatted and then enjoyed some pleasant mutual slow self-abuse. He wanted to fuck me. He had four condoms — *four, mind you!* — stuffed inside his towel. But even with the condoms, that seemed to go well beyond our ground rules on these matters."

"I would say, yes, getting pounded up the butt by a well-hung Thai lady-boy is well outside our agreed-upon parameters."

"I didn't think you'd mind. I just assumed that once you and Mango got into a cubicle, nature would run its merry course."

"Timothy, why would you assume such a thing? On those exceedingly rare occasions when I do anything like that at all I never mix work in with it. Well, once I did and regretted it, as you well know. Really. I'm...I don't know quite what to say."

"So you and Mango didn't do it?"

"Of course not!"

"Weren't you in the steam room just now? I thought I saw you both come out."

"Yes, but we didn't do anything together. Give me some credit."

"Anyway, I'm just doing what you always say. It's the Henry James dictum. When in Venice, one must always try the squid in its own ink."

"Oh, that. I forgot. I hope Kawee wasn't too squidlike."

"Not too. Just enough."

"Well, you do seem to be adjusting to Thai customs and mores nicely. I suppose I should be grateful after all your ambivalence and fretting about coming here."

"The only question in my mind is, why didn't we come to Thailand sooner? Don, I have to say, now I do see what the attraction is. The Thais are just so comfortable being who and what they are, and so totally laid-back about life's simplest pleasures — tasty food, sunshine, flowers and trees, affectionate and playful sex. I see why people come here and...well, fall in love with this gosh-darn place!"

So. What was this going to mean? And he hadn't even seen the reclining Buddhas yet.

"Look," I said, "I'm glad you've come around. Both the Thai Ministry of Tourism and I are pleased. But I've got work to do. For one thing, I have to go get my phone and call Rufus and tell him he doesn't need to follow Mango when he comes out. Mango, I'm pretty much convinced, had a falling out with Griswold over the particulars of their relationship, nothing more, and is in no way part of whatever trouble Griswold is in. Maybe," I added, "I should tell Rufus he should consider following *you* around for a few days. Who knows what you'll be up to next?"

He did not smirk this time, but he did chuckle peculiarly.

When I retrieved my phone from my locker and told Pugh he could call off the stakeout, he said he was glad I had called and that he had been trying to reach me. He said a famous Thai soothsayer had died early that morning in a fall from a Bangkok apartment building, and there was reason to believe that the seer had had some connection to Gary Griswold.

CHAPTER TEN

"Khun Khunathip's," Pugh said, "is a death that will reverberate. Thai television will be all over it an hour from now, and tomorrow the Bangkok newspapers will be draped in jasmine and marigolds. This is a man whose counsel was sought by ministers of state, by generals of the army, by girl groups in hot pants. It's been rumored that even Jack has had his astrological chart blessed by Khun Khunathip."

We were seated in the front seat of Pugh's Toyota, parked in the soi outside Paradisio with the air-conditioning blasting. Timmy and Kawee had slogged through the heat over to Griswold's apartment to wait for me while I tried to figure out where they — and I — would be safest from whoever it was in Griswold's life who now seemed to be going around causing people to fall over railings and die.

I said, "Who is Jack?"

Pugh winked at me. "I hope you won't think less of me."

"Why would I not continue to hold you in high esteem?"

"Jack is how His Majesty the King is referred to by people I know who wish to discuss him in less-than-reverential tones and not pay a price for their insolence."

"I wasn't aware such people existed in Thailand."

"They do. But it's a crime to insult the king. People have gone to prison for it. *Lèse majesté.* You no longer run into this concept all that often in the twenty-first century. Not outside of Thailand."

"But flippantly calling King Bhumibol 'Jack' would seem to qualify as a slur, wouldn't it?"

"The queen," Pugh said, snickering now, "is Jackie. And the crown prince is Jack Junior."

"And the royal family has consulted this now-deceased famous soothsayer?"

"I have heard that this is so. I realize it sounds eerily like *Macbeth*. Or *Lear*. Or *Duck Soup*."

"Rufus, what did you major in at Chulalongkorn University? And Monmouth College? And let's not leave out Duke."

"I majored in English, minored in criminology. Does that explain a few things, Mr. Don?"

"It's a start."

"The thing about Khun Khunathip," Pugh went on, "is that the guy was good. His track record as a prophet was far better than most. This was partly a consequence, I believe, of his intuitive grasp of the way human lives are intertwined with astral forces most of us lack the subtlety of mind to discern. But it's long experience, too. Khun Khunathip had been a successful seer in third-century BC Nepal — what is now the Kingdom of Nepal — as well as in Mayan Mexico a millennium or so later. So the guy has simply had the time and opportunity to really get his shit together."

I looked over at Pugh, who remained poker-faced. His Toyota had a seated Buddha figure behind the steering wheel obscuring the speedometer, and some kind of stony doodad dangling by a pink string from the rearview mirror.

I said, "So I guess Mr. Khunathip will be sorely missed by many."

"He will."

"But only until he turns up elsewhere in time and geography to resume his career as a seer?"

"That depends. Khun Khunathip's karma could include some slippage, if I read this guy correctly. His returning as a moody bacterium on a monkey's hangnail cannot be ruled out."

Pugh went on to explain that his police sources had phoned him about the seer because they knew Pugh had been making inquiries about Gary Griswold. His sources had told him that Griswold's name had not turned up in any other context but that he figured in the fortune-teller's financial records. A Bangkok Bank check for the baht equivalent of six hundred fifty thousand US dollars had been made out to Khunathip and drawn on Griswold's account. The notation in the seer's records said the amount was a "fee."

I said, "How come the cops are so interested in Khunathip's financial records? In your mind, does this confirm that they suspect foul play?"

"Naturally they suspect foul play. That's what the police are in the business of suspecting. It must be said that the lives of the Royal Police of Thailand bustle with far more compelling pastimes, such as entrepreneurial activity. But foul play is still a thing that interests them in an offhand way, and this death looks funny. Khun Khunathip was not an imbiber, so an accidental tumble eighteen stories from his apartment balcony at three twenty a.m. is not a likely scenario. Was he watering his plants and slipped? The police think not. Suicide also appears unlikely. Khun Khunathip was a confident and contented man, according to his soothsayer colleagues. He was not at all displeased with his being afforded the opportunity to live out his present-day putrid corporeal existence consorting with the likes of generals and rock stars, not to mention Jack and Jackie. He showed no indication of wishing to take premature leave of any of that. That pretty much leaves getting tossed."

"So," I said, "will tomorrow's newspapers be burning up with speculation as to who might have done the tossing?"

Pugh snorted with amusement. "Oh no. First, it must be determined who the likeliest suspects are. Then, depending on who they are and on their exact position in Thai society — and depending on no other thing, really — speculation will or will not be permitted. Stay tuned, Mr. Don. Just you stay tuned."

I said I would do that, but meanwhile it seemed more urgent than ever that we locate Gary Griswold and help him extricate himself from whatever terrible trap he apparently had been caught in. That is, find Griswold plus his thirty-eight million, or whatever was left of it.

I told Pugh that Griswold had been sending Kawee money each week via motorbike messenger. I suggested that the next time the messenger showed up, we intercept him and use whatever means practicable to get him to lead us to Griswold.

Pugh liked that idea and told me again he thought I was much more competent than the other drunken-stumblebum farang PIs he knew in Bangkok. I thanked him for the compliment.

I phoned Kawee on his mobile and learned that the messenger's visits were not entirely predictable, but he usually turned up on a Monday or Tuesday in the early evening. And if Kawee wasn't home, the messenger would leave the envelope with the whiskey seller who had a stall at the end of the soi.

Kawee said Timmy wanted to speak with me and put him on the phone.

"I don't know what this might be worth," Timmy said, "but Kawee showed me the crate in a ground-floor storage room where Griswold kept some of his excess belongings. There was a laptop computer inside its carrying case inside the box. I brought it upstairs for you to have a look at."

"Excellent. Great. Was there anything else of interest?"

"Not so far as I could tell. It was mostly books and empty suitcases."

"Guard that computer with your life," I said, "until I can get over there. I'm going to check e-mails at the Internet café by the Topmost, and then I'll be right over."

I told Pugh what Timmy had found, and he said, "Now you guys are cookin' with gas."

Pugh drove me the few blocks over to the Topmost. While he drove, he took a call from a friend at AIS, Kawee's mobile phone service. Pugh learned that the digital Skype phone through which Griswold communicated with Kawee was on an account at an Internet café in On Nut, in eastern Bangkok, on the way to Suvarnabhumi Airport. Pugh said that within three hours he would have a surveillance team in place inside and outside the café, with each team member carrying a copy of the photo of Griswold that Ellen Griswold had provided for me.

"We're on our way," I said to Pugh.

"Ih." This was the common Thai word, or just sound, that was somewhere between an exhalation and a grunt, and whose meaning seemed to land somewhere between "yes" and "I acknowledge that at this moment you physically exist in my presence."

I said, "Your team will tail Griswold if he shows up at the café, but they won't spook him, right?"

"Ih."

Pugh said he needed an hour or two in his office, about a mile away on Surawong, to bring his team together and get photos of Griswold copied and distributed. I said I would stay at the Internet café until he picked me up, that I needed to check my mail. And anyway I wanted to do some online digging.

The Internet café was a small storefront family operation, with eight or nine computers and farang tourists and Thai teenagers seated at several of them. Two of the owners' kids were snoozing on straw mats in the middle of the floor, and a middle-aged Thai woman sat operating a sewing machine just inside the front door. Here was an Internet café where you could check your MySpace or Facebook accounts and have your hemline lowered at the same time.

My Hotmail account was up to here with the usual crap, but my eye snagged on EllenG1958, and I clicked open the message. It read:

Dear Don,

This is to thank you in advance for everything I am assuming you have done to locate Gary, but it turns out that all your good exertions have been unnecessary. We have heard from Gary, and he is perfectly okay! Isn't that terrific news?

Gary is fine, his assets are intact, and he is just incredibly embarrassed over his being out of touch and with all the fuss that's been raised. You must have been closing in on him, because he heard about your being in Bangkok and your searching for him on Bill's and my behalf. Gary is feeling like such a dope at this point, in fact, that he would rather not see you personally and urges that you settle up with any expenses incurred in the course of your investigation and just come on home to Albany — where spring is finally showing signs of breaking out!

Look, I know. You're saying, what kind of BS is this? So let's just cut to the chase. What I'm saying to you is, I accept Gary's explanation for his freak-out — it had to do with a personal rather than financial crisis — and Bill and I are choosing to wrap this up. It's my money, so it's my call. Enjoy a few more days in the Land of Smiles, if you like, on my nickel. And be assured that the terms of your contract with me will be honored in all respects.

Let me know, please, that you have received this message, and reply with an Albany ETA when you have one.

Thanks again for your professionalism and for your keen interest in my incorrigible ex-husband's continued well-being.

Fondly,

Ellen Griswold

I closed and saved the message, logged off, and then sat there, the meter running at sixty baht an hour, about a buck seventy-five. One of the kids asleep on the floor behind me moaned, in the grip of a nightmare, I guessed. I sat for a while longer. The air-conditioning was far preferable to the pounding heat outside, though the café smelled of German underarm deodorant and Thai fish sauce.

I got up, paid my fee, and went outside. Now Bangkok felt not so much molten as molting, as if, in the heat, the city was shedding its skin or other outer layer in my presence, and what was now exposed was formless and incomprehensible to a wandering and lost farang like me. I loved Bangkok, but it seemed to be making a fool of me. I wished I knew why. What had I done to it?

Oh, but wait a minute. Now I had a rational thought. The thought was this: *No, it's not Bangkok that's jerking me around in some cruel and unusual way. Nuh-uh.* It wasn't the *place.* Bangkok itself was just a large, traffic-choked Asian city full of basically nice Thai people — drive-by shooters notwithstanding — who loved to laugh and believed in ghosts and ate great food. No, it was not Bangkok making an ass of me. Of course it wasn't. What a silly thought. It was the Griswolds.

I looked around and then ducked into an alleyway leading to a couple of laundry service holes-in-the-wall. They were closed on Sunday and the area was relatively quiet. I had Ellen Griswold's cell number and dialed it, 001 for the US, then the area code and number. It was six fifteen p.m. in Bangkok and — swiftly doing the math — seven fifteen a.m. the same day in Loudonville, New York.

"This is Ellen. Please leave a message."

Beep.

I cut the connection and put my phone away. I walked out and stood on the sidewalk for a few minutes — or was it fifteen? — and then walked over to the Topmost. I retrieved the room key, took the elevator to the unlucky sixth floor, went into 606, and lay down on the bed with a mild headache. I lay there for half an hour or so. Then I took an aspirin and walked back over to the Internet café.

When I Googled Khun Khunathip, the Thai soothsayer, I got over a thousand hits. The man was indeed a big deal. There were news photos of him at Buddhist New Year outdoor gatherings bestowing tidings of good luck on the throngs. In his company on other occasions were ministers of state, princesses, movie stars, industrial magnates. Several news stories reported Khun Khunathip's acumen in forecasting the military coup of a few years earlier that sent the thought-to-be-corrupt but still democratically elected prime minister into exile and installed the junta that had run the country until recently. You had to wonder if the seer's prescience about the coup came from charting the heavens or from a discreet phone call.

Although Khun Khunathip seemed to be the foremost figure in the pantheon of Thai soothsayers, his was a crowded field of practitioners. One survey said about a quarter of Thais regularly sought life guidance from a *mo duu*, or "seeing doctor," on matters ranging from family to love relationships to money to auspicious dates for marrying or having children. Some of the seers were neighborhood men and women, often with humble stalls outside Buddhist temples, who charged several dollars for a consultation. Others were big-time operators who advised the high-and-mighty and collected substantial fees for themselves or for temples whose abbots were in a position to dispense next-life merit points to present-life sinners.

Among the other celeb seers was one Pongsak Sutiwipakorn, who had failed to predict the last military coup but had made headlines much more recently when he had publicly forecast yet another — upcoming — coup by the end of April. A third popular seer, Khun Surapol Sutharat, got the press's attention by insisting that his charts offered incontrovertible proof that there would *not* be a military coup anytime soon. A fourth seer, Thammarak Visetchote, had recently been making a name for himself by advising a group of younger army officers who were known to be fed up with their older commanding officers and with the old guard's corrupt ways. Seer Thammarak's specialty was numerological forecasts. Again, I wondered how much these guys had in common with Nostradamus and how much with Karl Rove.

I printed out some of the data on the seers and stuffed the pages into my pocket before venturing outside and walking around the corner to the food stalls on hectic Rama IV Road. The sun was setting, but the traffic-fouled air was still suffocating. I thought Timmy and Kawee might appreciate some eats, so I picked up some cold diced pork salad with lime juice and galangal, a bag of cooked jasmine rice, and a half liter of fish soup in a plastic sack. For a snack, I had some pineapple chunks on a stick, passing up the deep-fried cicadas.

When I walked back to the Internet shop, I saw Pugh there looking up and down the street. His car was illegally parked, half on the narrow strip of sidewalk and half sticking out in the soi, and plainly he was looking for me. When he spotted me, he urgently beckoned. As I walked up to Pugh, I could not tell what the look on his face meant, only that his news, if any, was going to be bad.

CHAPTER ELEVEN

"Both of them?" I said. "They took both Timmy and Kawee?"

"I'm afraid so, yes, Mr. Don."

"But why Timmy? They may think Kawee can lead them to Griswold. But what's the point of dragging Timothy along? To me, that doesn't add up."

We were in Pugh's Toyota banging along Sathorn Soi 1 toward Griswold's condo. The call had come to Pugh from one of his innumerable police department snitches — the Johnny Walker brigades, he had called them — alerting him that four armed men had arrived at Griswold's building half an hour earlier. They had pistol-whipped the security guard and ordered Mr. Thomsatai to take them up to Griswold's apartment and let them in. They then forced the condo's two occupants, a Thai lady-boy and an older farang, to leave with them in the black SUV they had arrived in.

I said, "Thomsatai. That degenerate. They bought him."

"Possibly."

We lurched around the corner onto Soi Nantha. The sun was down now, and the sky was infused with a gold even richer than that of the spires on the temples over near the king's palace along the Chao Phraya River, a mile or two north of us. Pugh slowed a bit for the speed bump behind the Austrian Embassy, then hurtled past Paradisio, its entryway thick with Sunday day-off comings and goings.

"But it was Thomsatai who phoned the police?" I asked.

"He had to. The security guard would have notified his superiors, who would have acted. They have a reputation to protect, for business reasons."

"And the guard is okay?"

"Apparently."

"That's good. It means they are not simply gunning people down. They want to get what they want to get. In some cases, anyway."

Neither of us spoke out loud of the balcony-plunge deaths of Geoff Pringle and then the famous fortune-teller.

I asked if anybody got a description of the car.

"Generally, but no tag number. The traffic police have been alerted to watch for a black four-by-four with tinted windows containing four men and their two abductees."

"Is anything likely to come of that?"

As Griswold's building came into view, Pugh said, "It's a pricey car. Some enterprising officer might view it as a mark for a quick two-hundred-baht hit and then discover it has captives inside it. We would need good luck for that," Pugh added, and tooted his car horn three times, one for the Buddha, one for the Dharma, his teachings, and one for the monks who preserve the Buddha's wisdom.

We pulled in behind a cop car that was parked in front of the apartment building, pink bougainvillea petals from a nearby bush already gathering on its blue hood. A second car from GUTS security services was parked nearby, and a new younger and bigger guard stood watch at the sentry hut. A few of the building's occupants and some neighbors had gathered, but they seemed to be keeping their distance.

"There must have been witnesses," I said, as we headed into the building. "There was still some daylight when they did it."

Pugh said, "Do you really think any of these people would describe what they saw, and by so doing establish their existence inside what most of my fellow countrymen regard as the diseased and capricious minds of the police? Dream on, Khun Don, dream on."

A plainclothes detective and his uniformed associate had Mr. Thomsatai in a cubicle off a polished marble lobby of the type that once must have housed royalty but was common now in luxury apartment buildings. Was there a finite supply of marble in the world, as with fossil fuels? This was surely the case, but which would run out first? If Timmy had been there, he would have had an informed opinion on this question. But he wasn't, and I wanted to strangle to death until he lay in a heap on the shiny marble floor whoever had taken him from me.

Mr. Thomsatai glanced at Pugh and me when we came in, then away. This guy was guilty of something, probably practically everything. Why had the condo association hired this conscienceless crook? Thomsatai had violated two of the five explicit moral precepts of Buddhism — no lying, no stealing — and yet here he was, playing the aggrieved victim. I did not, however, walk over and kick him hard, as I was impelled to do.

Pugh politely *wai*-ed the plainclothes officer — raised palms together, a small bow — and the cop wai-ed him back. A round-faced man in his forties with an expertly shaped pile of gleaming black hair on his head, the detective was the senior Thai in the room, but he plainly knew and respected Pugh, for his abilities perhaps, or his Johnny Walker.

Pugh introduced me to the two cops as the "boyfriend" of Timothy Callahan. It was given as a neutral description and received that way. Pugh also told Detective Panu Pansittivorakul that I was a private investigator searching for a missing American, Gary Griswold.

"I am aware of that," Panu said with no particular expression. "How are you making out with your search, Mr. Don?"

"Nothing yet," I said. "But we have some ideas. I think we can assume that this abduction is in some way tied to Gary Griswold's having gone into hiding. Has anybody IDed any of the four goons?"

"Unfortunately, no. We have descriptions, but no one recognized any of them. Not the security guard, not Mr. Thomsatai."

I said to Thomsatai, "Could one of them possibly have been the unfriendly man on the motorcycle who paid you to phone him when Mr. Gary came around? He sounds like a good bet to me — the sort of man who, if there was a good kidnapping in the works, wouldn't dream of being left out. Wasn't Mr. Unfriendly Motorbike perhaps one of the four?"

Thomsatai looked up and lied so unconvincingly that beads of sweat popped out on his forehead. He was his own human polygraph. "No, no. I would recognize that bad man. These men were others. No motorbike man, no, no."

Pugh motioned for Panu to step aside and spoke to him quietly. I couldn't hear what was said, but the detective nodded at the uniformed officer. The cop then walked over and picked up a fat Bangkok telephone book from a desk and smashed it against the side of Mr. Thomsatai's head.

Timmy wasn't there to object, so I had to do it. "Rufus, don't, please. What happened to the elephant and the grasshopper?"

"Who were they?" Panu demanded of Mr. Thomsatai, who sat looking stunned and close to tears. Panu then switched to Thai and barked a string of orders I could not understand. The cop picked up the phone book again, and when I stepped in his direction, Panu snapped something to Pugh in Thai that from his body language plainly meant, "Get this farang dickhead out of here."

Pugh, not looking as embarrassed as I wanted him to, indicated that I should follow him out of the cubicle.

That's when Mr. Thomsatai said, "Yes, now I remember! Yes, yes, one of them was the man on the motorbike who was looking for Mr. Gary."

I looked at Pugh in a funny way whose meaning he correctly understood to be, "Can we trust any of this?"

Then my cell phone rang. I checked the number but the caller's ID was blocked. They all watched me — they knew it wasn't going to be a lovely invitation for Sunday brunch, and I knew it too. As Panu pointed and the uniformed cop quickly led Mr. Thomsatai out of the cubicle, I flipped open the phone.

"Hello."

"Don?"

"Yes, yes."

"It's Timothy."

"Timmy, can you talk?"

"Well, yes. That's why I'm calling."

"Of course. So what's the deal?"

"The deal is, they want Griswold. They will trade Kawee and me for Griswold."

"I see."

"That's about it. I'm not supposed to say any more. Oh, except for one thing."

"What's that?"

"They said I should tell you that we are on the fourteenth floor."

"Uh-huh. Okay."

"So that's about it, I guess. God, it's good to hear your voice."

"It's so good to hear yours."

"Just...please get Kawee and me out of this, if you can. Okay?"

"We will, we will. Can you tell me anything more about where you are?"

"No."

"Is Kawee okay? Are they treating you well enough?"

"Yes. We're both all right. So far. But one of the gentlemen hosting us just handed me a note asking me to tell you this. You have forty-eight hours to hand over Griswold."

"I understand."

"The note also has a big 'fourteen' on it. As in fourteenth floor. Get it?"

"I sure do."

"I'm supposed to hang up now. Bye."

"Good-bye, Timothy."

And then he was gone.

I repeated the conversation to Pugh and Detective Panu. "They're on the fourteenth floor somewhere. We're supposed to believe, apparently, that if we don't hand over Griswold within forty-eight hours, Timothy and Kawee will be shoved off a high balcony."

Pugh and Panu looked grim. "So sorry," Panu said.

"How many buildings are there in Bangkok fourteen or more stories high? Any idea?"

Pugh and Panu looked at each other. "Many hundreds," Pugh said. "Twenty-five years ago this would have been easy. Today Bangkok is Houston or Miami in that regard."

"Yes, but all you have to do is check all the fourteenth floors in Bangkok. That limits it, right? Even if there are, say, thirty-five hundred buildings with fourteen floors, you'd need only thirty-five hundred or, even better, sixty-five hundred officers to do a sweep. That doesn't seem insurmountable, does it? How many cops are there in Bangkok?"

Again, both Pugh and Detective Panu looked at each other gravely, and then at me. Panu said, "It's a matter of priorities." He gave a wan apologetic shrug.

"What we're talking about here," Pugh said, "is a déclassé Thai lady-boy, a nobody. And Mr. Timothy is a mere tourist, less than a nobody in Thailand. While it is true that tourists are gods in Thailand collectively speaking, individually they do not merit a tremendous amount of interest, particularly by the police. Am I putting that too harshly, Khun Panu?"

"A little, perhaps."

I said, "What if we paid for the services of the police? Would that help? Perhaps some senior officer, a captain or even general."

"It wouldn't hurt," Pugh said and glanced at Detective Panu, who shrugged mildly.

"Okay, you locate that official and I'll come up with the payoff. How much are we talking here? Twenty cases of Johnny Walker? Sixty? Or is it cash — US dollars? Euros?"

Panu said, "Bahts make a nice gift."

"How many bahts?"

"I've heard that fifty thousand can be helpful. That's about sixteen thousand dollars, I believe. Unless the US dollar has grown even weaker in the past hour."

"It's not just a question of national pride," Pugh said. "The baht is currently a sounder currency than the dollar. So your client, Mrs. Griswold, will provide the funding for this additional expense?"

I told them about the e-mail from Ellen Griswold calling me off the case because, she claimed, she had heard from her ex-husband, and he insisted he was in no danger and was merely embarrassed over some personal matter.

"Therefore," I said, "any further expenses will have to be met by Gary Griswold himself, who plainly *is* in big trouble. What this means is, we have to find Griswold fast. Then, (a) extract cash from him to pay off your for-profit police department to prod it to do its job, (b) find out from him what the hell is going on here so that we can help get him out of the rotten situation he's in, and (c) — if those two approaches fail — have Griswold in hand so that we can trade him for Timmy and Kawee and hope that he can hand over to these people, whoever they are, whatever it is they want from him, thus keeping Griswold from being shoved off a balcony."

Pugh said, "I like your *tour d'horizon*, Mr. Don. It's dead-on. And your willingness to sacrifice poor Mr. Gary, if necessary, in order to save your boyfriend and the katoey is admirable. There are degrees of innocence in this complex situation. And Mr. Gary, should he perish, would be fulfilling a karma plainly nudged into existence by his own klutziness. Not that we shouldn't do everything we can to save this wayward farang's sorry ass from whatever *mishigas* he has waded into of his own volition."

"Timmy, of course, would have a few choice words for me if he were here," I said. "He's a bit of a moral absolutist. He would allow for no cold-blooded choices of the type I have described. But let's just get him back, and then he can lecture all of us to his heart's content."

Pugh said, "And what if Mr. Gary is unwilling or, God forbid, unable to underwrite our efforts and those of the hardworking Royal Thai Police? What if we track him down and he laughs in our faces and tells us all to go do what is anatomically impossible for most people — not that there aren't exceptions to that rule at certain clubs I could mention in Surawong? Or what if we locate Mr. Gary and he is penniless? This could get complicated, I think."

"If Griswold can't produce whatever cash that's needed, then I'll go down to the ATM on Rama IV Road near the Topmost and stand there for half an hour with my MasterCard pumping bahts into a bag. That won't be a problem. Please go ahead right now and make whatever sleazy arrangements are appropriate with your sleazy police department's sleazy higher-ups."

Pugh and Panu both squinted at me and nodded.

I remembered Timmy's warnings to me about getting mixed up in this case. Timothy, the grounded one. Timothy, the sensible one. Timothy, the seer.

CHAPTER TWELVE

"So, Bob. What's the deal with the Griswolds? What I'm dealing with here seems to be not exactly what it seemed to be when you sent Ellen Griswold to me to track down her wayward ex-husband and wayward current brother in-law in Thailand." I explained what had transpired in the previous twenty-four hours and asked the lawyer, "So, what I want to know from you is, can the Griswolds be trusted, or what?"

I had reached Chicarelli on the golf course Sunday morning in Clifton Park, near Albany. When I called his house, his wife was reluctant to violate the sanctity of Chicarelli's Sabbath golf game by blabbing his cell phone number for a business matter. But when I said the urgent situation I was calling about had to do with the Griswolds, a name of consequence in Albany, she recited the number pronto.

"They've got Timmy? Christ, Strachey, have you notified the US embassy? They've gotta bring in the FBI, would be my thinking. Going at this on your own sounds very risky to me."

"It may come to that, but my Thai sources say the cops here are more effectively inspired by cash than by hectoring from farangs in suits. There's a big DEA station here, but I'd probably have to convince those guys that there's a major heroin shipment involved in order to get their attention."

"You might want to consider saying just that."

"I might, in the end. For all I know at this point, it could even be true. But what about the Griswolds? What's the story with them? Ellen sends me flying over here and gives me pretty much carte blanche to do anything I can to save her ex and his thirty-eight mil. Then she e-mails me some lame crap about he's A-okay, it's all a misunderstanding, and come on home. Plainly the guy really is up to his ears in some stinking mess involving influential fortune-tellers and who knows what kind of criminal weirdos. It seems like half the goons in Bangkok want to get hold of Griswold and...I hate to think. Give him a shove. My question to you is, why would Ellen call me off? What's her game here? It's possible that Gary lied to her about being safe, but why would she be so ready to believe the lie? Bob, I'm confused."

There was a long pause — was Chicarelli taking time out from my call to pick some grass off his four iron? — and then he said, "I shouldn't be telling you this." More silence.

"Yeah?"

"It could be financial."

"Uh-huh."

"Bill Griswold has serious money troubles, I've heard from people who would know. It's possible all of a sudden that maybe the Griswolds think they cannot afford you."

"That sounds unlikely. I'm a monetary tiny speck in their scheme of things."

"No, this is big and it's significant. There's a hostile takeover underway at Algonquin Steel. A holding company operating out of the Caymans is busy rolling up shares in the Griswold's zillion-dollar family store. Bill Griswold is fighting it, and there's a high probability that the family's assets will be tied up in litigation for years to come. Bill and Ellen may land on their feet eventually, but the family well is going to be shallow-bordering-on-dry for the foreseeable future. All this just developed on Friday, so that could help account for Ellen's change of plans."

"I was somewhere over the Pacific on Friday. At least she didn't call the airline and demand that they turn the plane around."

Chicarelli laughed once. "She might have. That's Ellen."

"Anyway, what you're suggesting doesn't sound right. It's not like the Griswolds are suddenly penniless. And surely Ellen would not cut her ex-husband off if she believed he was in real danger. And again, if he contacted her and told her he was not in any danger, why would she believe that? She thinks he's borderline bonkers these days. It's possible, I suppose, that he's got some scheme in mind to save himself, and my poking around is screwing that up somehow. But if that's the case, why wouldn't Griswold just explain that to me, and I'd have another helping of fried crickets and then head home. No, there's something screwy about the way all the Griswolds are behaving. Anyway, now I have no choice but to get to the bottom of the entire bizarre mess and get Timmy out of Thailand. You know, he didn't really want to come here. He thought it would be dangerous. I talked him into it."

"People by the thousands go there and have a wonderful time," Chicarelli said. "Isn't Thailand called the Land of Smiles?"

"That's what I told Timmy. It's true, too. But nobody, Thai or otherwise, who has anything to do with the Griswolds is smiling these days. What's that about? That's what I want to know."

"Jeez, Strachey. Now I'm sorry I ever sent Ellen to you. I figured: Thailand. Gay. Free ride. Big bucks. I thought I was doing you a favor. And I was helping out Ellen, too. She's somebody you don't want to make unhappy if you can avoid it."

"She's formidable. Though I kind of like her, even if I don't quite trust her."

"This didn't come from me, but did you ever hear the stuff about Ellen and the demise of Bill's first wife?"

"What stuff is that?"

"Sheila Griswold, Bill's ex, was a vindictive lady who made a career of making his life miserable after the divorce. Hounding him endlessly for more, more, more. I knew Sheila's attorney, Hal Woolrich, a total scumbag who's now in Waterbury for tax evasion. Anyway, Sheila disappears on a Caribbean cruise and a lot of people thought she went overboard with a little help from others on the boat. Among the merrymakers on the ship that night were Ellen's personal trainer, Duane Hubbard, and Hubbard's boyfriend, Matthew Mertz. They were pretty scuzzy characters. Mertz had a history of coke dealing and at least one assault conviction. Word got back to Albany — probably by way of Woolrich — that these two were on the ship when

Sheila disappeared, and a number of people who knew the situation wondered if maybe Bill and Ellen put those two up to turning poor Sheila into shark bait. Anyway, there was never any evidence and, because of jurisdictional confusion, no investigation to speak of."

"Ellen told me," I said, "that her husband was a suspect in people's minds in his ex's disappearance, but not that she was. This is quite a fascinating family you've gotten me involved with, Bob."

"Yeah, well, Strachey, you send them a billable-hours statement the first of the month and payment arrives by the end of the month. Or has so far. Just how fucked-up the Griswolds may be, I don't really know. But Christ, if I'd ever thought Timmy was going to get hurt on account of the Griswolds, I would never have sent Ellen to you. This just stinks to high heaven, and I am so, so sorry."

"Timmy hasn't gotten hurt on account of the Griswolds. He's gotten hurt because of me. So, what became of these two characters, the personal trainer and his beau, Hubbard and Mertz?"

"I have no idea. Would you like me to find out?"

"Nah. There's no real need to know. This all happened — what? Fourteen or fifteen years ago?"

"Something like that."

"If you can easily track these guys down, do. Otherwise, I've got plenty of other unsavory characters to keep my mind occupied. What you might do, though, is try to get an explanation from Ellen as to what's going on here. What did Gary actually tell her yesterday that made her fire me from the case? I've tried phoning her and will try again, and I'll e-mail her too. Maybe she'll open up to you."

"Possibly. Though in my dealings with Ellen over the years I've sometimes wondered if she wasn't holding back on a few important details of whatever it was."

"Now you tell me."

"Yeah, well. Have you ever had the perfect client? What you're always dealing with are human beings. It's a hazard of the workplace OSHA can't seem to do anything about."

I gave Chicarelli my Thailand cell phone number and asked him to call me anytime he developed any clue at all as to what the Griswolds were up to. He wished me luck springing Timmy and Kawee. I said, "Do you believe in lucky numbers?"

"No. Can't say that I do."

"Me neither. I've always believed that when good things happen in circumstances that are beyond our control, that's what we call luck. Likewise with bad things. The Thais believe that events can be manipulated through managing the symbols of luck — rituals, amulets, wielding the right numbers, prayer. I would try any of that if I thought it would help keep Timothy safe. But now I look around me here — at the shrines, the temples, the stupas, the spirit houses — and none of it seems like anything that will help bring Timmy back. In fact, it all feels like it's part of what took Timmy away from me and put his life in danger. And I feel as if I'm not only in danger of losing Timmy, but that I'm losing Thailand, a place I love. It's awful."

"Get Timmy back," Chicarelli said, "and I'm guessing your love of Thailand will follow."

"Yeah," I agreed. "First things first."

CHAPTER THIRTEEN

When General Yodying Supanant of the Royal Thai Police declined to order all of the fourteenth floors in Bangkok searched without payment in advance of the fifty-thousand-baht fee he charged for this service — he called it a "gift" that would go toward a new wing for a Buddhist monastery in Ubon Ratchathani — I rode with Pugh over to the ATM around the corner from the Topmost with a Robinson's Department Store shopping bag Pugh had in his car. It took awhile for me to repeatedly insert my MasterCard and extract a total of fifty thousand baht from the machine, including time-outs to stand aside politely and allow others who wished to use the ATM to withdraw their more modest amounts.

Pugh sat nearby on a stool at an espresso stand and sipped coffee from a tiny paper cup. Two young woman had set up their own miniature Starbucks-like operation, about four feet by four feet, the electric coffeemaker powered by a cable that ran up the side of a building and vanished into the fat spaghetti maze of black wires strung just above the sidewalk along Rama IV Road. I remembered Timmy's story of one of the earliest Peace Corps deaths. A volunteer was killed not by a wild animal or an obscure tropical disease but by electrocution while playing poker with four Thais during a thunderstorm. I recalled this as a characteristically Thai way of dying prematurely, and now I could add defenestration to any such list.

As Pugh sat watching me extract currency from a humming and blinking machine on the side of a building, it occurred to me that he might be wondering if he would be left in the lurch, now that Ellen Griswold was about to sever my expense account bounty. I assured Pugh that he would be paid, no matter what. He said, "I only doubted that for a nanosecond."

Detective Panu refused to participate in the delivery of the "gift" to General Yodying — having made the initial setup calls, Panu then pointed out to me in a dignified tone that bribery was illegal in Thailand, and he had no intention of physically handling the tainted bahts — so Pugh said he would make the delivery. We swung by a police station on Sala Daeng Soi 1 and Pugh pranced in with the shopping bag and out again in less than a minute.

I said, "Will this guy follow through?"

"I believe so."

"It's a lot of money."

"Is Yodying a crook? Without doubt. But for the moment he is our crook, Khun Don. He's what we've got."

"Rufus, you're so reassuring."

We had used the scanner at the Internet café/seamstress shop and e-mailed Timmy's passport photo to the general. Within a matter of hours, supposedly, a police sweep of all the fourteenth floors in greater Bangkok would be undertaken. Each cop would be armed with a picture of Timmy and a description of Kawee down to the fuchsia toenails.

I said, "So, are there also six hundred judges issuing several thousand search warrants for all those fourteenth-floor apartments and offices?"

"No," Pugh said. "You would have to pay extra for that. But don't sweat it."

Pugh took a call from Jampen Noo, his field supervisor. She told him the surveillance team was in place inside and outside the Internet café in On Nut from which Griswold placed his phone calls to Kawee. If Griswold showed up, they would snatch him and hold him as unostentatiously as possible in a van parked nearby until Pugh and I could get there.

Meanwhile, Pugh and I headed back over to Griswold's condo to look for the laptop computer Timmy said he and Kawee had found in Griswold's ground-floor storage bin. Mr. Thomsatai greeted us with a deep and respectful wai and the phoniest Thai smile I had ever witnessed. Why was this guy not behind bars? That was going to have to wait, along with a number of this case's other nagging deferred matters.

We looked through the storage bin and found nothing there of use. More art books. A couple of empty canvas travel bags with Miami-Bangkok airline baggage tags still affixed. There was also what looked like a bike-riding helmet.

I asked Thomsatai, "Does Griswold have a bicycle?"

"Mr. Gary have bike. Good bike. Italian. But it is not here. I think he took it to where he go."

Pugh said, "I'll tell my crew to watch for a possible arrival at the Internet café by bicycle." He made a quick call and did so.

Up in the apartment, the rooms looked surprisingly undisturbed, given that a forced abduction had taken place there several hours earlier. Apparently Timmy and Kawee had not put up a struggle. If the goons had guns — which they did, according to both Thomsatai and the pistol-whipped security guard — resistance would have made no sense. I didn't know about Kawee, but Timmy was nothing if not sensible.

To our amazement, a laptop computer lay on Griswold's desk. Presumably, this was the one Timmy and Kawee had retrieved from the downstairs storage area. So, the kidnappers seemed to want Griswold himself and not necessarily the kind of information he stored in his computer. What did this mean? Or, did the boneheads simply forget to bring the device along?

Pugh and I messed around with the MacBook Pro but couldn't come up with a password that would get the thing up and running. We tried all the obvious stuff: *Mango*, and the earlier Thai boyfriends; plus *Buddha*; *Dharma*; *Sangha*; Griswold's birth date; *Toot Toot*, Lou Horn's art gallery; *Algonquin*; and a lot of other details from Griswold's daily existence. We even tried *bicycle* and *cruising speed* and *past lives*. Nothing worked.

Pugh said, "I know a guy who can get into this. I'll call him."

"How soon can he do it?"

"Soon."

Pugh had the computer whiz on his speed dial and spoke to him in rapid Thai.

"How come the cops didn't take the computer with them?" I said. "This place isn't even being treated as a crime scene."

"Like I said, it's a low-priority matter. A lady-boy and a tourist."

"Timmy warned me about this aspect of Thailand."

Pugh said nothing, just indicated that I should take a seat while he took care of something. I remained standing, though, while he went over to Griswold's shrine. A box of matches lay nearby on a table, and Pugh used one to light several candles and a couple of joss sticks in front of the shrine. He had one of the photos of Timmy that we had e-mailed to the police, and Pugh leaned this picture against the shrine next to the candles and the incense. He sat himself down on the straw mat in front of the shrine, his legs crossed and back straight. He bowed his head. The serene Buddha figure looked out at Pugh, its left palm raised in the "do not be afraid" *mudra*.

I stood awkwardly for a few minutes, then walked over and slid open the door to the terrace. The night heat slammed into me, dulling my senses. I held on to the railing and looked down at the parking lot and gardens far below. When I turned away from this abyss, I noticed that a few leaves had fallen off the orchid and azalea plants on the terrace, and I picked up the leaves and dropped them into the crocks holding the flowers. The watering can nearby was about half full, and I watered the flowers and the bamboo plants.

When I reentered the apartment, Pugh was still seated silently in front of the Buddha, the candles flickering and the incense smoking up the room. I went over and sat down next to Pugh, also in the lotus position. I felt a twinge of something in my back, so my position turned into something a little more nasturtium-like. I sat there with Pugh for some minutes trying to lose my fear, as Pugh apparently had done in the presence of the Buddha. I envied Pugh and loved the way his connection to a world far beyond the mundane gave him courage and clarity of mind. Sitting there with him, I myself was much calmer now than I had been earlier. But I was still scared to death.

§ § § §

We waited for word of the police sweep of fourteenth floors all over Bangkok in Pugh's office on Surawong. At midnight, the Sunday night traffic down below was still bumper-to-bumper, though not so noisy as it might have been. I remembered how in the '70s Bangkok streets were always impossibly clogged and endlessly frustrating and how the Thais nonetheless rarely honked their horns. To blare one's horn merely out of impatience was to demonstrate *jai rawn*, a hot temper — literally hot heart — and what every Thai aspired to and valued above all was *jai yen*, a self-possessed inner being and a cool demeanor.

This was in contrast to the Vietnamese in Saigon who leaned on their car and motorbike horns nonstop and seemed always intent on trying to run one another off the road and smashing to bits a few pedestrians while they were at it. Later, when I thought back about Vietnamese driving styles — rude, cunning, tenacious — it did not surprise me at all that these people had won the war.

Pugh had had some rice and duck red curry with pineapple sent up, so I ate that wondering if Timmy and Kawee were eating as well. I supposed they were. Even the most sadistic Thai kidnappers, I guessed, would value good food and not think of depriving their captives of some flavorsome tom kha gai before throwing them over the railing of an upper-floor balcony.

Pugh's third-floor office was not far from Patpong, home to many of Bangkok's famous pussy shows, and it was across Tha Surawong from the entrance to Soi Pratuchai, a street of gay bars and fuck shows. Pugh said that when Timmy was free, he and I could drop by the Dream Boys Club and watch a show that was nearly identical to the Ziegfeld Follies of 1928, except the cast was all male and the performances involved the use of much more lubricant than was probably common in the Ziegfeld era.

Just after midnight, Pugh checked with his contact in General Yodying's office and learned that the sweep had been ongoing for over three hours but so far no trace of Timmy or

Kawee had been found. Residential buildings had been checked first; banging on the doors of residents after bedtime would not go over well and, Pugh said, might have cost me twice the fifty thousand baht I and the taxpayers of Thailand were expending on the operation. Fourteenth floors in hotels had also been checked, to no avail. Now office buildings were being combed with the help of the security services that watched over them.

I said to Pugh, "But what if some of these private security guys are working with the kidnappers? They'll alert the captors, or even cover up their locations. Then what?"

"It's a risk we run," Pugh said. "No dragnet is ever perfect. Yodying is relying on the surprise element, but it's not foolproof. Another possible loophole is this: many Thais of the upper social strata are likely to tell the cops doing the searching to sod off. There are many homes the police simply will not get inside of. We have to assume, however, that Timmy and Kawee are not being held captive in the apartments of Jack and Jackie, or of any real estate magnates or media tycoons."

"Really? Why should we assume that? Do Thai rich people have more delicate sensibilities than the American rich or the Estonian rich? I'll bet not."

"More refined, no. But careful, yes. Many layers of personnel separate Thai criminals in high places from Thai criminals at the operational level. I think, perhaps, that this type of arrangement is not all that unusual in much of the USA, is it, Mr. Don? New Jersey may be a little cruder and more direct than that. But even in Atlantic City the concept of plausible deniability is probably not unknown."

"Rufus, now you're making me nervous. Maybe this whole search is a waste of time. And a very expensive waste of time, at that. Jesus."

Pugh was behind his desk surrounded by rack after rack of computer discs. He had a couple of racks of music CDs, too, much of it Thai pop, a bit of Schubert lieder, some American C&W — Roy Orbison, Waylon Jennings, Patsy Cline. He said, "We have to explore every avenue open to us, Mr. Don. Do we not? We're covering the Internet café that Griswold uses. And tomorrow we can cover Kawee's apartment and the whiskey seller where Griswold's cash delivery moto-man makes his normal early-in-the-week drop-off for Kawee. Griswold's desktop may also yield up some answers, and we should hear from Khun Thunska, my computer guy, soon after sunrise on that particular front. There is also this to consider: the kidnappers will undoubtedly contact you again to arrange for the swap of Griswold for Timothy and Kawee. At that point, you might be able to convince them that we have been unable to locate Griswold but that we are busting our asses to do so, and can we have a little more time? So while uncertainty remains a constant, we know what we know. I do, of course, understand why you are fearful, but I want to tell you, Mr. Don, that hope springs eternal in this particular human breast, and we are a long way from being totally fucked."

At one a.m., we sent out for more curry. The restaurants were closed by now, but a street stall over on Silom, under the SkyTrain station, had some deep-fried water buffalo gums in a hot sauce that one of Pugh's crew thought we would enjoy.

While I ate, I tried Ellen Griswold again. She did not answer her phone, but this time I left a message. I said, "I received your e-mail firing me. Thanks for giving me some leeway in my return-to-Albany plans. That's nice, because we haven't seen the Emerald Buddha yet. Meanwhile, get this, Ellen: Timmy has been kidnapped by some very bad people who are after your ex-husband, and I need to talk with him immediately. Do you understand what I am saying, Ellen? Please explain this to Gary and tell him here's how he can reach me. You got Timmy and me into this, and now I am counting on you to help get us out of it. Please call me right away and tell me what you are going to do to help." I gave her my Thai mobile phone number.

I told Pugh what Bob Chicarelli had told me about the Albany Griswolds' sudden financial crisis.

"Interesting," he said.

"It is."

"The Griswolds may have seen this coming and were afraid Mr. Gary was going to lose his family boodle at the exact same moment theirs was in jeopardy."

"This occurred to me. Except, if that's true, then why have they called me off? They would want more than ever for Gary and his thirty-eight mil to remain intact and possibly available to save the family name and fortune. Not that Gary would necessarily be eager to be helpful. He and his brother were not close at all, and there was some actual bad blood, according to Gary's Key West friends."

"Griswold family ill will, or even strife, is yet another element that perhaps we should pay some attention to," Pugh said.

I agreed that we should just as Pugh's cell phone rang. He listened and said a few things in Thai. Holding the phone against his chest, Pugh said to me, "This is Captain Pirom, representing General Yodying. Regrettably, the police have had no success in ferreting out the captives. The search was not, however, as thorough as the general would have preferred. He is willing to do a second sweep in the morning of all the fourteenth floors in Bangkok. But this will tie up many resources, the captain says, so a second payment is being requested. They want twenty-five thousand baht. I am meant to tell you that because you are a repeat customer, that's a fifty percent discount." Pugh looked forlorn. "What should I tell the captain?" he said.

I leaned forward and peered into my fried water buffalo gums. I heard a voice in my head saying, "*Now* do you believe me?"

CHAPTER FOURTEEN

I woke up in need of a toothbrush, but it looked like a swig of hot sauce was going to have to do. I had slept for four hours next to Pugh on the straw mat on his office floor. I had dreams of falling, and I didn't think the dreams were symbolic.

Two of Pugh's staff — a muscular, elaborately tattooed young man named Ek and a middle-aged woman named Aroon who carried a bronze figurine of King Chulalongkorn in her shoulder holster — had slept on the floor in an outer office, and I greeted them as I went out to use the bathroom. Being Thai, they smiled. The tiny lavatory had a toilet, a washbowl, and a miniature shower in it. I tossed my sweaty clothes out the door and used all three appliances. I also borrowed somebody's toothbrush and honey-flavored Colgate, which wasn't all that bad.

Pugh had sent someone over to Starbucks on Silom for coffee for all of us, and while Ek and Aroon took turns using the shower, Pugh checked in with his surveillance teams. They said there had been no sign of Griswold. A call to the cops produced nothing new either. Pugh showered while I examined the shrine in the corner of his office — gold leaf had been freshly applied to the Buddha figure on the platform — and watched the Monday morning traffic build up down below on Surawong. Pugh came back looking neat and fresh, as if just back from a month in the Swiss Alps. I had never seen a Thai looking dirty or rumpled. The entire population of sixty million always appeared freshly ironed, and they were peculiarly odorless despite the heat. The Thais had a lot of water and they used it.

After Pugh hung up with the police, I said, "You know, maybe the kidnappers were smart enough to suspect we might have every fourteenth floor in Bangkok searched, so they're holding Timmy and Kawee on the thirteenth floor somewhere. If so, this is all a waste of time and our only hope is to find

Griswold and make the trade. Or at least find him and find out who these people are that he's gotten so pissed off, and then go after them as fast as we can."

"There are no thirteenth floors in Bangkok," Pugh said.

"All right, then, fifteenth. At least they didn't say ninth floor. I suppose all tall buildings in Thailand have no thirteenth floors and instead have five ninth floors, increasing the amount of good luck available to the population."

Pugh laughed. "Mr. Don, you seem bemused by our being a superstitious people."

"I guess I am. But nothing more than bemused. It's not condescension, I don't think."

"I'd say it is exactly that, but never mind. As I recall, buildings in New York City don't have thirteenth floors either."

"I am bemused by that also."

"And additionally, I suppose, by knocking on wood and avoiding black cats and keeping one's fingers crossed and not stepping on a crack so as to avoid breaking one's dear mother's back."

"All hokum. Tell me, Rufus. What happens to all those thirteenth floors that are left out of the tall buildings in Bangkok? Are the construction materials divided up among the government building inspectors for resale and monthly bonuses?"

He laughed. "No, we ship all the unlucky thirteenth floors to our impoverished neighbors the Cambodians. This might help explain their unfortunate history."

"Another flaw in this whole operation," I said, "is the likelihood that the kidnappers have their own police sources who have alerted them that a search of fourteenth floors is under way and they have simply moved Timmy and Kawee to any other high floor. Even if they didn't anticipate a dragnet, isn't it likely that friends in high places would have alerted them?"

"This is possible, though General Yodying is an honorable man who would do his best to protect your investment. I know he planned on deploying his forces and only informing them at the very last moment what their mission was to be."

Miss Aroon poked her head in and said that Khun Thunska, Pugh's computer specialist, was on his way over and would arrive shortly.

"Why isn't he phoning?" I asked. "Can we assume he didn't find anything useful on the laptop?"

"Perhaps he wants to show us something and explain it."

Now my cell phone rang. Was it Timmy? Or was it the kidnappers, with instructions for the swap we were in no position to carry out? Pugh watched me open the phone.

"Hello?"

"Don, it's Ellen Griswold. Can you hear me?"

"Perfectly. Thanks for getting back to me so fast, Ellen."

"God, I can't begin to tell you how sorry I am that this has all turned into such an incredible fiasco. Your boyfriend has actually been *kidnapped*?"

I briefly described the events of the past twenty-four hours. "They're holding this young Thai man, Kawee, too. A friend of Gary's. So we need to talk to Gary fast. How can we do that?"

"Oh, bollocks, I wish I knew. Gary called *me* on Saturday night, and said he'd heard from somebody that you had been to his apartment and were looking for him, and to please call off the dogs — that would be you — because he was perfectly fine, he said. He's just meditating for a year to recover from a series of unlucky love affairs, and you were interfering with his concentration. I have to say, I was not entirely convinced that he wasn't concocting a whole line of BS about meditating for such a long time. I've heard of people going off to a cave, literally or figuratively, and doing it for a month. But a whole *year*? Anyway, I felt I had to take him at his word that you would be making trouble for him somehow. I mean, he didn't sound at all frightened or upset. So that's when I e-mailed you. But now it looks like he really is in trouble, and God, now your

Timothy is too. How perfectly awful! I am so, so sorry, Don. So, what are you going to do?"

I didn't think she was making this up as she went. It was silly enough, but in its inane way it was too pat. I guessed she was referring to notes she had made. I said, "So, Gary phoned you? Where was he calling from?"

"He didn't say. And I didn't think to get a number. I was so startled to hear his voice, and so relieved."

"Did he say he would call again?"

"No, but it sounded as if he would eventually. He was emphatic in telling me not to worry."

"Who told him I was looking for him? Think about this. It's important."

"Just a minute." Now her voice was distant: "Amanda, no, you may *not* ride into Albany with Josh. You are not to get into Josh's car at all. Ever. Now, I *said* I would take you later. No, no. And don't use that language with me!" To me: "Don, can I call you back? This is all getting to be *way* too much!"

"No, Ellen, you cannot call me back. We have to talk now. What we have here is a life-or-death situation. Do you hear what I'm saying?"

"Yes, I hear you, Don." Distant again. "No, no, I said no, and no means no!" I heard a shriek in the background, as if intruders had broken in and shot someone. "Oh, goddamn it."

I said, "I have to ask you this again. I need very badly to know this. Who told Gary I was looking for him? Did he tell you this?"

"No, he didn't. And I didn't think to ask, not realizing at the time it might become important. Oh God, she is *impossible*. Are you and Timothy raising children, Don?"

"No."

"Listen, I do apologize. It's not that I don't understand that what you're going through is so much worse than anything I have to deal with here on boring old Elm Court Drive. It's just that I think I've told you everything I know. And if Gary calls again anytime soon, I'll make it clear to him that he must contact you immediately and impress on him just how urgent the situation is."

"You didn't give him my cell phone number when he called?"

"No, I didn't have it yet, I don't think."

"That's true. What I want to ask you to help me out with, Ellen, is this. I wish to continue in your employ until I get Timmy back at least. There are some expenses I'm running up in connection with his being released."

"What? Ransom? You're paying ransom?"

"No, they don't want money. They want Gary. Whoever the kidnappers are, they have offered to release Timmy and Kawee in exchange for our handing over Gary."

"Oh, good God. Well, you wouldn't do that, would you?"

"What I'm doing is, I'm working hard to get everybody's ass out of the fire intact. That is my intention. But I'm running up my accounts. For instance, we had to arrange for a search of a number of buildings in Bangkok, and it cost money."

"Well, just make sure you get receipts."

"Sure."

"And keep your costs down as low as you can. My cash flow situation is rather wobbly at the moment."

"Yeah, well, so is mine."

"Aren't the police involved? If someone is kidnapped, why not rely on the police instead of hiring private security at an extortionate rate?"

"In Thailand, it's complicated in that regard. Anyway, once I get hold of Gary" — I didn't add *and wring his neck* — "perhaps he can be persuaded to pitch in and help cover expenses. After all, it's his disappearance, so-called, that got me into this sulfurous quagmire in the first place."

"God, now I feel terrible about getting you mixed up in one of my family's typical messes. Listen, just do whatever you can to get Timothy safely back with you. That's the important thing. And that poor Thai man too. Have the kidnappers threatened them in any way?"

"Yes, they have. So I need your ex-husband's help as soon as possible. There's a deadline, which is later tomorrow. Gary will know who these people are, we can reasonably assume, and perhaps know where to find them. So I do need to talk to him, and fast."

"Well, I have total confidence in you, Don. Bob Chicarelli said you were a bit of a pain in the rear end sometimes but totally committed to whatever you took on and totally professional. You'll know what to do, if anybody will. Good luck, and do keep me posted. So, it sounds like you should have everything more or less under control by later tomorrow?"

"I certainly hope so, Ellen."

"I'll wait for your report."

I rang off and told Pugh what Ellen had told me.

"She's a doozy of a client," Pugh said. "How much did you get up front?"

"Ten K. But the plane tickets were forty-four hundred. So with the bribes to your police department, I'm already in the hole over nineteen thousand dollars. Plus what I owe you. Griswold's thirty-eight mil had better be largely intact. Southeast Asia is supposed to be such a bargain tourist destination. What am I doing wrong, Rufus?"

Grinning, Pugh said, "You've had a run of bad luck, Mr. Don, and you are defenseless in the face of it. Like most farangs, you rely solely on your brainpower and your financial assets, both of which are finite. I'm doing everything I can to compensate for your limitations, however, and between the two of us we're going to pull the rabbit out of the hat. So, do not despair, my friend, do not despair."

I looked at Pugh and said, "Rufus, I have no idea what you're talking about."

He guffawed. "You must be amazed that Thailand functions at all."

Miss Aroon came in leading another man into the office, and Pugh got up to greet him, smiling and bowing and wai-ing. Thunska Rujawongsanti, the computer consultant, was small and round, and appeared to be somewhere between the ages of fourteen and fifty-eight. He looked more Chinese than Thai. I knew that there had been a certain amount of intermarriage since the nineteenth century, when the Chinese began arriving in Siam in great numbers to — as a Chinese-Thai journalist had once explained it to me — teach the Thais how to count.

Khun Thunska had Griswold's laptop with him and opened it on Pugh's desk.

"So, what was the password?" I asked.

Thunska shrugged. "I have no idea. We just dispensed with that type of foolishness and spoke to this little honey of a Mac on a higher plane. It never knew what hit it."

I gave Pugh an Is-this-guy-putting-me-on? look, and he said, "No Thai juju was involved. Just some trade secrets and perhaps some Johnny Walker for a Mac company representative in Singapore."

Thunska acted as if he hadn't heard this. He was busy juicing up the Mac. He quickly produced an image on the screen and said, "I wanted you to lay eyes on this. I would have phoned it in, but you have to see this to believe it."

"Who is it?" I asked. "The foreigner appears to be Gary Griswold. But who are the Thais? One does look familiar."

Pugh said, "Oh, baby."

The photo was of three men standing with drinks in their hands on the balcony of an apartment. They were casually but elegantly dressed, and they were relaxed and smiling. The digital image seemed to be of an unremarkable social occasion until Pugh identified the two men standing with Griswold.

"The man on Griswold's left is former Minister of Finance Anant na Ayudhaya. He was removed from office in the coup last year but is generally understood to control the ministry under the current restored nominally democratic government. The man on Griswold's right is the one whose photo you have perhaps seen, Mr. Don. It is Khun Khunathip, the esteemed fortune-teller who fatally went over a high railing just two days ago. Perhaps it was the very railing he is leaning against in this photo."

"I believe, yes, that that is the unlucky railing," Thunska said. "You can make out the Westin Grande in the background, suggesting that this photo was indeed taken in Khun Khunathip's apartment in Sukhumvit."

I said, "This is big stuff, no? Shouldn't the police be told about this?"

Pugh and Thunska exchanged quick glances, and Pugh said to me, "Mr. Don, you are half right."

CHAPTER FIFTEEN

I walked down to an ATM on Surawong and withdrew another twenty-five thousand baht. I had nearly maxed out my MasterCard, so I started in on my American Express account. Pugh bundled the cash into a shopping bag and sent Ek over to the police station on Sala Daeng Soi 1 with it.

Pugh phoned his own police sources to check on the investigation into the death of the renowned seer, Khun Khunathip. Miss Aroon had brought up the morning newspapers, both Thai and English language, and while all the papers had the soothsayer's passing emblazoned across their front pages, none speculated on the details or meaning of his death. The great man had simply "died in a fall."

Pugh's police contacts told him that an actual investigation was under way, as opposed to a fake investigation. Pugh said this could mean that either important persons had nothing to do with the apparent homicide and wanted justice done, or that important persons had everything to do with the apparent homicide and they wished to gauge how much was going to leak out before they either declared the seer's fall accidental or found a hapless scapegoat from the Thai lower social orders to take the rap.

Ek drove Pugh and me inch by inch through the morning traffic miasma over to the Topmost so that I could change clothes and Pugh could fortify himself with the bacon at the breakfast buffet. On the way, we tried to work up a story I could tell the kidnappers so that we could buy time if we needed it. Nothing we came up with sounded any more convincing than the truth. Pugh said the kidnappers undoubtedly had their own police sources — some of them possibly the same as Pugh's — and the kidnappers would know that we had been unable to track down Griswold. They were simply using us to accomplish what they had been unable to do, thinking that we had better information than theirs and more resources. But we didn't.

I repeated to Pugh what I had told him earlier during an attempt to deconstruct Ellen Griswold's phone call. "It had to have been Thomsatai that tipped off Griswold that we were looking for him. If so, Thomsatai has to have a phone number or some other way of contacting Griswold. If we can get him to talk, Thomsatai has to be our most reliable route to Griswold."

"Possibly," Pugh said. "Though Griswold may have a friendly police contact who alerted him. As soon as I began asking the cops about Griswold, word would have spread. There's a network of gay police officers, to cite one possible mechanism for alarms being sent Griswold's way."

"There's no stigma attached to being gay in the police department?"

"There's some, but not a lot. Once in a while you hear about some prick senior officer who's hard on gays. Some of them picked up these bad attitudes from Christians or the Chinese or the US military. But most cops couldn't care less. When I was in the police, a bunch of us were at a drunken beach party where all the guys ended up naked in a heap on the sand screwing and getting screwed. It was like a kind of larky extension of that day's volleyball game, and everybody thought of it as just having a nice social occasion. Naughty but harmless. And nearly all those guys were straight, I think. The tops outnumbered the bottoms, as I recall, and I'm guessing that that's significant."

"I can see why Griswold emigrated here. Poor guy. He thought he was coming to gay paradise and ended up in some weird purgatory. What about Khun Khunathip? Do we know if he was gay?"

"I'd say no. Word gets around about the hectic erotic lives of Thailand's mighty. Khunathip was not a monk, but if I had to guess I'd make him for a celibate. He got off on celebrity and power, the ultimate getting-off devices even in our sanuk-loving society."

"And Khun Anant, Griswold's drinking companion on Khun Khunathip's balcony? Any chance he's gay?"

As Ek pulled into the driveway of the Topmost, Pugh said, "While I love the image of former finance minister and present-day molder of the Thai economy Anant na Ayudhaya on his back, heels to Jesus, while a senior vice president of the Commercial Bank of Siam, say, proceeds to make a strenuous deposit in his excellency's person, again I would guess no, he's not gay. The connections between Griswold and the soothsayer and the financier appear to be other than sexual or purely social. The confluence of Khunathip, Anant, and a mentally uncertain farang with thirty-eight mil in his pocket strongly suggests a financial occasion. And a major one, at that. That is why, Mr. Don, knowing what I know about money and power in Thailand and the lengths people will travel in order to get and keep money and power, I am truly shakin' in my boots." As he climbed out of the car and headed for the breakfast buffet, Pugh smiled tightly and added, "And how's it shakin' with you, Mr. Don?"

After I cleaned up and Pugh had his bacon, we drove over to Griswold's condo and again threatened Mr. Thomsatai with a telephone book. I wouldn't actually have hit him, and I guessed that neither would Pugh. Ek was stationed nearby, within sight of Thomsatai, and with his Buick Roadmaster chest and enormous upper arms adorned with inky images of hissing serpents, Ek made an impression. So the condo manager was forthcoming, bordering on chatty.

"Ah, Mr. Don, Khun Rufus. Have you been able to find Mr. Gary? I am so worried about him."

"We thought you might know where he is, actually," I said. "Or at least how to reach him by telephone. Or wasn't it you who tipped Griswold off that I was in Bangkok searching for him? You're the most likely candidate, what with hardly anybody else even knowing I was in town."

Thomsatai got on his might-have-a-stroke look and began to gush sweat. It was unclear, though, whether this was because he was about to tell a huge lie or because he thought we thought he knew something he didn't actually know and somebody might go after him again with a phone book.

He looked at us and said evenly, "The kidnappers offered me ten thousand baht if I told them how to find Mr. Gary."

Pugh said, "And you'll tell us for eight? Khun Thomsatai, keep this up and I may have to ask my assistant Ek to bring in the telephone company."

"No, no, that is not necessary. What I am saying is this: I was unable to sell them this information because I do not have it. I have no way of contacting Mr. Gary, and I have no idea where he is. What I am telling you is too, too true, of course."

I said, "How did the moto-bike man know that Timmy and Kawee were up in Griswold's apartment yesterday? That apartment is nearly always empty except when Kawee waters the plants and leaves offerings. But yesterday the kidnappers knew exactly when to arrive with Timothy Callahan and Kawee in the apartment but not Khun Rufus or me. Can you explain how they knew that?"

Now he started eyeing the doorway again, but Ek was standing in it. Thomsatai avoided looking at me, but he looked at Pugh, suddenly shook his head violently, and cried out, "I am sorry!" He began to weep quietly. Snuffling, he said, "My mother's water buffalo died. I needed money to send to my mother in Chiang Rai for a new buffalo. You understand this, Khun Rufus. I know you do." He snuffled some more.

Pugh gazed at him for a moment. Then he said to me, "That's a bar girl's story. When she has spent the rent money on clothes or she feels like she needs a flat-screen television, a bar girl whose imagination is limited tells her john that her mother's water buffalo has died and the poor old lady is going to starve without one."

I said, "Don't water buffalos actually die? It does sound like a serious matter in Thailand."

Now Thomsatai looked eagerly at me for the first time, apparently under the mistaken impression that I might rescue him.

Pugh said, "Being a farang, you wouldn't be expected to know this. But Thai water buffalo are immortal. And when they start breeding like maniacs after water buffalo rutting season, soon we have way too many of them and they begin to crowd us out of our villages. So we send the buffalo overflow to Laos. In Luang Prabang, they are trained to perform dressage for the tourists. Check out UNESCO's Web site. People come from all over the world for Luang Prabang's famous water buffalo dressage shows. It is plain, Mr. Don, that this man with his water buffalo sob story is lying."

Thomsatai got on a doomed look. He knew he was in the hands of madmen, and what was he going to do, call the police? He took a deep breath and said, "They phoned and asked me if anybody was in Mr. Gary's apartment. They said if I didn't tell them, they would drive a motorcycle over my face."

We waited for more, but that was it. After a moment, Pugh said, "Who phoned you?"

"The moto-bike man." Thomsatai was trembling lightly now.

"How did he know to phone you yesterday evening?"

"I don't know. He did not tell me."

"And you told him what?"

"That two men were in Mr. Gary's apartment. Kawee and Mr. Don's friend."

I said, "Why didn't you tell this to the police when they came here after the abduction?"

He looked at me stonily. "Because the man who called did not want me to tell the police, I think. He would hurt me if I told them."

"How would the moto-bike man know it was you who told the police what you had told them?"

Thomsatai looked over at Pugh as if to say, this farang is an awfully naive fellow. Pugh caught Thomsatai's meaning and looked at me and shrugged.

Pugh said to me, "We'll work this out ourselves. *Mai pen rai.*"

"What's mai pen rai?"

"Literally, it means 'It is not a problem.' The larger meaning in Thai thinking and culture is — if I may employ a New Jerseyism you will readily comprehend — whatthefuckyagonnadoaboutit. It's what is is. Don't sweat what you cannot control. In this case, what is, is we cannot trust the police. Mr. Thomsatai doesn't trust them, and neither should we."

"Even for seventy-five thousand bahts?"

"Oh, that's another story. Clearly we have outbid the opposition with that one. But that's for the performance of one particular service, a double sweep of fourteenth floors. Beyond that, we're not only on our own but moving into uncharted territory, what with a certain personage — the gentleman in the photo on the balcony — now very much in the picture. He also is a man who undoubtedly goes around singing 'The policeman is my friend.'"

Thomsatai jumped when Pugh's cell phone rang, and Pugh glanced at the phone to see who was calling. He said to me, "Speak of the devil."

CHAPTER SIXTEEN

The second sweep of fourteenth floors had been completed and no trace of Timmy or Kawee had been found.

Pugh said, "Sorry, Mr. Don. It was worth a try. Truly."

"Yeah, it seemed to make sense. I guess there are going to be just too many holes in a dragnet of this amorphous type."

"General Yodying is himself disappointed. He wants to take you to dinner at the Oriental Hotel when you have the time. Perhaps you view this as a mordant touch, bordering on the macabre. But the general's intentions are good."

"I've never been to the Oriental. Timmy wants to go there. Maybe we'll all go."

"I'm sure General Yodying will be happy to include Mr. Timothy once he is safe and sound."

"Timmy told me a story about Noel Coward at the Oriental. The manager phoned him and asked if it was true that there was a gentleman in his room. Coward replied, 'Just a moment and I'll ask him.'"

Pugh laughed and said, "There is much entertaining farang lore in Bangkok. We Thais know it too. We are as amused by visiting farangs as you are by one another."

"I know that Thailand was never colonized, thanks largely to the cleverness of King Chulalongkorn. Maybe that's why foreigners here are seen mainly as sources of amusement, in addition of course to serving as reliable sources of hard currency."

"Yes, and more importantly the latter. We are good at providing our own laughs. But hard currency from the West is needed to keep our upper classes roaming about in automobiles built in Bavaria and sipping satiny fluids distilled in Scotland."

"If you were a wealthy foreigner, Rufus, and showed up in Thailand with thirty-eight million US dollars and were going to invest it in a sure thing that was legal — no heroin, no arms smuggling, no adult or pedophile international sex trafficking — what would that investment be?"

"A legal investment? Hmm. Tourism infrastructure? Computer technology? Transportation? Perhaps entertainment — such as Hollywood movie palaces the likes of which L.B. Mayer is surely swooning over, if somehow his soul is extant in Bangkok today in some sentient form. Or grandiose retail outlets would perhaps be the smartest investment of all. An American journalist once told me he had been in Thailand for several weeks but had not yet been able to figure out what was percolating inside the minds of the Thai people. I told him, oh, that's easy. Going to the mall. That's what modern Thais spend much of their spare time thinking about or doing. Going shopping. The writer was disappointed, I think."

"And which of these investments that you have listed would provide the quickest return?"

Pugh looked doubtful. "None of the above, Mr. Don. Sorry. If you're talking getting your money back in months or even a few years, no such investments are likely to pay off that fast. Land deals, of course, can be ways of making a quick killing in Thailand, as in most places, if you are privy to inside information on some government project — a highway, an airport, a SkyTrain extension, say. But you said legal investment, and using insider information, while common here, is against the law. And it sounds as if Mr. Gary Griswold is a far better Buddhist than are some of Thailand's leading lights who were raised in clouds of incense with garlands of marigolds dangling from every orifice. You believe him to be a truly moral man, and perhaps he is that. Of course, there are legal gray areas available to investors here, also. And perhaps Mr. Gary was not too pious to eschew one of the murkier financial pursuits to be found here in the kingdom."

"Like what?"

"For instance, real estate development that's not meant to result in actual finished construction. Investors are lined up for, say, a large condominium project. A construction company is formed that embarks on the project and inflates its start-up costs by a thousand percent. All the condo units are sold for tidy sums, many of them to unsuspecting foreign retirees. Escrow laws here are weak, so the organizers of the project put up part of the building, then abandon the skeletal structure and walk away with millions. You see these half-finished concrete towers throughout Bangkok. Attempts have been made to tighten the escrow laws, but powerful people who profit from these corrupt but barely legal schemes have so far prevented the laws from being updated. It's a way of raking in big money fast, and perhaps someone talked Mr. Gary into investing in one of these cunningly conceived scams."

"Maybe. Though with his family history, Griswold would likely know the difference between ethical and nonethical business practices. And surely he's been around Thailand long enough to grasp what's a sleazy con job and what isn't a con job within the local context. No, I'm inclined to think that whatever he was planning to invest in was on the up-and-up, or at least was presented to him in a way that allowed him to think it was."

"Mr. Gary is apparently a far better Buddhist than many of us whose Buddhism one would reasonably expect to be more organic to our daily lives."

"Yes, unless he's fooling us all. That's a possibility, too."

"This has occurred to me also. I hope you won't be too disappointed if we track down Mr. Gary and he turns out to be a cad. Or at least a bit of a pill."

"If Griswold was a scheming big jerk, it would certainly make it easier to exchange him for Timmy and Kawee. There is that."

"This is a very Thai way of looking at it, Mr. Don. Now you're talkin' turkey."

Suddenly I saw Timmy's face, his eyes narrowing with disapproval over my brazen moral relativism, and I wanted to hold him and beg him not to judge me so harshly. And I wanted to beg his forgiveness for bringing him to this benighted land of violence and superstition. Then I heard him say, "Violence and superstition? You'd better be careful not to compare Thailand to the land of the NRA, Pat Robertson, slavery, Jim Crow and Rush Limbaugh." It was at that point that I asked him to please just shut up for one minute so that I could simply luxuriate in my profound relief over his being safe and well and once again by my side.

§ § § §

Pugh and I joined his team for the stakeout at the On Nut Internet café from which Griswold made his phone calls. Pugh had an illegally parked van with tinted windows situated half on the sidewalk directly in front of the café. A uniformed cop stopped by for a handout and was soon on his way. The place was in the shadow of the towering concrete On Nut SkyTrain station. This was the terminus of the Sukhumvit Road line, and whenever a train pulled in crowds came down the steps and dispersed up and down the street, many of them passing within inches of where we waited and watched. A few people went into the Internet café and sat down at computers. Nearly all were Thais. One was a male Westerner in sandals, cargo shorts, and a Jacob's Pillow Dance Festival T-shirt, but he wasn't Gary Griswold.

Pugh had the air-conditioning humming and sent out for eats from a nearby food stall. We had some nice pork larb and green papaya salad. I was so comfortable that I drifted off into semiconsciousness for an hour or so. To the extent that I was conscious, I tried to come up with another way of locating Griswold — or Timmy and Kawee — but I could not. There was one other avenue of hope. It was Monday, so I knew there was a fifty-fifty chance that the moto messenger that Griswold sent every Monday or Tuesday evening with cash for Kawee's housekeeping and other expenses would likely show up within a few hours at Kawee's room or at the whiskey seller's stall down the soi from his place. Pugh had additional crews covering both locations.

I gave some thought as to how I might be able to pay Pugh for his extensive services in the event I never saw another dime from any of the Griswolds. That was going to be a sizable dilemma. I did recall that I was in Timothy's will, but that thought didn't help.

By early evening there was no sign of Griswold, and Pugh said, "Let's you and I head over to Kawee's place. That looks like a better bet at this point. The moto messenger with Kawee's stipend may well know where Griswold lives, or at least where he is likely to turn up. Ek and Noo can keep an eye out here."

"What if," I said, "Griswold only shows up at a particular place once a week to hand over the cash delivery? The moto guy may know when and where that is, but what if Griswold won't show himself there again until next week?"

Pugh shrugged. "Then we go to Plan B."

"Which is?"

"We kidnap former Minister of Finance Anant na Ayudhaya, and in order to find out what he knows, Ek goes after him with a telephone book."

"Is that really feasible?"

"No. Not for us it isn't. Not exactly."

I let that go and followed Pugh out of the van onto the baking sidewalk. We climbed the steps of the SkyTrain station, and Pugh changed enough baht notes into coins to extract from the ticket machine two passes to the Sukhumvit station a couple of miles away. At the end of the workday, there weren't many passengers on our car riding toward central Bangkok. Most people were heading the other way. The car was pleasantly frigid. One elderly woman was speaking Thai into a cell phone while everyone else sat mute. The view out the windows was more Miami Beach–modern, except for the occasional temples with their whitewashed stupas and golden spires.

When the train stopped briefly at Ekamai station, I asked Pugh about the big bus station we could see down below on our left.

"That's the Eastern Bangkok bus station. If you're going to Pattaya or on to Cambodia, that's where you go to get the bus."

I imagined Elise Flanagan with her Antioch alumna group down below us climbing onto a coach three weeks earlier and then spotting Gary Griswold at the Thai-Cambodian border. That is, spotting either Gary Griswold or Raul Castro.

We sped across one of the city's few remaining canals, and I caught a quick glimpse of houseboats lining the dark waterway. Might Gary Griswold be hiding out on one of them, I wondered? Or might Raul Castro?

We arrived at Sukhumvit station and were headed down the long flight of steps to the busy commercial neighborhood below when my cell phone rang. I wanted to believe it was going to be Ellen Griswold calling me back with news of her ex-husband's location and his eagerness to help us free Timmy and Kawee and his profuse apologies for getting us into this goddamn mess in the first place.

We halted on the midlevel platform, and I stood out of the way of the surging crowds as best I could.

"Hello?"

"Donald, it's Timothy."

"Oh God."

"They told me to call you again."

"Yes. Good. Are you all right?"

"So far. But I'm supposed to remind you that now you have just twenty-four hours. You have until just after the sun sets tomorrow. They said they will not do what they have to do with us in the daylight. Do you understand what I'm saying? We're on the fourteenth floor."

"Yes, I understand."

"They will phone you this time tomorrow. And you will tell them that you have Griswold and are ready to hand him over."

"What is it they want with Griswold?"

"I don't know. Anyway, I am not allowed to tell you anything else."

"Okay."

"Just get us out of this Millpond hell, will you?"

"We're trying. Do they know we're having trouble finding Griswold?"

"They seem to know that. And they said you should try harder."

"Oh."

"I have to hang up now."

"Okay. Good-bye, Timothy. I heard what you said."

"Good. Bye, Don."

I looked at Pugh and said, "I know where they are. Timmy told me where they are."

I repeated the conversation to Pugh and added, "Timmy said he was in Millpond hell. Millpond is the name of an Albany, New York development company that tried to put up a mall on some suburban farmland a number of years ago. That project fell through, but eventually the company got hold of the farmland when the elderly owners moved into Albany, and then Millpond started building a group of luxury condos on the land. But the company was way overextended, and it went bust in the Poppy Bush recession. The unfinished condos stood vacant for years — an eyesore and an attractive nuisance for kids liable to break their necks climbing around on the tall concrete shells. These buildings were just like the unfinished condos you described to me here in Bangkok. I believe that Timothy and Kawee are being held on the fourteenth floor of one of them."

"This is possible," Pugh said. "These structures have security services meant to look after them. But security services perhaps can be bought — or simply replaced by the building's owner. Or the owner may not even know what's going on in his building. Or it may not even be known who the owner is."

"How many of these unfinished tall buildings are there in Bangkok? You told me earlier that they're all over the place. But I've only seen a few."

"You're right, Mr. Don. More than a few is more than enough, but I'm guessing there aren't more than a dozen. And not all of them will have fourteenth floors. So that will narrow it down somewhat. I can readily find out from people I know in the city building inspector's office how many such abandoned buildings are out there and exactly where they are."

"Can you get this information fast? Won't those offices be closed for the day?"

"For a fee, someone can speed back to the office and look up this data. Though then, of course, we run into our next set of difficulties."

"Which are?"

"Arriving at the correct building to effectuate a rescue and having either Timmy or Kawee shoved off the balcony, and then the captors threatening to kill the remaining one unless we produce Griswold and let them all go on their way."

"You think they would do that?"

"Of course. Why not? I think these people are not such good Buddhists."

CHAPTER SEVENTEEN

The first thing I realized was, they will kill Kawee first. He was a mere Thai lady-boy, and under the present circumstances, Timothy had greater bargaining value. I was ashamed that this realization came to me with a certain amount of relief.

Pugh got on his cell and called somebody who gave him a number, and then he called somebody else. After hanging up, he told me he would have a list of unfinished and abandoned tall buildings in Bangkok within two hours. He made another call and asked Ek to assemble a team of men and woman with, as he put it, "military skills and experience." I thought of my American Express account limit, and I wondered if maybe I could simply borrow the money for a sizable military operation from China, like Bush.

The last dull orange light of day faded out as Pugh led me away from Sukhumvit Road and down a mixed commercial and residential soi. The air was still ferociously hot, and within minutes my shirt was soaked through again. Pugh's dark face shone with a light sheen, but below the neck he didn't seem to be sweating at all. How did the Thais do that?

We passed Indian tailor shops, gold and gem emporiums, restaurants, flower stalls, bars and massage parlors. A number of the masseuses who were camped on stools outside their storefronts gabbing with one another or watering their plants grinned at Pugh and me and chimed, *"Hallo, massaagge?"* The curbside food stall aromas of chicken sizzling on grills with lime juice and herbs would have been pleasing under better circumstances, but now the smells were just cloying. How could Thai normal life dare to go on so cheerfully, so deliciously, when elements of Thai society that were completely rotten were threatening to kill two gentle and decent souls?

We entered a lower-rent district of three- and four-story concrete apartment buildings with drying laundry hanging over the balcony railings next to the flowering plants. Pugh stopped at a van parked on the street and the waiting driver opened the window. Seeing me, the driver told Pugh in English that one of Kawee's roommates said the moto man who delivers money to Kawee had not yet turned up, and if he arrived and Pugh's crew somehow missed him the roommate would notify the van on his cell phone. The roommate, an older katoey named Nongnat, had said she was worried about Kawee. Sometimes Kawee stayed out overnight with a new boyfriend, Nongnat had said, but not without phoning first. Pugh's people did not tell Nongnat that Kawee was being held hostage, thus avoiding any off chance that certain elements of the police might learn of the abduction and decide to meddle unhelpfully.

Pugh led me down the soi to where it ended at a chain-link fence along an expressway. Propped up next to the last apartment building on the block was a tin-roofed bamboo shanty that had a big open-front window and a counter. The place apparently served as a neighborhood convenience store. You could get Colgate, condoms, a variety of beverages — including one made of bird saliva, according to the colorful sign next to it — as well as under-the-counter whiskey that Pugh said was distilled nearby in somebody's flat.

Another of Pugh's fleet of vans was parked nearby, and he checked in with the driver. The moto money man had not turned up at this location either, and the whiskey seller had been put on a retainer to make sure he pointed out the man if and when he appeared.

We were headed back toward Kawee's apartment when Pugh's cell phone rang, and after a brief exchange in Thai he indicated that we should pick up the pace and trot.

"The moto man has arrived at Kawee's room with Kawee's money from Mr. Gary."

"Oh, terrific. Does he know where Griswold is?"

"Not exactly."

"Thailand seems to be the land of not exactly."

"Exactly."

"So if Griswold is sending Kawee's weekly payment, apparently he knows nothing of the kidnapping."

"Yes, unless he is simply — what's the term? — keeping up appearances."

"We can ask him about that."

Now even Pugh was sweating a bit. The moto man was standing next to his bike in front of the entrance to Kawee's building. He had on a dark jacket, impractical in the heat, it seemed, but apparently a fixture of every Bangkok motorcycle-taxi driver's getup. He had the serene look of a man who lived in chaos but had mastered the ability to float though it. The katoey Nongnat had come downstairs and was also calm but worried looking. She had the sloe-eyed, elegantly honed good looks of a honey-colored *Vogue* model who happened to have a prominent Adam's apple.

Pugh spoke with both of them in Thai and then told me that the moto man, Pichet Suthat, had indeed seen Gary Griswold just an hour earlier. Griswold had phoned him to arrange for the weekly pickup of an envelope — Pichet apparently did not know that it contained cash — and he had met Griswold at the corner of Sukhumvit Road and Ekamai Soi 63 near the Ekamai bus station. It seemed possible that this transaction had been taking place even as Pugh and I paused overhead at the Ekamai SkyTrain stop.

Pichet said he did not know exactly where Griswold lived, but he thought he had seen him a few times coming out of an apartment block just a short way up Soi 63 from Sukhumvit Road. We hired Pichet on the spot to take Pugh there, and we flagged down another moto taxi for me to ride. Nongnat asked in English where Kawee was and why we were looking for him. Pugh told her that Kawee was in some trouble and might need help, and we were friends of Gary Griswold prepared to do what we could. Pugh asked Nongnat if she knew where Griswold lived. She said no, and now she was even more worried about Kawee, she told us, and insisted on climbing on the second bike behind me.

Nongnat had on pink shorts — avoiding the need for womanly sidesaddle on the motorcycle — and pressed herself up against me as we took off. Her floral aroma as she nuzzled the nape of my neck was distinctly feminine, though as the motorcycle bounced and swayed and stopped short a couple of times it soon became apparent lower down that Nongnat was biologically still male. Once when I shifted in my seat a bit — I was also concerned that I might alarm or embarrass the moto driver I myself was wedged up against — Nongnat gave me a playful poke at the base of my spine and chuckled sweetly.

Pugh had arranged for his two surveillance vans in the neighborhood to follow us to Griswold's supposed residential block, even as his team at the On Nut Internet café maintained its vigil, and a separate flying squad was assembling under Ek's direction for an assault on abandoned tall buildings across Bangkok.

Traffic along Sukhumvit Road was heavy under the elevated SkyTrain line, and we bobbed and weaved among the cars and tuk-tuks, pausing only briefly for traffic signals and once detouring around a jam-up by jouncing over the curb and pinballing among the pedestrians, narrowly missing several. I thought of big Yai, who had run down a complaining Austrian tourist on the sidewalk and then turned around and driven over the prostrate and injured Viennese a second time. I wondered if soon I would meet sociopathic Yai face-to-face.

Pichet led us to the apartment building he thought Griswold might be living in. It was one of the posher ones in the neighborhood, not far from a cineplex and a couple of big international chain hotels. The lobby had a security door, but Pugh bounded off Pichet's bike and followed a man who looked like Wayne Newton into the lobby and then held the door open for the rest of us. The two vans pulled up out front, and one of Pugh's drivers joined Pugh, me and Nongnat as we approached a uniformed security man who appeared around a corner looking alert. Pugh spoke to the guard in rapid Thai and I heard him mention Gary Griswold.

Pugh said to me, "No Griswold here, he says, but let's try this." Pugh pulled a photo of Griswold out of his pocket and showed it to the guard.

The guard's face showed instant recognition, and he said, "Ah, Mr. Gray."

"Mr. Gray?" Pugh said.

"Mr. Gray Winsocki. Fifth floor. You want me call up to him? But I think he not here."

"Where is he?" I asked.

"Bicycle. Mr. Gray go out on bicycle. His bike not here."

I said to Pugh, "So he's likely to be back, right? He won't be biking to Cambodia or anything like that, it looks like."

The guard said, "Bangkok not so good for bicycle. Too much car. Too much motorbike. But Mr. Gray, he like bicycle. He go fast around cars. I think he come back later."

Pugh indicated to the guard that he'd like to speak with him privately, and they walked over to an alcove.

Nongnat said to me, "Kawee okay? I worry Kawee. Kawee say Mr. Gary good man, but why he hide? Why he change name? Farang not change name, just Thai."

"These are exactly the questions Khun Rufus and I hope to have answers to soon. Within minutes, with luck."

Nongnat wrinkled her elegant nose. "Mr. Gary he trouble. I tell Kawee he big trouble."

"Why did you think Mr. Gary was trouble?"

"No fuck, just pray. I tell Kawee be careful this type."

"Yes, that is a universal basis for caution."

Pugh and the guard came back and Pugh said, "This gentleman has refused us admittance to Mr. Gary's flat. It seems that one of life's most challenging quests is finished for us, Mr. Don. We have found an honest man. This dude won't let us into Griswold's place even in exchange for a substantial consideration. Well, fuck 'im if he can't take a bribe. Meanwhile, however, he is granting us permission to hang around here and nab Mr. Gary when he turns up again. Which my disappointingly ethical friend here expects to be soon. Mr. Gary normally takes his bike out for no more than a few hours. So I suggest that we position ourselves discreetly and wait."

It was mid-evening now, with daylight gone and less than twenty-four hours left before the kidnappers' deadline. Pugh's driver stayed behind in the lobby, and the rest of us went out front, and Pugh and I got into the air-conditioned van. Nongnat went down the street for some food and came back with jasmine rice and yellow curry with fish and bamboo shoots. We ate it eagerly — I was hungry by now and so no longer found the local food smells off-puttingly indifferent to our plight — and Pugh spelled his man in the lobby while he came out and also ate with steady concentration. This man observed his food admiringly as he ate it. It seemed as though any second he might actually speak to the rice and curry approvingly, even tenderly. The food was Thai all the way, and so was he.

At ten thirty Griswold still had not returned, and we were all wondering about that. What was he doing out riding his bike around Bangkok this late at night? But a call came in from one of Pugh's operatives, reporting that the list of abandoned partially constructed buildings at least fourteen stories high was on its way to where we were stationed. The list was expected within fifteen minutes, so Ek was summoned and told to wait up the street with his SWAT teams.

When the list arrived in a shoulder bag carried by a tiny young woman on a motorbike, Pugh and I got out and carried the bag up the soi to meet Ek. He had a convoy of three large four-by-fours, the type of swaggering road hogs Timmy would have immediately labeled socially irresponsible. Timmy, however, was not there to complain.

Some of Ek's small army of muscular guys in T-shirts and cargo pants got out of the SUVs and stood on the sidewalk looking formidable, even menacing, just as a male farang on a bicycle rounded the corner from Sukhumvit Road, approached our assemblage, seemed to take in the scene at a glance, and quickly swooped around and began peddling furiously back up the soi. Pugh saw this and yelled something in Thai to the girl on the motorbike who had brought the bag. She was off like a shot after the man on the bicycle, and we jumped into the van and took off after both of them.

Pugh's driver was so reckless that a couple of the taxi drivers we cut off actually honked their horns at us hot-heartedly and glared as we lurched down Sukhumvit Road. Within a block, we spotted Pugh's little moto woman, who had knocked Griswold off his bicycle and was wrestling with him on the sidewalk in front of a 7-Eleven. We pulled up, hopped out, elbowed aside a dozen or so alarmed bystanders, and hauled both Griswold and his bike into the back of the van. We required privacy for what was about to transpire, so we sent Nongnat back to her place with Supornthip, the moto driver who had chased down Griswold. They climbed on Supornthip's bike and sped away, and we took off close behind.

Griswold, who I recognized from his photographs, was in spandex biking shorts and a tank top, and he carried a shoulder bag, which Pugh wrenched away from him as one of Pugh's muscle guys, who had the word Egg stenciled on his T-shirt, wrapped plastic handcuffs around Griswold's wrists. Sweaty and decidedly nonaromatic, Griswold said nothing but was breathing fast. His bike helmet had slipped down low over his forehead, and Pugh carefully removed it and set it aside. Under his gleaming mess of helmet hair Griswold's eyes were wide open, and he kept glancing at me.

Pugh gave the driver some instructions in Thai, and that's when Griswold, apparently understanding Pugh's words, said evenly, "Not a good idea."

"Why should we not take you to your condo in Sathorn? It is your real home."

Griswold studied us and said, "Who are you? Before I say anything else, I need to know that."

"We are not your enemies. We are your friends," Pugh told him and then instructed the driver in English to take us to Pugh's office in Surawong, and to use the garage entrance.

Griswold took this in and then looked at me curiously. "Yeah. Okay. I think I understand what's going on here. You — Mr. Buttinski-Farang. What's your name? Is it what I think it is?"

"Donald Strachey. I'm a private investigator. I was hired by your former wife and current sister-in-law Ellen Griswold to find you and to protect you if necessary, and to persuade you to stop acting like a ninny."

Griswold laughed mirthlessly. "Ah, yes. The Albany private eye. I've heard about you. I thought you went home. You were supposed to fold up your tent and carry it back to the Hudson Valley. And yet here you are. I really need to talk to my former wife about her lax hiring practices." He shook his head and pushed some sweat off his forehead with the backs of his cuffed hands.

"You are in spectacularly big trouble, Griswold. You do grasp that, do you not?"

"Am I in spectacular trouble? Well, yeah, I guess I am. How thoughtful of you to fly all the way across the Pacific Ocean to point that out to me. Thanks loads."

My impulse was to grab the sarcastic asshole and bash him one, but I wasn't sure what all he knew. And of course, Timmy would have disapproved of my striking a pacifist — if Griswold really was that. I seemed to be surrounded by peace-loving Buddhists who found room in their hearts to smack people with phone books, and others who hurled soothsayers and farang retirees off balconies.

I said, "My partner — boyfriend — Timothy Callahan has been abducted by violent criminals. This is entirely your fault, Griswold. These criminals are people who are in fact looking for you and have not been able to locate you — because you are hiding out from them — and they want to swap Timothy and your young friend Kawee for you. If recent events are any guide, once they get hold of you these people intend to toss you off a tall building. So we have developed two plans. Plan A is to rescue Timmy and Kawee and then to protect you. You'll be happy to know that handing you over to these goons is only

Plan B. But before any of us carries out any plan at all, we need badly to understand exactly who and what it is we're dealing with here. Griswold, you have some extensive explaining to do. You can begin when I say go. Go."

He looked surprisingly at ease. Griswold's breathing had evened out now, and he lay on a straw mat in the back of the van with his head propped on a sack of rice. As I spoke, he listened carefully, his mouth dropping open when I told him Timmy and Kawee had been kidnapped and the kidnappers were willing to release the two once they had taken possession of Griswold. Unless he was faking it more brilliantly than seemed likely, Griswold was hearing about the kidnappings for the first time.

"Oh no," Griswold said. "Poor Kawee. This is awful. He's such a sweet-natured soul."

"Apparently that is the case. And I can tell you that Timothy Callahan is a nice guy, too. So let's get them both back real, real fast."

"I was so naive," Griswold said and shook his head. Then he looked up at me and said, "Please tell me. What is Timothy Callahan's birth date?"

I thought, Oh, good grief, here we go. "I'm not telling you that. We're not going to screw around with any astrology bullshit. What we're going to do is get to the point, and we are going to do so starting right now."

Griswold gazed up at me serenely. I was pathetic in his eyes. A rationalist, a literalist, a lost soul. He said, "I'm just trying to get some perspective on where you and your friend fit into all of this. Nothing more."

Then Pugh said, "I too am interested, Mr. Don. If you revealed to us where and on what date Mr. Timothy was born, this could help clarify the larger picture. I appreciate and respect your Western rationalist outlook, but just indulge us. And then we can proceed using more universal means. Phone books or whatever."

Pugh had used the word *us*, meaning Griswold and himself. What was going on here? Wasn't Pugh in a very real sense *my* contract employee?

I could hear Timmy snickering over all this, but I could also hear him bellowing, "Just tell them what they want to hear!"

I recited the year of Timmy's birth and told Griswold, "Timothy was born in Poughkeepsie, New York, on November eleventh, at ten fourteen a.m. So?"

The van was making its way through the Monday night traffic northward and westward toward Surawong. We were traveling at a normal rate of speed now, observing all the traffic laws, blending in, not attracting attention.

Pugh and Griswold looked at each other and then at me.

Pugh said, "It would help if a professional did Mr. Timothy's chart and blessed it. But even without that, I do believe that there is hope."

Griswold nodded in agreement. "There's a good chance that you can pull off a successful rescue. The date today is four-fourteen, a numerologically benign period for a Sagittarius. However," he said, "if the rescue doesn't work, I think I can work something out with these people. I'm quite certain I know who they are — or at least who they represent — and there's some chance I can make a deal with them and save myself as well as Timothy and Kawee."

This didn't sound right. If there was a way for him to negotiate with these people, why wouldn't he have done it sooner? I said, "So, who are they, and what would this so-called deal be?"

Pugh said, "Please do tell the truth, Mr. Gary. We will be very pissed off if you lie through your teeth and this quickly becomes apparent, which surely it will. Egg won't like it either, I am thinking." We all looked over at nicely toned Egg, who sat rock still, glowering at Griswold.

"I'm familiar with the Five Precepts, Khun...?"

"Rufus Pugh."

"I do understand, Khun Rufus, that to tell an untruth is reprehensible. And much more important than irritating you or your muscular young friend here, it would put me at grave risk of offending the spirit of the Enlightened One."

Pugh smiled weakly. "Said like a true farang dilettante Buddhist. No Thai would utter any such words. We would say if we lie, we might later turn into a buffalo turd and the ghost of our mother might slip and fall on us and break some bones. But never mind. You seem to get the point about truthfulness being an all-around better approach than going around telling big whoppers. So let's have it."

Griswold lay back now and looked up at the ceiling of the van. He was either organizing his true thoughts or he was formulating some cunning net of falsehoods that would have his late mother turning fecal-footed cartwheels in hell.

He said, "I reneged on a financial agreement in which I was to be the prime investor. A number of people had already put money into the same project. And when I unexpectedly decided to pursue an entirely different project and backed out of the original scheme just before I was to transfer my funds, the first project collapsed before others could get their money back and they lost many millions of dollars. And now a major group of losers blames me instead of the group that cheated them. They want me either to reimburse them — which I am not about to do — or they want me to die horribly as a warning to others not to trifle with them. It's as simple as that."

True or not, this sounded plausible. "So why," I asked, "don't you simply leave Thailand? If this is such a dangerous place for you, why are you choosing to hang around Bangkok?"

"To complete an extremely worthy nonprofit project," Griswold said. "When this project is done, I might leave Thailand for another Buddhist country — Laos, maybe, or Cambodia, despite my having been Thai myself in several past lives. Or I may remain here and let my karma play out in a way that would lead to my remaining safely in Thailand, my truest home, although in a form that might be other than human. To the extent to which any of these matters is within my control, I haven't yet decided how I will choose."

I noted Griswold's fine Italian bicycle in the back of the van, scratched and bent from having been whacked by the motorbike, and his helmet on the floor next to him. While I was thinking *brain damage*, I saw Pugh gazing at Griswold, rapt and solemn. A minute earlier, Pugh had been dismissing Griswold as a silly farang dilettante, and now he was looking at him as if he was some kind of spandexed holy man.

I said, "So what was the scheme that went awry, and who are the people who are mad at you?"

"There is no need for you to hear the particulars," Griswold said. "It had to do with currency speculation and involved certain insider information. I have to admit that the scheme was ethically borderline, but I saw it as justified by the opportunity to invest the proceeds in meritorious works on a very large scale."

Timmy's voice again in my head: "A Buddhist Augustinian. How unusual."

I said, "And what makes you think you might talk your way out of having these people who think you screwed them make a violent example of you?"

"I can tell them I'm going to cut them in on a new deal I've come up with that they will find irresistible. I know these people. The proceeds from this project will mainly benefit humanity. But even twenty percent should be enough to get these people off my case for the time being. And all we need, really, is a little time."

"And that new deal would be what?"

"I just can't go into it. Sorry. My partners would consider it a breach of confidentiality. Let's just say it has to do with international finance."

I had gotten a C in economics at Rutgers and looked at Pugh for help. I didn't even know what questions to ask. Pugh was still studying Griswold and looking impressed. Where had all this guy's Thai street savvy gone?

It hadn't gone anywhere, for now Pugh looked hard at Griswold and said, "Former Minister of Finance Anant na Ayudhaya. Is that thieving crumb-bum your partner in this so-called humanitarian venture, or was he a partner in the deal that went sour?"

Griswold froze ever-so-briefly. He recovered instantly and said mildly, "Why would you possibly assume anything like that? How bizarre that you would think that."

I said, "We got into your laptop. There's a picture of you together with this ex-minister and Khunathip the seer. I expect you know what happened to Khun Khunathip. So what's the story of you three looking like you're jollying it up at some Cornell class reunion on Khunathip's balcony?"

At the mention of Khunathip's name, Griswold seemed to breathe a little faster. Or was it the mention of a balcony? "That was a social occasion. I'm impressed by your chutzpah, Strachey. Getting into my computer was really an extraordinarily sleazy thing to do."

"Griswold, I was simply trying to save your dumb ass. That's what I was hired by your sister-in-law to do. Of course I was going to look anywhere that might offer any clue as to what kind of idiotic mess you've gotten yourself into. Anyway, what was your relationship to Khunathip the seer? The police say you turned up in his financial records. You paid him a fee, so-called, of six hundred fifty thousand dollars."

Now Griswold looked grim. "The fee had nothing to do with the investment. That was simply my payment for a series of readings this extremely keen-minded and profoundly far-seeing man did for me over a period of more than a year. His sad fate had nothing to do with any of that. Khun Khunathip should not have died. That was just so, so wrong."

"Was he killed by the same people who are after you?"

"He was a party to the original currency speculation scheme. He invested in it. In fact, it was Khun Khunathip who led me to it in the first place. When I came up with a much better investment project — one that was not only financially sound but morally uncompromised — and I pulled out of the currency speculation scheme before actually transferring any cash, Khun Khunathip tried to get his money back, too. It was about one million US, I believe. When the original investors refused to give the million dollars back to him — they laughed at him and called it overhead — he became uncharacteristically angry and did new astrological charts for each of them, and then cursed the charts. Then he sent each member of the investment group the cursed charts. Apparently the investors then hired their own astrologer, whose charts indicated that Khun Khunathip would have to be killed in order to erase his curses. I have to admit that I brought a certain amount of naïveté to all of this, but I was shocked that Khun Khunathip didn't know any better than to cross these ruthless and powerful people. This is an aspect of Thai society I failed to appreciate when I came here, and I have to say I still don't know what to make of it."

The van was stalled now in a big jam-up at Silom and Rama IV Roads. We had been stuck for several minutes, but there was no honking and there were no muttering drivers sticking their heads out their windows to see what in God's name the bloody holdup was. People sat quietly in their air-conditioned cars or in their fuming tuk-tuks. A low-fare, un-air-conditioned municipal bus idled nearby, and the steaming passengers sat by the open windows uncomplainingly inhaling that evening's portion of each person's annual allotment of small particulates.

Pugh said, "Khun Gary, welcome to Paradise. Like any paradise where human beings are present, Thailand is complicated. Mark Twain said, 'Heaven for climate, hell for society.' Here the two exist in a kind of rough harmony. As you seem to have discovered."

I said, "What about Geoff Pringle? You know about him, I take it."

"I read about him online in the *Key West Citizen*. For reasons of keeping up appearances for the farang tourists, I suppose, there was no report of Geoff's death in the Bangkok newspapers, either Thai or English editions. I was very, very sorry to learn of Geoff's passing. He was once a good friend of mine. It was Geoff who turned me on to Thailand in the first place. But he was one of the people who lost money in the currency speculation scheme. He blamed me, which was totally fair. I had gotten him into it originally. Geoff, however, made the mistake of pestering both the Ministry of Justice and the US embassy about his losses — he believed that he had been swindled, and of course he had — and it must have become apparent that he was going to be a troublemaker on a scale somebody high up didn't want to be bothered with. So Geoff had to go. It's one of the Thai business practices that I have to say I'll never get used to."

I said, "And now back to former Minister Anant. Where does he fit in here? Was he one of the participants in the original currency speculation scheme that was called off, or is he involved in the new project that's going to accumulate both vast wealth and karmic merit?"

I could all but see the wheels turning inside Griswold's head. Before Griswold could come up with some half-truth or bald-faced lie, Pugh said matter-of-factly, "It was both. Khun Anant was involved with both schemes, the dubious one that was abandoned and got two people killed, and the supposedly worthy project that is ongoing and hasn't gotten anybody killed just yet. Am I right, Khun Gary?"

Griswold peered down at his handcuffs and said nothing.

CHAPTER EIGHTEEN

Up in Pugh's office in Surawong, Griswold described for us his worthy project. It was a massive complex of temples, monasteries, and Buddhism study and meditation centers to be built on a drained cobra swamp on the outskirts of Bangkok near the new airport. A kind of Buddhism theme park would adjoin the main campus to help educate many of Thailand's fifteen million yearly foreign tourists about Buddhism. The monks from next door would participate in "monk chats" with the visiting farangs, explaining the tenets of Buddhism. Griswold said he had borrowed this last idea from an existing monastery in Chiang Mai, in northern Thailand, but his monk chats would be conducted on a much larger scale. Griswold himself would finance the construction of the complex, and the new business scheme he was planning along with Thai investors would serve as an endowment for the institution for decades or even centuries to come.

Pugh said, "Your audacious plan is largely meritorious, Mr. Gary. You are to be commended. It will be compromised, of course, if you are flung off the side of a high building before your project reaches fruition."

"That's one reason I'm trying to stay alive. Not just for myself but for the Sayadaw U Winaya project. That's who the project will be named after."

Pugh nodded approvingly, but I was in the dark. Griswold saw my puzzlement and explained. "A sayadaw is the abbot of a monastery in Burma. Sayadaw U Winaya was the revered abbot of the Thamanyat monastery in southeastern Burma until his death several years ago. He was a supporter of democrat Aung San Su Kyi and an opponent of the evil junta that rules the country so savagely. After his death, the monk's corpse was placed in a glass box and put on display in a shrine near the monastery, and was believed by Burmese Buddhists to have supernatural powers. Pilgrims came to Thamanyat from all over the country. The paranoid ruling generals feared the dead monk's magic and were probably behind the theft of the corpse by armed and masked intruders two years ago.

"At U Winaya Park, we'll have a replica of the great monk's corpse in a box of glass and gold. It will serve as a place of solace and spiritual power, not just for Thai pilgrims but for millions of Burmese refugees who had fled the horrors of their homeland. It's just barely possible that this project could go forward without me. But I'm providing most of the financing, and even more importantly the endowment cannot be set up without my guidance. So it's best, Strachey, that not only should Timothy and Kawee be rescued, but that I also should continue breathing and walking around upright, if at all possible."

It all sounded grandiose to me, out of scale for a philosophy with simplicity and humility at its moral core. But Pugh was looking thoughtful and approving, so who was I to judge?

"How," I asked Griswold, "were you planning on overseeing this huge project while you were in hiding? That sounds all but impossible, especially in a business culture that you don't know as intimately as you know your own."

"Later this month," Griswold said with quiet smile, "I won't be in hiding anymore."

"Oh? Why is that?"

"On April twenty-seventh, a number of changes will come about in Bangkok. And among those changes will be the effective removal of the leader of the original investment group. He will no longer be in a position to either hurt me or even hassle me."

Pugh said, "Nine."

"Not only," Griswold said, "will two and seven add up to nine, but my sworn enemy in all of this will on April twenth-seventh have been in his present position for exactly six years. And his wife will turn sixty years old on that day. They are finished. I will be free."

By now I expected Pugh to swoon over all this numerological mumbo jumbo — lucky nines dueling with unlucky sixes — but he just looked at Griswold peculiarly and said nothing. We were heading up Surawong Road now, nearing Pugh's office.

I asked Griswold, "How come you've been hiding out for six months, not just from these people who are after your ass but from all your friends and family back home? You could easily have been in touch by e-mail or even phoned people once in a while without compromising your safety. Your friends in Key West have been worried sick about you, and so have your brother and sister-in-law in Albany. That all strikes me as unnecessary and, if I may say so, pretty selfish for a practicing Buddhist."

Griswold's face hardened now. "Something happened six months ago that changed the way I see my life. This was a personal blow, nothing business related. But afterward I needed time to clear my mind of all the impurities I could possibly rid myself of. I have been mostly meditating for the past six months and attempting to restore a kind of karmic harmony in my life and in the lives of others."

"Did this have something to do with Mango?" I asked.

Griswold gave me a funny look. "Mango? How do you even know about Mango? Oh, I guess you would. You've spoken to Ellen and you've broken into my laptop, and you've probably been through my tax returns and my garbage pail. No, it had nothing to do with Mango. Mango was a beguiling man I thought for a while I might make a life with, until I found out he had several other lives going on at the same time, including one as a money boy. Another of his lives was accumulating real estate in Chonburi with his Thai lover, a man named Donnutt, who is also a very busy and accomplished money boy. In fact, Mango wasn't the first Thai man who turned out to be more interested in my bank account than anything else about me. I'm a bit disillusioned in that department, I have to admit. Thais are so sane about sexual orientation but far too casual about relationships. I know I'm an anachronistic joke in this regard, but I want the kind of marriage my parents had, except with a human being of the same sex. Others, I know, share this old-fashioned view, and it's what I'm holding out for and what I believe I'll have some day."

"Thailand might not be the best place for that, Griswold. Relationships are far more fluid here," I said, "more accommodating of human nature and the varieties of human need. Maybe you should have run off instead to North Korea or Idaho. It's not too late, of course. So what was this life-changing event six months ago, if not romantic?"

The van pulled into a parking garage next to Pugh's office, and Griswold said, "None of that is anything you need to concern yourself with in the present circumstances. Though you'll learn about a number of aspects of it soon enough."

I supposed I was going to have to wait for some more nines to turn up.

Two men met us at one of Pugh's reserved parking spots, and they along with Egg led Griswold through a passageway to Pugh's building and up to his office." Pugh and I followed, and soon he slowed our pace a bit until we were out of earshot of Griswold and the others.

Pugh said to me, "Griswold knows his numerology. A big man — the head of the investors who got screwed and are after Griswold — is going to take a fall on April twenty-seventh. But Griswold, I believe, gave something away. The esteemed seer Surapol Sutharat will lead a birthday blessing ceremony on that date on the plaza in front of the Central World Mall that will be open to the public and will be attended by many thousands of merit-makers. It will be one of the major socioreligious occasions in Bangkok to mark the beginning of Songkran, the Buddhist new year. The television newsies and the Bangkok papers have been burbling over with reports on this upcoming solemn event. And the star birthday girl, Paveena Hanwilai, is the wife of a considerable personage in Bangkok, a man whose name will ring a major bell with you, Khun Don."

Pugh had stopped walking and was looking at me now, and I asked him, "Who's that?"

"Paveena Hanwilai is the wife of Police General Yodying. She's a Bangkok A-list celeb from an aristocratic family — distantly related to Jack and Jackie, as she likes to remind folks — who gets her name and her picture in the papers regularly. She's often seen in the company of soothsayer Surapol at merit-making rituals at temples and upscale shopping centers around Bangkok. Of course, there could be another wife of a Bangkok pooh-bah with a sixtieth birthday on April twenty-seventh. I'll ask Khun Thunska to hack into city records and do a quick search for other April twenty-seventh sixtieth birthdays. But present circumstances do strongly suggest to me that Paveena is our gal and General Yodying is our boy. I believe I assured you earlier that General Yodying was our crook, not someone else's. You have my sincerest apologies for that miscalculation."

I thought about this and said, "So, can I get my twenty-four thousand dollars back?"

"Retrieving your money is the least of our worries," Pugh said. "Yodying is no doubt in touch with the kidnappers, perhaps even directing them. It's good that we did not involve the police in the rescue effort we have planned."

"You mean the rescue effort that might result in Timmy or Kawee getting thrown off a building as a warning to us to back off?"

"Yes, that very rescue effort. But we now have enough information to deal with that particular thorny aspect of this complex situation. Knowledge is power, after all."

"I love your bromides, Rufus. I find them soothing. Back in New Jersey, I may someday endow a bromide center at Monmouth State and name it after you."

"Thank you, Khun Don. You are a kind man."

CHAPTER NINETEEN

Griswold phoned somebody he refused to identify to us and tried to make a deal. First he offered 20 percent of the new project, then 30, then 40, then 50. He told whoever was on the other end of the line that that was as high as he could go. He had told us before placing the call that offering 90 percent would have been fine with him — after all, he'd be in the clear with these people as of April 27 — but that doing so would arouse suspicions about his sincerity. Also, he was unwilling to describe to the kidnappers the exact nature of the new can't-go-wrong project, and that probably did not inspire confidence.

Griswold hung up after a few minutes looking pale and exhausted. "I'm sorry. They said no deal. They want me. I suppose they think they can torture me and make me pay them back the money they lost, and then they'll kill me as a lesson to others not to fuck with them."

I said, "Why not just give them the money? Three lives are at risk here. How much did they lose?"

"Forty-three million US. I haven't got that much. And what I do have I will need for the Sayadaw U project. And also to right a wrong that has festered for far too many years."

He sat there beside Pugh's desk in his shiny biking outfit, reeking of stale sweat, and suddenly I wanted to pick him up and toss him out a window myself. Here was a man who had employed six month's worth of meditation to empty his mind of impurities and locate the peaceful core within, and yet he was going around wreaking bloody havoc wherever he turned. His wheel of life was like some kind of rampaging buzz saw.

Surprising both Pugh and myself, I said, "Griswold, you really have to consider giving yourself up to these people. Maybe your present life just isn't going to work out for you. Plainly, your heart is generally in the right place, and if I understand the rules of reincarnation correctly, you've earned a pretty good karmic report card overall. You've donated to lots of good causes over the years — Amnesty International and so forth, and I'll bet the Democratic Senatorial Campaign Fund. And your Buddhist study center and theme park, even if it never gets built, will surely earn you about a zillion points for good intentions. Your next life is bound to be both noble and cushy. So maybe the right thing for you to do is to just call it quits for this particular incarnation and let Kawee live out his current putrid existence as he sees fit, and the same goes for Timothy Callahan. Just give yourself up and let the karmic chips fall where they may. What do you think?"

Griswold sat glowering at me — he really would have to speak to his ex-wife about the hired help — but Pugh looked bemused.

Pugh said, "Khun Don, there is a certain Buddhist common sense to what you say. But I am thinking that it really need not come to that."

"So what do you have in mind, Rufus?"

"We can talk some more about that. Meanwhile, let's get Khun Gary spruced up a bit and into some fresh duds. Egg has some clothes in the outer office that should fit you, Khun Gary. There's a shower, and if you like we can call in a masseur and send out for a sack of grasshoppers in fish sauce for you to nibble on. Be assured you shall have whatever your heart desires, short of absconding. Egg will be following you wherever you go and he will not hesitate to crack a few ribs to sustain your cooperation. You are an extremely valuable property for us, so there's no chance we can allow you to slip away. For now, Egg, please remove Khun Gary's handcuffs."

Griswold's look softened, and he said, "This has turned into quite a mess, I know. I do apologize for that. It's not at all what I had in mind."

"Apology accepted," Pugh said. "Think nothing of it. Oh, there is one thing you can do to express your regrets in a more tangible way, and your doing so will be appreciated all around. Your former wife has discharged Investigator Strachey and will shortly cease paying his fees and underwriting his expenses. He has already spent many thousands of dollars trying to save you from a particularly unattractive form of dying fairly young. Acting as Khun Don's subcontractor, I also have incurred expenses. If you could kindly cough up about fifty K, this would go a long way toward easing any remaining bad feelings in this room. We know you're worth about thirty-eight mil, so fifty thousand would be no skin off your back. How about it? Good form is always appreciated in Thailand, as I'm sure you know. Economic justice is farther down on our list of social graces, but we here in this room like it, and we happen to own your sorry ass."

All serene again, Griswold said, "I can help you out, yes." He was back in Lady Bountiful mode.

"It would not be a charitable contribution, Khun Gary. It would be a fee for a service rendered. That service being: preventing three people, one of whom would be you, from meeting the same sad fate as Khun Khunathip and your old friend Geoff Pringle. Though please do understand. While we are professionals at bailing out the hapless, we can only do what we can do. Your coughing up the fifty K in the next half hour, if you please,' does not guarantee success. We will, however, do our darnedest."

"The next half hour?"

"There are banks nearby. Or if you have a cash stash — which surely you must — you can direct us to it."

Griswold said, "Get me my bag."

Pugh had already been through Griswold's shoulder bag. It contained a bottle of water, some vile PowerBar sort of thing with a Malaysian label, and Griswold's wallet. Griswold selected an ATM card from the six or seven in his wallet and wrote the password on a piece of paper Pugh provided.

"If you think you might help yourself to a million or two I've got sitting around in that account," Griswold said, "you can forget it. That account holds no more than US seventy thousand dollars."

"And your withdrawal limit is?"

"There is no limit."

"Khun Gary, you are a god."

"No, just a good businessman."

I said, "And the son of Max and Bertha Griswold. That helped."

At the mention of family and money, Griswold grew solemn. "Yes, my parents worked hard and became wealthy, and I was the beneficiary of nearly half their wealth. I have never felt anything but grateful for, and unworthy of, my inheritance. And I've always tried to share that wealth in a responsible way. And I intend on continuing to do so if I possibly can."

"This is where our interests intersect," I said. "Keeping you alive to perform more good works, and keeping Timothy and Kawee alive so they can scratch around in the dust in their far humbler ways."

"You're a somewhat bitter man," Griswold said. "If you remain in Thailand, I could direct you to people who would help you do something about that."

"My bitterness is temporary, and my bitterness is rational. It has to do with the possibility of the sweet man I have made my adult life with ending up as a pile of broken bones and useless bloody tissue on a Thai sidewalk or roadway."

Griswold looked momentarily stricken and said, "You know, my parents died in a fall. In an airplane that crashed."

"I heard about that. From Lou Horn."

"Oh. Lou. How is he? Is Lou all right?"

"Yes, except for wondering why you totally cut him off and acted like you had just..."

I let the words hang, and Pugh said it. "Fallen off the face of the earth."

"All that will be cleared up soon enough," Griswold said. "I do feel very, very bad about the way I treated my old friends."

"You should."

"I really need to get a competent reading soon. All this falling. It's hard to believe. My parents. Khun Khunathip. Geoff. And now these threats against Kawee and your boyfriend. It's just too much falling to write off as what most people might call coincidence."

"You're a faller too, Griswold. A couple of years ago you fell off your bike. And got a good whack to your noggin. Don't leave that one out."

"Funny," Griswold said. "Lou and my friends Marcie and Janice in Key West talked about that. A bike accident. But I really have no memory of it happening."

By now, Pugh had one of his crew in the office and was instructing her on how and where to extract the fifty thousand dollars worth of baht from an ATM. Griswold began to make a move toward the outer office and the bathroom when Pugh asked him to wait just one moment.

Before Griswold left the room with Egg at his side, Pugh said, "In addition to the funds, I need one other thing from you, Khun Gary, if we're going to fish your butt out of the soup. I need to know who exactly we are dealing with here. I have reason to believe that Police General Yodying Supanant is the head of the investors who got screwed and who want you to make good on their lost investments. Am I correct?"

Shaking his head, Griswold said, "Oh God. I should never have mentioned that part of it. You know about Paveena and her birthday celebration, don't you?"

"I read the *Post*, just like you."

"Yes. Damn. But it's just as well. I suppose you do have to know everything if you're going to get all of us out of this fuck-all with no more falling from high places."

"Precisely. And no more of this falling-off-the-face-of-the-earth hugger-mugger."

Griswold was led out of the room, looking dazed.

As soon as Griswold was gone, Pugh got on the phone with Khun Thunska. He asked him to do a quick check of computerized city records of who in Bangkok besides Paveena

Hanwilai would have a sixtieth birthday on April 27 and had a powerful husband.

Next, Pugh called Ek and they had a quick exchange in Thai. Pugh explained to me that he had instructed Ek to locate the abandoned building in which Timmy and Kawee were being held. A helpful employee in the Bangkok building inspector's office had come up with a list of nine buildings that fit Timmy's "Millpond" description. Ek would narrow the list down through surveillance and trustworthy contacts at security firms, but he would not act until told to do so by Pugh. Pugh told me he now had a plan for rescuing Timmy and Kawee that involved some risk for them and for us, and would have repercussions we would all have to cope with.

I said, "So, you don't like my idea of having Griswold turn himself over to the kidnappers and leaving it up to him to talk his way out of this? I thought you might see a kind of karmic logic to that one."

Pugh shot me a quick, tight smile. "It wouldn't work. They would likely grab Griswold and renege on their promise to release their captives. As Khun Gary predicted, they would torture him and extract as much cash from him as they could in a short time. Then they would throw all of them off a building — Griswold, Timmy and Kawee — as a kind of fuck-you gesture to all of us. Then the police would miraculously appear on the scene and arrest you for some type of visa violation and me for trout fishing without a license. A financial settlement of perhaps fifty K or so would soon be agreed to, and we would both be released. Life would go on for me, and you would be placed on a Lufthansa flight for Frankfurt in the middle of the night, coach class. So, Khun Don, commonsensical as your ostensibly hardheaded formulation might be on its face, you'd better forget it. Here in the Land of Smiles, it just ain't gonna fly."

I said to Pugh that if my desperate, fatalistic and admittedly selfish solution was not the answer, then what was? The scenario he laid out for me over the next three minutes sounded outlandish, although it occurred to me that it would not have surprised Timmy.

CHAPTER TWENTY

Time was running out for Timmy and Kawee, and my fear kept me awake as I lay on a mat through much of the night in Pugh's office. He slept nearby, as did Griswold. A large man named Sek had been brought in to watch over Griswold, who, as I lay trying not to tremble, snored grotesquely. I could hear snoring from the outer office, too. It was late Monday night now, but even with the air-conditioners whirring I could hear the fuck-show and pussy-show crowds exiting the nearby clubs and moving noisily about in the street below. Eventually I sank just below the surface of consciousness for a few hours. I might have sunk even deeper had Pugh not jostled me just after six in the morning with a cheery, "Rise and shine, Khun Don, rise and shine. Time to head on out and find the bad guys and put up your dukes."

Somebody went over to Silom for coffee, and Griswold was led into the outer office where he was to wait for further developments under Sek's supervision.

Coffee, pineapple chunks and rice gruel arrived, and Ek soon called and told Pugh that he had located the building where Timmy and Kawee were most likely being held. It was one of two unfinished and abandoned fifteen-story condos in a complex off Rangnum Road about a mile north of Siam Square. Ek had learned from a source at one of the security services watching over Bangkok's abandoned high-rises that the guards at one site had been instructed by an agent for the building's owner, a bank, to take a few days off and had been replaced by unknown amateurs who were described by one security officer as "gangsta boys."

Pugh put Ek on hold while he took a call from Khun Thunska. While I listened in on an extension, the computer ace reported that nearly a thousand women would turn sixty in Bangkok on April 27. He said he would go over the list more thoroughly over the next few hours, but a preliminary once-over showed that only one of these women was wed to a Bangkok big shot. That was Paveena Hanwilai, wife of General of the Royal Thai Police Yodying Supanant.

Pugh got Ek back on the line and said, "Time to move."

§ § § §

We headed north toward Rangnum Road in two vans. A broad-shouldered youth named Nitrate drove the one with Pugh, me and Miss Aroon. She was dressed in shorts and a tank top and appeared ready to don the costume she would need for the rescue operation. The van following us held Griswold, Sek, Egg and four well-toned young men who normally performed in the gay fuck show at Dream Boys but also moonlighted as muscle boys for Pugh. Pugh said only two of them were gay, but the money at Dream Boys was good, and life in show business beat driving a truck around in the heat. I watched these guys load lengths of rope into their van before we left the office, along with several bamboo poles.

The morning traffic was thick and moved in fits and starts. Pugh said he remembered that when he was a boy large herds of cattle were driven up Rama IV Road to the city's main slaughterhouse, and now it often seemed as if the city hadn't modernized at all but had just substituted Toyotas for cows. We could have taken the speedy SkyTrain up to Rangnum Road, but our flying squad needed more flexibility than that afforded by public transportation.

It didn't much matter that our progress was slow. We didn't need to be in place at Rangnum Road, Pugh said, until eleven o'clock, when Ek would arrive with his own captive, the soothsayer Surapol Sutharat. I asked Pugh about seer Surapol's public prediction that no coup could be expected in Thailand anytime soon, when apparently some change of government that would send General Yodying packing was in the works for April 27.

"It's disinformation," Pugh said. "That's how these guys work. Their charts may show one thing, but publicly they say whatever their clients want the public to hear. It's soothsaying-slash-spin."

"But this other seer, Pongsak Sutiwipakorn, has forecast a coup before the end of April. What's his deal? If he has a line to the coup plotters, why are they giving the game away? Isn't surprise a crucial element in any government overthrow?"

"It's swagger. When upper-echelon Thais brazenly tip their hands, it's the same as when lower-class Thai men rip off their shirts and brandish their ogreish tats to give opponents the heebie-jeebies. Much of the time, however, this tactic is bluff. But you can never be sure if it's real or not, so you're never sure how or even whether to respond. It's part of what makes civic life in Thailand so endlessly fascinating."

"Griswold is apparently convinced that a coup is imminent. How else would he know that General Yodying is going to lose his job on the twenty-seventh?"

"Former Finance Minister Anant would know such things if he was involved in the conspiracy. And soothsayer Pongsak would know from consulting his charts. Whether it's a coup or an unfortunate accident on April twenty-seventh that causes General Yodying to — dare I once again use the word *fall?* — either way he seems to be a goner, practically speaking."

I recalled the long-ago days of the old O'Connell Democratic machine that befouled civic life in Albany for much of the twentieth century. It, too, routinely played rough, although surely it would have met its match tangling with Minister Anant, General Yodying and the politico-soothsayers of Bangkok. The civic reformers who finally succeeded at de-corrupting Albany in the 1980s would have been eaten alive by this Thai crew. And tossed over a high ledge near the top of the Al Smith State Office Building.

We parked both vans in a soi a couple of blocks from the condo complex. A Burmese travel agency was on one side of us and a small open-front restaurant on the other. Some of the cooking was being done in raised kettles on the sidewalk, and the air was hot and rich with the aroma of the chilies, cardamom and cinnamon in a Massaman curry. It was only just after ten, so the rescue crew climbed out of the vans and headed to the restaurant for a snack. Despite the tension generated by our task, the several men and one woman were kidding around in the Thai manner, joshing one another and casually ha-ha-ing. It was as if all the good food Thais ate produced not just generally good health but good humor, too.

Pugh also got out of the van and found a flower seller nearby. He bought a garland of jasmine blossoms and walked over to the spirit house in front of a store that sold running shoes and flip-flops. Pugh placed the garland before the Buddha figure, wai-ed the statue, and bowed his head for some minutes. He had placed his cell phone next to the garland and other offerings that had been left by others: candles, rice, a cardboard carton of guava juice. He wasn't planning to leave the phone behind, I surmised, but wanted to have it handy in case Ek called.

At ten to eleven, Ek did call. At Pugh's signal, the rescue crew quickly gathered around him for their instructions. He spoke to them in Thai. Most of them spoke some English, but it was limited and there was no room for misunderstandings or screwups. And they were no longer kidding around.

The group broke up into units of two each. One pair carried the ropes and bamboo poles. The men wore cargo pants and T-shirts and could have passed for construction workers or window washers.

Pugh, Egg, Griswold, Miss Aroon and I walked a bit ahead of the others on the opposite side of Rangnum Road. When we reached the private soi leading to the abandoned condo complex, my heart began to race and my impulse was to sprint into one of the buildings and tear up fourteen flights shouting Timmy's name. I took a deep breath of the muggy Bangkok air and maintained my steady pace next to Pugh. I saw Ek's four-by-four parked up ahead next to one of the tall concrete shells, as well as other vehicles I did not recognize. One was another dark SUV and then a blue Mercedes. A motorcycle was parked behind the Mercedes.

Ek stood in the entryway to one of the buildings with two more of Pugh's operatives. He beckoned for us to move with him into the shadows. He said, "That one," and indicated the structure forty or fifty feet across the driveway. We moved forward a few steps and peered up, and I could sense that, like me, everybody was counting to fourteen.

When the men with the ropes and bamboo poles arrived, Ek signaled for them to follow one of his team into our building. Miss Aroon joined this group now and was handed a bulging Central World shopping bag by Ek. I watched as all of them entered a stairwell and disappeared.

We were far enough off Rangnum Road that passersby would not be aware of anything out of the ordinary going on in the complex. We had the privacy we needed to do what we needed to do. Just as the kidnappers had the privacy they had needed to hold Timmy and Kawee captive for the previous forty hours, and the privacy they would need to hurl them off a fourteenth-floor balcony after sunset.

I said to Pugh, "Where's the seer? He's up where Ek is heading?"

"Khun Surapol was snatched as he approached Wat Mahathat, his neighborhood temple, for morning prayers. He was told that he was needed to bless a construction project and would soon be released and even amply rewarded. Then Ek and his lads hauled him over here and marched the eminent seer up to the fourteenth floor of this building. Its balcony looks directly across to the balcony of the condo where the captives are being held."

I stepped into the sunlight and looked up again, and wondered if we shouldn't be rigging circus trapeze nets around the building across the way. I guessed, though, that no net would support an adult plummeting from fourteen floors up. I said, "Wouldn't the kidnappers have spotted us by now?"

"It doesn't matter. They may phone General Yodying, but he will be neutralized within a matter of minutes."

"Rufus, I'll have to trust you that you can get away with this."

Pugh said, "Ih."

After a few minutes, Pugh's cell phone chirped. He spoke briefly in Thai, then said to me, "That was Ek. It's time to make our move."

At Pugh's signal, Sek and Egg accompanied Griswold out from the shadows. Both men wore shoulder holsters containing long-handled Chinese revolvers. We walked across the unfinished driveway and entered the second unfinished apartment building.

Pugh said, "Let's you and I, Khun Don, lead the way and make a memorable first impression on these boorish fellows."

In what would have been the lobby of the apartment building, we passed the two openings to the empty elevator shafts. All around us was raw concrete with its limestone smell. It was damp in the Bangkok pre-monsoon humidity and smelled like the inside of a wet cave. It took me back to my spelunking days in college, and I wondered what in the world I had in mind back then crawling around in those claustrophobic spaces, cold and muddy, and in danger in the rainy spring months of being crushed or, more likely, trapped and drowned. Which was the most awful way of dying? Drowning? Being compressed and suffocated? Falling? As we climbed upward and passed the exposed elevator shafts on each floor, I thought to myself, Don't fall, don't fall, don't fall.

We were all getting winded in the heat, except for Griswold, the manic cyclist. He was more fit than any of us and probably had never smoked. Pugh, Sek, Egg and I were soon panting, and I finally got to see a Thai perspire. I thought of Timmy and Kawee, who two days earlier had been force-marched up these same stairs, probably unsure whether once they got to where they were going, they might be hurled down an elevator shaft or off a balcony.

Pugh was quietly counting off the floors. When he got to the twelfth, he said, "Fourteen is next."

Sek and Egg had drawn their revolvers by now and were following Pugh, me and Griswold closely. As we turned onto the stairs leading to the fourteenth floor, four men appeared above us and we stopped. Two of them held guns, and the other two held good-sized bamboo canes.

There was a rapid back-and-forth in Thai between Pugh and one of the men holding a revolver. He was large and sullen, and I thought, yes, finally, the knocker-over of Austrian tourists.

As we climbed the final flight of stairs, I said to Pugh, "That's Khun Yai?"

"The one and only."

We were led into what would have been — and I assumed what might one day still become — a large fourteenth-floor apartment. The place was set up like a campsite. Camp stoves were on a table in one corner next to a portable refrigerator. I could smell the soup in a pot. Straw mats were spread around on the floor. There were gas lanterns atop a pile of crates next to a card table with stools around it. Apparently we had interrupted a poker game, for four hands lay facedown around the table with a pile of bahts in the middle..

With two of their men pointing guns and two of ours doing likewise, any shoot-out would have been short and ugly. Everyone in the room must have been acutely aware of this, though nobody lowered his revolver.

I saw no sign of Timmy and Kawee and figured they were in another section of the apartment.

Pugh said something in Thai, and Yai apparently indicated that one of his goons should go and fetch the captives. One of them kept looking at Griswold and then down at a photo he had, apparently to make sure we had not delivered a fake Griswold. It was plain that Pugh had done what he had told me earlier he was going to do. In Thai, he had informed these men that we were turning Griswold over to them in return for Timmy and Kawee. He said Griswold was not resisting because he now realized it was his fate to pay for his sins. He had caused important men to lose both money and face, each an unforgivable violation in the Thai moral universe. And he knew he would have to pay, and he was prepared to do so.

Griswold said nothing. Apparently he was fluent in Thai, for he followed the conversation with a look that was fascinated though faintly bug-eyed.

Big Yai got on his cell phone to somebody — General Yodying? — and seconds after he rang off, one of the gang came back leading Timmy and Kawee. Their hands were tied behind their backs and they were bound at the ankles too, so they had to take little dainty steps. They weren't in the clothes I had last seen them in but were in cargo shorts and T-shirts. They were both sweating. Timmy's hair was a rat's nest and Kawee's lip gloss looked chewed off. On the front of Timmy's yellow T-shirt were the words *Thailand — Land of Smiles*.

When Timmy and Kawee saw us, their faces fast-forwarded through shock, relief, joy, apprehension and fright. Then they just stared at us, hyperalert.

I said, "We're getting you guys out of here. It won't be long now."

"And with hours to spare," Timmy said. "Thank you for that."

Yai indicated that his gang should free Timmy and Kawee from their bonds. They quickly did so, using sharp knives from the food preparation area to slice through the ropes. Timmy and Kawee began rubbing their wrists and moving their legs about, as if they were warming up for a ping-pong tournament. Next, Yai directed two of his men to tie Griswold up.

That's when Pugh said something in Thai that made Yai look out the door to the balcony with a start.

We had a clear view across the way to the second building in the condo complex. From the balcony opposite us, two people were dangling. Each was upside down. Ropes were tied around their ankles, and the ropes were attached to bamboo poles held in place by four of Pugh's men, Nitrate, Ek and two others.

One of the dangling people was Khun Surapol Sutharat, the seer who had been providing ace astrological advice to the kidnappers. The other dangling person was a middle-aged woman in a fashionable Siamese gold-colored blouse and long green skirt, the skirt now semicomically bunched up above her waist, exposing the woman's black panties. Someone had lowered a cell phone on a wire to Khun Surapol and we could see him frantically trying to hold it up — down, really — to his ear.

Pugh took out his own phone and hit a speed-dial number. After a moment, he handed the phone to Yai and gestured toward the dangling soothsayer. "Somebody wants to palaver with you," he said.

Yai spoke some Thai into the phone and then listened. He looked confused, bordering on panicky. It didn't help his frame of mind when the men holding the bamboo pole across the way began to bob it up and down, as the seer and the woman next to him gesticulated and clawed at the side of the building.

Yai took out his own phone now and frantically dialed.

Pugh said, "Tell the general that that is his wife Paveena Hanwilai over there, the birthday girl herself. If you and the general don't do as we say, we'll drop her skinny ass fourteen floors to the pavement below. And Khun Surapol will accompany her soul to paradise or to purgatory or to Newark Liberty International Airport — wherever. In any event, both of their corporeal worldly remains will leave an impression, for the general and for many others in the vicinity of Rangnam Road."

Now Yai spoke into his phone in rapid Thai. He scowled furiously then said in English, looking at Griswold and me, "Wait."

The general was no doubt phoning his wife to see if she had actually been abducted. She had in fact been snatched, Pugh had told me, from Wat Mahathat, where she prayed each morning with her soothsayer. She was not, however, hanging from a pole across the way. She was locked in a janitor's closet in a disused primary school next to the temple, minus her cell phone, her skirt and blouse and — just to play it safe — her black underwear. To preserve her modesty, Mrs. Paveena had been provided a large plastic garbage bag with a hole on top for her head to stick out and holes on the sides for her arms. The woman dangling next to Khun Surapol in Paveena Hanwilai's garments was Miss Aroon — who had never been an acrobat exactly, but had for a time some years earlier fired ping-pong balls from her vagina to the cheers of drunken tourists at a club in Patpong.

Suddenly Yai was listening closely on his phone and nodding. He soon said something to Pugh in Thai. Pugh smiled amiably and said — I knew this much Thai — "*Capkun kap*, Khun Yai." Thank you so much, Mr. Yai.

Then Yai narrowed his eyes and hissed out two or three more brief sentences. Pugh shrugged and said something that from his look could have been "I'll take note of that."

Pugh said to me, "Mr. Yai has informed me that today the general is going to release all of us. But by the end of the month he will have killed every last one of us. What do you think of that?"

"I find that pronouncement unsettling, Rufus. What do you think of it?"

"Well, I think the general has another think coming."

Griswold had followed all this with a look of bemused fascination. Kawee looked more or less relaxed by now, too. Timmy just looked queasy.

CHAPTER TWENTY-ONE

The first shots were fired at our minivan no more than fifteen minutes later as we drove south on Ratchaprasong Road. Nitrate sensed what was about to happen when motorcyclists pulled up on either side of us simultaneously. As he gunned the engine, I caught just a millisecond's glimpse of the raised long-barreled revolver pointed at my side of the van. Nitrate did an instant U-turn — southbound traffic was heavy, northbound lighter — and shot northward. The second van in our convoy followed, and I could hear shots fired behind us.

Ek, in the seat behind me, had shoved open his window and was ready to fire at anybody within sight who was firing at us, but Pugh said something in Thai and Ek held his fire. Pugh told me, "We're not gonna kill anybody on the street. We'll get on the expressway. No motos are allowed on the expressway."

Pugh was on his cell phone now, consulting the second minivan, driven by Egg. Griswold was in the second van, Timmy and Kawee were in ours. Kawee was taking all this in with a look of intense curiosity. Timmy just looked numb.

Still on his phone, Pugh said to us, "Egg's van took fire, but no one was hit."

Timmy was next to me, clutching my thigh. Kawee, on the other side of Timmy, was hanging onto an armrest and looking this way and that.

One of the motos came at us again from the left. As the driver raised his arm, Ek veered into him hard, and the attacking moto went over on its side and slid at high speed into the oncoming southbound traffic. There was a lot of crashing and banging behind us, but Ek straightened out the minivan and sped ahead. The other minivan was close on our tail, with the expressway entrance just ahead.

At the last second, Nitrate swerved onto the freeway, where motorcycles were not permitted. The second van was keeping pace with us, and so was the second moto guy, not a law-abiding citizen. As we shot down the ramp and onto the expressway, the gun-wielding cyclist was making a pass at the van Egg was driving. I turned around and watched as Egg slowed briefly, and an object shot out the side window of the second minivan and hit the moto gunman hard on the side of the head. The object splattered and the motorcycle flipped end over end, its driver doing cartwheels parallel to the vehicle, a horrifying choreography of metal and flesh dancing in tandem along a long ribbon of concrete.

Kawee exclaimed, "Oi, oi, oi. He in hell now."

Timmy had been looking more traumatized by the minute, though I knew he would survive all this when he peered over and said to me, "I feel as if I've gone to the movies for a picture I really wanted to see, and first I had to sit through an entire day and a half of noisy, stupid trailers for movies I would not dream of paying money to look at."

"It's the story of your life with me, Timothy. You moved in with Marcello Mastroianni and woke up with Bruce Willis."

He laughed lightly.

I asked Pugh, "What was it that hit that guy on the bike?"

"Miss Aroon's durian. Normally I discourage my employees from carrying this large, spiky, melonlike fruit along on operations. Some Thais find its pungent smell enchanting, and some Thais — like most farangs — consider its stench revolting. But Miss Aroon needs her durian and usually has one stowed under the seat of the vehicle she's in. She had one along today, and of course, she has a strong right arm and impeccable aim."

One of the Thais in the car said something in Thai that made the others guffaw. Pugh said, "He asked, 'How do we know she used her arm?'"

We had slowed to a normal speed now and the other minivan was close behind as we moved steadily eastward and then, I noted on the overhead signs, southward. Pugh's phone sounded and he spoke briefly and then instructed Ek to pull over to the shoulder of the highway. He did so, and the second minivan followed us. I looked back to see the guardrail-side door open on the other vehicle, and the soothsayer Surapol Sutharat step out and stand by the roadside. Then the door closed and both vans drove on.

I said, "Do you think Khun Surapol predicted this turn of events, Rufus?"

"He would have had an inkling. The man is not stupid. He's corrupt, but not entirely incompetent with his charts."

"So now what? Do we ride around on the freeways of Bangkok until April twenty-seventh? We'll run out of gas."

"Nope. Not necessary. What I think is, we all deserve a few days at the seashore."

"Sounds good. Can we pick up our bathing suits at the hotel?"

"No, Khun Don. I am sorry. We must proceed directly to Hua Hin. It is a pleasant town a few hours' drive south of Bangkok on the Gulf of Thailand. Hua Hin is such a desirable getaway spot that Jack and Jackie themselves have quite an impressive palatial hideaway there."

"Well, if it's good enough for Jack."

"Others will be in danger, also, and will need to join us there. In fact, I must make some calls now. My wife and children will be along, as well as my girlfriend Furnace, a delightful woman you will enjoy tremendously. Furnace will, of course, be housed separately from the rest of us, though with luck your paths will cross. Kawee, you should invite Miss Nongnat to visit. And it might be wise for Khun Gary's old paramour Mango to attend our seaside holiday also. The general is sure to be ripshit over today's developments, and his agents will tend toward impatience and extreme violence toward anyone who might be expected to know of our whereabouts."

Pugh got on his cell phone and made several calls in Thai. This was the first time since Timmy's rescue that we could speak with each other without the risk of gunfire erupting, and the first thing I said was, "Okay. Yes. You were right."

He said nothing.

"I'll spend the rest of my life making this up to you, Timothy. You name it. It's yours. Plus, of course, I'll listen to you in the future when you talk sense. Really, I'll try harder to do that."

He was breathing evenly but was still sweaty and didn't smell so great.

I looked across Timmy and said to Kawee, "I'm really so sorry I got you two into this. It must have been very frightening."

Kawee said, "We think we die."

"Yes."

"I tell Timothy he live better life next time."

"I know he'd like some improvements."

"He say okay. But he ask if you be there, too."

"In his next life?"

"Yes, he want next life with you. You his soul mate, he say."

"That would be my preference also. What did you tell him? Will we be together?"

"Yes, maybe. But maybe not human. Maybe you both snake."

"Two snakes?"

"Timothy and Donald spirit in snakes. Or other animals. All depend on karma."

"If we were mammals, it might be okay. We'd manage. Mammals with small brains and large penises."

Timmy was too polite and respectful toward other decent people's deepest beliefs to roll his eyes, but I knew he was doing it mentally.

Finally, Timmy said, "Kawee was very thoughtful and supportive during our captivity, Donald. He enlarged my perspective."

I wondered if he had also massaged his prostate, but this was no time for that discussion. I said, "How so?"

"I just have a better understanding now of the way the human mind can both retreat into itself when that's the only way it can stay safe, and at the same time how any one mind is only a temporary partial manifestation of something far larger and longer lasting."

"Oh. Well, good. Except, that doesn't sound Buddhist. It sounds Jungian."

"You and your Western insistence on labels. God."

"Are you putting me on?"

"Yes, a little. But, really, Kawee did help me with the whole idea of acceptance. Acceptance of how temporary any one human life is, and how the transitory nature of life should be nothing to fear. There's actually something quite beautiful about it. All that gorgeous fluidity."

Pugh was in the front seat with Nitrate, who was driving, and when Timmy said this, Pugh reached over to the steering wheel and hit the horn three times.

CHAPTER TWENTY-TWO

The compound where we took refuge in Hua Hin — which, Pugh explained, was spelled Hua Hin but pronounced *Wah-HEEN* — was a few miles south of the town center near Monkey Mountain. This was a high hill overlooking the Gulf of Thailand where monkeys frolicked on the grounds of an old temple. Pugh suggested that Timmy and I have a look while we were in the vicinity. But he said not to get too close to the greedy and always-quarreling monkeys, a few of whom were deceased former officials from the Thaksin Shinawatra administration.

Timmy said, "Do you really believe that's true?"

"Of course," Pugh said. "This is known."

The compound, a quarter mile off the main road and a few hundred yards from the beach, was owned by an anti-Samak, anti-Thaksin businessman friend of Pugh's who owned about fifty 7-Eleven franchises and a Hua Hin hotel that catered to German tour groups and, Pugh said, served the greasiest schnitzel south of Bangkok.

Pugh's friend, Sila Chusuk, was vacationing with his family in Switzerland and we had the run of his two commodious guesthouses. These were rambling, tile-roofed stucco structures with big louvered windows that were sealed shut now for the hot season and with central air-conditioning keeping everything crisp. There was a pool in the palm-fringed flower gardens at the back of the walled compound, with fuchsia blossoms floating in it the color of Kawee's toenails.

We had stopped in town to buy some light clothes for Timmy and Kawee — Pugh said we would not be calling on Jack and Jackie, so beachwear would do — and some toiletries, and of course, food. The Thais had missed their lunch, so a stop was made out on the main road to pick up soup and rice. As soon as we arrived at the compound, Pugh and his crew served up the take-out savories and went at them. Nobody had a lot to say. They were all just happy to be alive and enjoying another good meal. The same was true of Timmy, Kawee and me — and presumably Griswold, although he had precious few words to offer any of us.

Upstairs, Timmy and I shared a room, Pugh was next door, then Kawee and Nitrate, then Griswold, Egg and Ek. Griswold bore constant watching, Pugh and I agreed. While Timmy took a long shower, I noted on my cell phone that Bob Chicarelli had called from Albany during the rescue while I had left my phone in the van. It was just past four in the afternoon in Thailand, predawn in the eastern United States. I returned the call, but Chicarelli didn't answer and I guessed he was asleep. I left a message, saying we had rescued Timmy and Kawee from the kidnappers, that Griswold was with us, and we were in hiding until some loose ends got tied up. I didn't mention that the loose ends included a Thai police general who was intent on blowing all our brains out. For reasons I couldn't quite articulate to myself, I hesitated before asking Chicarelli to notify Ellen and Bill Griswold that their family member Gary was now safe and sound. But they had to be told — originally I had been hired to find him, after all — so I told Chicarelli to inform the Griswolds we had Gary with us but that there were still plenty of nettlesome unanswered questions as to his past activities and future intentions.

After Timmy's shower and then mine, we heard a commotion outside our room and went out to find Griswold throwing a hissy fit at Pugh.

"Although I don't object to your men watching over me to see that I don't bolt," Griswold was saying, "you have to understand that I am *not* going to run off. What I *do* object to is their listening in on all of my telephone conversations and — good grief! really! — taking notes on whom I speak with and what I say. You are not doing yourself or me any favors by butting in this way, Rufus, and I am telling you that it is a great big pain in the neck."

Pugh said, "Khun Gary. Do you have secrets from us? We are your friends."

"It's not a question of secrets, Rufus. There are no great secrets on my part. It is a matter of simple privacy. I must be in touch with business associates to complete the Sayadaw U project, and some of this involves sensitive information and delicate negotiations involving people who would not be at all pleased to be eavesdropped on."

"I'm sorry you consider our watchfulness intrusive. We are all in this together, after all. When I say that, I don't mean the part about your worthy project. I mean the part about keeping you from being hurled from a high place, as well as the part about keeping your head from being made to explode. We do need to be all on the same page in that regard, Khun Gary. So I hope you will indulge us in this small way and let us keep track of your activities in a manner consistent with personal security professional standards."

"Rufus, you're quite the bullshit artist. Did anyone ever tell you that?"

"Let me think."

I said, "Griswold, I, for one, don't trust you at all. You have a track record of flying off the rails and causing all kinds of ridiculous trouble, and you are definitely going to be monitored. So get used to it."

"I'm a little unclear," Griswold said, "exactly what your current role is here, Strachey. As I recall, didn't my sister-in-law shit-can you? I think you told me that yourself. Hence, your extortionate request for fifty thousand dollars to underwrite what looks to me increasingly like a mere seaside vacation."

Now Timmy spoke up. "Well, it certainly has not been any kind of sun 'n' sand holiday for me, Gary. Or haven't you noticed that?"

"Well, I am sorry about your being kidnapped. Really, I am. It must have been a horrible ordeal. But the fact is, Timothy, you did not need to come to Thailand in the first place, and I can't imagine what you thought you were getting yourself into. Surely you must have done enough research to know of the violently inclined criminal elements in Thailand and about the corrupt police forces. Or didn't your friend Donald inform you about any of that?"

Timmy snorted with what could have been amusement.

"What's so funny, Timothy? And you know, you both are now free to leave Thailand at any time. Khun Rufus could drive you over to the ferry terminal and put you on a boat for Sihanoukville in Cambodia, and you could travel on to Phnom Penh and be on your way out of Southeast Asia by this time tomorrow. There's really nothing holding you here as far as any of the Griswolds are concerned. Am I right?"

Pugh said, "We've got your fifty K, Khun Gary. You hired us to protect you until April twenty-seventh. Remember?"

Griswold bristled, but before he could tell us all to take the fifty thousand dollars and shove it, I said, "Griswold, were you in Cambodia about two and a half weeks ago?"

"Yes, I was. Why?"

"What were you doing there?"

"Why do you ask? How would you even know that?"

"Elise Flanagan saw you."

"That *was* Elise Flanagan. Oh God! I thought I saw her and she spotted me. At the Aranya Prathet border post. What the hell was Elise doing entering Cambodia? She can barely find her way from Key West to Homestead."

"Elise was on her way to Angkor Wat with a tour group. And you?"

"I was on my way back into Thailand on a visa run."

"A what?"

"It's hard for foreigners to obtain a long-term visa in Thailand. The Thais like to be able to keep the worst of the riffraff from overstaying their welcome in the Land of Smiles — penniless ravers and druggies and notorious pedophiles and so on. So in order to stay here, most farangs must have the means to leave the country every three months and then reenter with a new visa. It's a kind of racket, actually. The government charges you for the visa, and airlines and tour operators make out even better. Me, I just hop on a van at Ekamai, read for a couple of hours, and then cross and recross the border. You can do it really fast by paying an extra twelve dollars for VIP treatment, so-called. That means the Thai operators stand in the visa queue for you and bribe the Cambodian immigration officials for fast service. In hot weather like this, it's a bargain."

"Well, it's the only way your friends in Key West knew you were even alive," I said. "They were hugely relieved, but confused too. Anyway, what happened six months ago that sent you careening into oblivion? It would certainly help us decide what to do next if we had a clearer picture of what precipitated all this weird to-ing and fro-ing in the first place."

Griswold's look darkened, and he was about to say something and then didn't.

I went on, "You e-mailed Janice Romeo that you had had a disturbing reading from a soothsayer. Was that Khun Khunathip?"

Griswold nodded. "Yes. It was."

"Janice says you told her that the seer predicted bloodshed in your life, and he said that great sorrow was in store for people close to you."

Griswold grunted. "Well? Was he right, or wasn't he?"

"And that's why you disappeared? Because of this astrological forecast?"

"No," Griswold said. "Khun Khunathip's reading was just the beginning."

"The beginning of what?"

"Of a chain of events that led eventually to the Sayadaw U project."

"You're leaving some stuff out, it seems."

"You bet I am."

"Why?"

"It is very dark."

"Enlighten us. It can only help."

"Not yet."

"Okay, when?"

"April twenty-seventh."

"That's a week and a half away. Today is the fifteenth."

"That's right. One and five. That is six."

"Unlucky six. Okay. What about tomorrow, the sixteenth. That's a one and a six. Which equals seven. Isn't that better?"

"Better but not best." He looked at Pugh. "Am I right, Khun Rufus?"

"Right as rain," Pugh said and gave me a look that said not to worry, we would find a way to squeeze it out of him.

CHAPTER TWENTY-THREE

Timmy and I walked over to Monkey Mountain to watch the sunset. A long concrete staircase led up to the temple atop the hill. Most of the gray monkeys were swinging in the trees at the foot of the staircase next to the food stalls, or scampering around on the ground gobbling up bits of food left by tourists. One of the bigger monkeys was hissing and squawking at the smaller ones and grabbing their food.

I said, "I'll bet that guy was Prime Minister Thaksin's minister of defense."

"Or head of his police."

There were a few other farangs climbing the two hundred or so steps, and a number of Thais. The Thais appeared to be couples and small families who had come to pray or for an outing with a view. We could see two men on motorcycles stopped down below, but they didn't seem to be paying any attention to us.

As we approached the summit, Hua Hin was now visible to the north, spreading westward from a long arc of sandy beach. The high-rise hotels along the water and the green hills inland gave the place a mini-Rio look, though instead of a huge cross overlooking the town there was a Buddhist temple, and now we were approaching it.

The place had the customary Buddha figure on a platform in a cozy room, with candles flickering and floral and other offerings below the altar. This gold-leafed Buddha was seated in the lotus position, palms pressed together in a wai, and he was smiling in his serene way.

I said, "You go into a Christian church and an agonized Jesus is stuck up on the wall looking like a bit player in a Wes Craven horror flick. You go into a Buddhist temple, and this guy really gives you a feeling of peace. I like this better."

Though long-since lapsed from the Mother Church, Timmy stiffened and gave me one of his looks. "If the Buddha had been crucified by the Romans, he might not look so thrilled with his circumstances either. But, lucky for him — and for much of Southeast Asia — he was not."

"True enough."

"But I do share your deep good feelings about the Buddha, Donald, and about Buddhism. Even if I don't believe in reincarnation, or in a system of rewards for good behavior that feels to me as if it's organized a little too much like the Delta SkyMiles program — still, Buddhism is so wonderfully enveloping with its philosophy of acceptance and tolerance, and its rejection of violence, and its aesthetic of simplicity. I'm so glad I came to Thailand — even though I came closer to dying here than I ever thought I would at this stage of my life."

We walked over to the parapet, where the setting sun was putting on its gaudy show over the hills to the west.

"I was so afraid for you," I said. "Pugh thought we could rescue you, but he wasn't sure we could do it in time. And after what Yodying's goons did to Geoff Pringle and to Khun Khunathip, we knew what a cold-blooded bunch they are. It was your presence of mind, really, and the Millpond reference, that made the rescue possible."

"Well, it was your presence of mind to pick up on the hint that saved Kawee and me. As soon as I understood that you had heard me, I knew we were going to be okay."

"Really? I wasn't all that confident."

"I told Kawee that you had the information that would free us, and he said yes, he could tell that you were a man who was up to the job because you reminded him of a kind of gay Bruce Wayne."

"That's a bit confusing."

"Anyway, he really was prepared to accept whatever his fate might turn out to be. He said he had long ago accepted that suffering was central to being human, and also why should he be afraid of anything he couldn't control? His calm in the face of danger was really amazing. And while I didn't follow all of his logic, I saw how his belief in an ongoing cosmic continuum of life gave him strength and confidence, and just being tied up in the same room with Kawee gave me strength and confidence, too."

"So those goons didn't... You know...beat you or anything?"

"No, they didn't. And they fed us decently, too. I can't really complain about our treatment. Except for having to crap in a bucket. I wasn't crazy about that."

"But the heat and the tedium must have been pretty grueling. What did you and Kawee find to occupy yourselves with in that room for a day and a half?"

"Oh, we just fucked and whatnot."

"I wondered about that."

"I thought you might, after that Paradisio episode. No, really, what we did was, we basically just talked about how much we liked our lives and how lucky we had been with so many things in our lives up till that point. Except for one thing, in Kawee's case. When he was seventeen, he had a boyfriend back in his village who died of malaria. The kid was Burmese and went home to visit his family in Shan state and got sick. Burma has no health care system to speak of, and the guy was too weak to make it back to Thailand, and he just died. Kawee says this guy, Nonkie, was his great love. Some day, Kawee told me, he wants to visit Shan state, because a Burmese friend who was there told him that Nonkie's ghost had been asking people traveling to Thailand to find Kawee and invite him to come over. Kawee said he would have gone by now, but it's hard to get a visa. And anyway once you're inside Myanmar the military government could grab you and put you on some forced-labor road-building project. He wants to see Nonkie's ghost, but he doesn't want to get trapped inside that sad country."

The sun was gone now, but the entire western sky was aflame over southern Thailand and Lower Burma and the Andaman Sea beyond.

I said, "Has Kawee seen ghosts before? He might be disappointed. I know Thais believe in them, but I've never actually met a Thai who has run into a ghost."

"Kawee told me about his uncle who was in the hospital with several cracked ribs after he fell off a logging elephant. The doctor showed the family the uncle's X-ray, and they all saw his *phee* on it. That's his ghost."

"I wonder if Griswold believes in ghosts. He seems to be a genuine convert to most of the bigger ideas here, both Buddhist and the old superstitions like astrology and numerology that got dragged along when Buddhism spread eastward from India."

"But if in a previous life Griswold was Thai himself," Timmy said, "and was Buddhist, then he's not really a convert. The unfortunate diversion from his true path was his being born to Max and Bertha Griswold in Albany. He must have done something really nasty way back when to have been karmically punished by ending up for a while in the steel business in Albany. Oh, you know what? There's something Kawee said that might help explain it."

"What?"

"Kawee said Griswold once told him that somebody else in his family had committed a very great sin. It was something so terrible that Griswold himself would have to help compensate for it with offerings and with meritorious works in order to protect his soul and the souls of family members."

I said, "I don't think that in Buddhism you can be punished by being born into the wrong family on account of sins that that family hasn't even committed yet at the time of your birth. Buddhism is fairer than that, more morally logical."

"But what if the sin was committed before you were born? By your parents or grandparents."

"There's only one way to figure this out. We have to ask Griswold. It may be part of what set him spiraling off into la-la land six months ago — hiding out and plotting whatever it is he's plotting."

"You're just going to ask him about it outright? Good luck with that."

"I realize I may have to wait until April twenty-seventh."

"Donald, that's twelve days from now. I have a feeling you're going to have to get a handle on all this well before then. Surely General Yodying isn't so dumb and incompetent that he won't track us down here. And if he does, we might not be so deft and clever and lucky the next time."

"True. But I'm sure Pugh has a Plan B and a Plan C and a Plan D. It's how he thinks. To be on the safe side, though, maybe you should head home, Timothy. I'm sure Pugh could get you over to Cambodia, and you could fly home from Phnom Penh, just like Griswold said."

Timmy looked back at the temple. A couple of elderly monks in their orange robes were walking inside followed by three young novices. The gold leaf on one of the smaller Buddha images in an outside alcove was glowing now in the last tangerine-colored light, and the sea beyond looked so soft that you could float out over it, suspended by particles of light, and drift down for a swim and then have a nice green curry along the beach.

Timmy said, "I may not make it to magical April twenty-seventh. But for now, I want to stick around. Despite what happened to me, I like this place."

"Me too," I said. "All we have to do to really enjoy Thailand is keep from being hurled into our next lives prematurely."

"Okay, let's do it that way, if we can. Survive first, and then take on whatever pleasant features Thailand has to offer next."

"Deal."

CHAPTER TWENTY-FOUR

The two motorcycle guys at the foot of Monkey Mountain were not assassins. They were moto-taxi drivers, and since it was dark now Timmy and I hired them to take us back to the compound. My phone rang just as we reached the house, and it was Bob Chicarelli.

"Can you hear me, Strachey?"

"Perfectly."

"Good, because you'll want to know about this. Are you still working for any of the Griswolds?"

"Yes, but not Ellen and Bill. Nothing has changed since they pretty much cut me off yesterday morning. According to Ellen, I'm supposed to tie up any loose ends here and then head home. But now I'm working for Gary Griswold. I'm helping protect him — for the moment anyway. He's not too crazy about having me around, either, so there's no telling how long this job — if you can even call it a job — is going to last. Why do you ask?"

"It's just as well that you're not counting on Bill and Ellen for fees or expenses. Algonquin Steel has been in total turmoil over the last twenty-four hours. The Albany Griswolds are struggling to retain control of the company, with this offshore group buying up shares by the shitload. Whoever the buyers are, they're paying premium prices and money seems to be no object to these people. So just do understand that Ellen is going to be plenty distracted until all this comes to a head at the company's annual meeting at the end of this month, when it is very likely that Bill will lose control of the company. I don't know whether any of this affects what you're doing over there, but since I basically got you into this I thought you should be kept up to speed."

"Yeah. This might be helpful, I'm beginning to think."

"Hey, Strachey, that's great news that you were able to spring your boyfriend and that Thai kid. How did you pull that off?"

"It's this Thai PI, Rufus Pugh, I'm working with. He knows his way around Bangkok the way you know your way around Albany. Except he's also got muscle-boy gunsels and acrobats and an arsenal of smelly fruit. Tell me something, Bob. You said Algonquin Steel's annual meeting is at the end of the month. Do you mean the very end, like April thirtieth?"

"No, I think it's the twenty-seventh."

"Uh-huh. What do you know about the group that's trying to take over the company?"

"Nothing, really. I'm told they're based in the Caymans. But that's probably just a front, and the buyers could be anybody anywhere in the world."

"Is Algonquin in such good shape that it would be all that desirable to foreign investors? Why is the company suddenly so red-hot?"

"That's a bit murky," Chicarelli said. "Algonquin is solid and profitable and I would say an excellent long-term investment. But it's not so flashy that anybody is likely to make a quick killing on it. The company is almost blue chip—like in the way it's likely to keep paying out modest but dependable dividends for decades to come."

"It sounds as if Algonquin would make a nice conservative addition to any institutional endowment."

"I'd say so, yes. But I doubt if it's Yale or the Ford Foundation that's going after Algonquin now. Whoever these buyers are, they are very, very aggressive."

I asked Chicarelli if he had informed Ellen Griswold that her brother-in-law Gary had been located and, at least for the moment, was in Pugh's and my protective custody.

"I left a message with Ellen, but I have yet to hear back. Which is odd, since it was her hiring you to find the guy that got all these strange turds flying around in the air in the first place. I'm assuming she's pleased but currently distracted.

Maybe she'll call you directly when she has a spare moment. Meanwhile, if I find out more, should I call you and let you know?"

"Yes. By all means."

Timmy was laid out on a chaise back in the poolside gardens, studying the night sky. The stars were blurry in the warm haze but offered up the same northern hemisphere constellations visible in upstate New York.

I said, "Are you attempting to discern your future up there?"

"Yes. The stars are saying: Timothy, tonight you will get a good night's sleep."

I sat down and told him about my conversation with Bob Chicarelli. "I do believe," I said, "that Gary Griswold is behind the attempted takeover of Algonquin Steel. Probably in partnership with Anant na Ayudhaya, the ex–minister of finance Griswold was going to do the currency speculation deal with and then didn't. Once they get hold of Algonquin, they can donate it to the Sayadaw U Buddhism center Griswold is sponsoring, and it will support the center in perpetuity, or at least as long as capitalism lasts. Griswold builds the center, and he and these Thai investors keep it solvent. It's good for Buddhism in Thailand, and Griswold and his cohorts earn so much merit they'll be sitting pretty for tens or even hundreds of lives in the future."

Timmy sat up but looked puzzled. "That is very weird."

"It's the best explanation we have for the timing of Griswold's big investment project and its coming to fruition this month. It also explains his secrecy. He doesn't want us to find out about it, because he thinks we might blab to his brother and sister-in-law, and for some reason he doesn't want them to know that he's the man behind the takeover."

"Jeez, Donald. It's his own family. What could possibly be going on that would lead Griswold to force his own brother out of the business their father founded? I know this kind of thing happens in families — all-out bloody wars, even, over control of a family business. But don't we know that Griswold actually washed his hands of Algonquin Steel several years ago?"

"Kawee told you there was some kind of Griswold family sin that he said he had to atone for. It might have something to do with that."

"You mean he's both atoning and getting even?"

"It's not that rare a combination in family affairs."

Several figures approached us across the tile terrace behind the guesthouse where most of us were staying. None of them was Griswold. I wanted to tell him that I had figured out how he was planning on financing his Buddhist center. And I wanted to assure him that since he — not his sister-in-law — was my client now, I was not about to spill the beans. Unless, of course, he was planning on misbehaving in some annoying way and somehow putting all of us in immediate terrible jeopardy yet again.

Pugh, Kawee and Mango joined us by the pool. Mango had just come by bus from Bangkok, and Pugh said Miss Nongnat had also arrived. "She's upstairs powdering her nose," Pugh said. Pugh's wife and children were on the way and would arrive soon, and his girlfriend Furnace was in a friend's house up the road with Miss Aroon keeping her company.

"Have you had rice yet?" Pugh asked and said that Ek had gone into town to pick up some eats for everybody.

Nitrate brought drinks out — beer, Coke, fruit juices, bottled water, and bird-spit beverage. Timmy asked, "How do they get the birds to spit into that small container? Are there bird charmers who make a profession of this?"

"When elephant mahouts grow old and are forced to retire," Pugh said, "many of them switch careers and become bird mahouts. It's so much less rigorous a life. As with the elephants, a bird mahout develops a long-term relationship with one bird and can make it spit into one of these little bottles on command."

The Thais all had a good laugh over this, and they seemed pleased when Timmy laughed too.

"No, really," Pugh said, "the birds use their saliva as mortar when building their nests. The nests are filched — regrettably for the birds, I must say — and then boiled, and the resulting fluid is the basis for this tasty beverage."

I had a beer, but Timmy tried the bird-spit juice and said, "I guess this is as close to kissing a bird as I'll ever get."

"That depends on how long you remain in Thailand," Pugh said, and the Thais all laughed, though I wasn't sure why.

Mango had come out into the hot night wearing a skimpy yellow bathing suit. As the rest of us sat drinking and kidding around, he approached the pool, and I fully expected him to execute a perfect godlike swan dive. Instead he climbed onto the diving board and jumped in holding his nose. He came to the surface glistening in the moonlight and then hoisted himself out of the pool and — with the un–self-consciousness and easy grace of a gifted athlete — remounted the board and jumped in again holding his nose.

I wondered if there might be some tension between the two when Griswold came out and encountered the man with whom he was once in love and who had, Griswold believed, destroyed that love with Mango's devotion to Donnutt and with his money-boy activities involving a number of other farangs. Pugh said, however, that Griswold had gone into town with Ek and Egg to use the Internet café and look at documents from the other investors in the Sayadaw U project. So we had at least a brief reprieve from any awkward meeting between the two.

Any worries over a confrontation soon became moot, however. Pugh took a call from Ek, who said that outside the Internet café, as they were leaving, Griswold was admiring the rented bicycle of a Swedish tourist, and suddenly grabbed it, jumped on, and sped off. They chased him on foot, but Griswold was both deft and fast on the bike, and they lost him. Once they retrieved their van, Griswold had already been lost in the crowds of tourists pouring in and out of the Hua Hin hotels, bars, massage parlors, and schnitzel joints.

CHAPTER TWENTY-FIVE

Pugh sent several of his men into town to search for Griswold, and he called people he knew and trusted to be on the lookout for a sweaty farang on a stolen bike. Griswold was carrying next to nothing with him, but he did have his shoulder bag with his multiple ATM cards. He did not have his passport with him, however, and he would need that to check into a hotel. Unless, of course, he crammed his bag full of bahts at an ATM and bribed his way past a desk clerk. Griswold could also, Pugh said, phone someone he knew and trusted to come and pick him up. Plainly he had friends in high places in Thailand. Those people presumably could keep Griswold safe until April 27 when General Yodying supposedly would be neutralized.

"But what about us?" was Timmy's reasonable question to Pugh. "We aren't exactly off the hook, I don't think."

"No, Mr. Timothy. We are indeed still very much up shit creek. Even if we were to inform General Yodying that Khun Gary is no longer in our custody, he would be unimpressed. First, he might not believe us. Second, it is not Khun Gary running around loose that the top cop desires, and we are the enablers of Griswold's freedom. Third, there is the not inconsequential matter of our having snatched the general's missus and left her stranded in a closet clad only in a garbage bag. I think that that monstrous affront alone is the main reason he plans on drilling holes in our souls before hurling them — and their present corporeal manifestations — into a hell beyond our imagining but not quite beyond his."

I told Pugh about the phone call from Bob Chicarelli and my belief that Griswold and some Thai investors were behind the takeover of Algonquin Steel. "So Griswold, I think, is so obsessed with this corporate raid and using it to punish his brother, and to atone for some long-ago Griswold family sin, that he'll do anything to be able to operate freely until the twenty-seventh of this month."

"Ah, yes," Pugh said. "Two and seven." He seemed to think this explained a lot.

Ek appeared with the take-out food he had picked up before Griswold bolted. As he spread the containers of rice and soup out on a table near the pool, along with spoons and chopsticks, Ek spoke to Pugh in Thai in a tone of self-deprecation and apology. He was plainly mortified that he and Egg had let Pugh get away, but Pugh spoke back to him consolingly.

Pugh said in English, "Ek blames himself for Khun Gary's flight. But it was a collision of karmas — his bad, Griswold's good — and he is not to blame. Not, at least, in the present circumstances. I told him, however, that he should (a) make an offering to the spirit of the Enlightened One at the earliest opportunity, and (b) get his ass back out there and drag that SOB Griswold back here pronto. The guy couldn't have gone far. Though first, of course, Ek must have rice."

We all dug in, the Thais considering their food as they ate it as if it was both fun to eat and holy.

Kawee had stripped to his thong and had been enjoying a swim with Mango, and soon they both came over to the table for some eats. Noting the uncommonly large bulge in skinny little Kawee's thong, I glanced at Timmy, who nodded, and I thought, Holy Moses.

Ek ate quickly and soon left to help with the search for Griswold.

Pugh said, "The chances are good that if Griswold has phoned someone in Bangkok for assistance, it will take two or three hours for them to get somebody down here. Word is out around Hua Hin that we are looking for Griswold. This could speed locating him, but it also runs the risk of one of Yodying's local admirers being tipped off as to our presence and also to Griswold's being on the loose."

I said, "If Griswold has friends in Bangkok who can protect him in these circumstances, why couldn't the same people have protected him while he was hiding out over the past six months? There seems to be a piece of all this that we don't yet know about."

"A single piece? Khun Don, you are such an optimist."

While we all ate, the Thais who had known him talked about Griswold and what a bundle of contradictions he was to them.

Pugh said, "He was a man of the mysterious Occident."

Kawee told about how he had met Griswold at Paradisio and how Griswold had been forthright in telling him that he was attracted to very butch men and Kawee was too feminine for them to have any kind of sexual relationship. Kawee said this even as he stood up to reach for more rice and his enormous bulge all but brushed my nose. He went on to tell in his breathy voice how he and Griswold had become friends, based on their spiritual quests and yearnings, and that each had learned from the other's stories of suffering in life and how each had come to understand how suffering is the beginning of wisdom. Kawee told of losing his friend Nonkie to malaria, and he said Griswold told of losing his first Thai lover to a disease with similar symptoms: fever, chills and weakness. They commiserated with each other, and they learned to fully appreciate what they had when they had it but also to accept the transitory nature of all things.

I said, "Griswold had a Thai boyfriend who died? I didn't know that."

"It was long time past," Kawee said. "Maybe eighteen fifty-eight."

"Back when he was Thai himself?"

"Of course."

Mango recounted the sad tale of his time together with Griswold, whom he admired for his spiritual depth and searching, and told of the breakup over the question of sexual fidelity. "I was too sorry for the bust-up," Mango said. "Mr. Gary was nice man and good lover. Also, he very rich. Lot of money is big plus."

I said, "Apparently something else very bad happened soon after you two broke up, Mango. Something that actually changed the way Griswold saw his life."

"Yes, and that was when bad men find me and ask me where Mr. Gary go. Bad luck for me. Bad luck for Mr. Gary. Khun Khunathip saw it in chart. Sadness and blood coming. Soon they come."

Kawee said, "Mr. Gary too sad for Mango, too sad for other things. Then also everything be worse. That when two farangs come."

"Two Westerners?"

"Two farangs come and Mr. Gary crying. Too, too sad when farangs come from America."

"Two Americans made him cry? What was that about?"

"I don't know," Kawee said. "He no tell me. But two men come. Then Mr. Gary change big investment plan. He go bank every day. He meditate at *wat*. Soon he leave condo and hide. He change. He angry. He sad. I make offerings and I water plants."

"Did you ever meet these two men?"

"One time."

"What were their names?"

"They no say. They not nice. They say, where good gay massage? I say where and they go. My friend Tree say they try fuck him no condom. He say no, and they no tip."

Pugh asked, "Were these men living in Thailand or visiting?"

"Just come from America," Kawee said. "Then go back America. They no stay long. Two days, maybe three."

I asked Kawee to describe the two. Doing so was beyond the limits of his English, so he did it in Thai and then Pugh translated. "The men seemed to be in their early forties," Pugh said. "Definitely American — Kawee knows the accents of the Westerners who sojourn in Thailand — and a bit rough around the edges. Not the sort of international business types you might expect to come calling at Griswold's condo. One was a dark-haired man who had bleached his hair blond. They looked like they had been muscle boys once but were over-the-hill. Drinkers, too, Kawee believes, with unmistakable beer breath at high noon. Shady characters, it seems, and I suppose we can surmise, intimately connected with whatever sent Khun Gary spinning off into financial, spiritual and personal mysterious activities the minute these two nasty pieces of work left town."

I asked Kawee if he knew where these men had been staying in Bangkok. "At the Malaysia Hotel," he said. "First Malaysia, then Grand Hyatt. They move, they tell Mr. Gary. I hear them say this, and they laugh."

"The Malaysia," Pugh explained, "is a midrange tourist hotel not far from the Topmost. The Grand Hyatt is what the name sounds like. It's a high-end international business travelers and tourist hotel near Siam Square. Apparently these scruffy characters were upwardly mobile even during their brief, unpopular stay in Bangkok."

Timmy said, "It looks as if Griswold may have given them money. Or they must have gotten it from somebody else during their short stay in Thailand. Could they have been investors in the currency speculation scheme that was abandoned, and they were the first ones to demand and receive their money back? Though, from Kawee's description, they don't sound all that Wall Street."

I said, "The currency speculation deal was just local, I'd guess. Wouldn't you say, Rufus?"

"If the esteemed former minister of finance was involved, the scheme likely involved only a prestigious circle of Thai scalawags. In any case, investors in that unfortunate incident lost all their dough. And those who complained got a nice shove from a precipice for their trouble."

"But," Timmy said, "maybe these visiting Americans were the first ones in line and they threatened Griswold. He paid them off with his own money and then went into hiding before the other ripped-off investors went wild."

"The timing is wrong for that scenario," I said. "We're confusing cause and effect. Griswold pulled out of the currency speculation deal, causing it to collapse, just after these guys showed up and may have received money from him."

I asked Pugh if he could use sources in the banks where Griswold kept his money to check on large withdrawals or transfers around the time of the visit by the two Americans.

"That would be illegal," Pugh said. "Banking privacy laws preclude any such inquiries."

"Yes, but can you do it?"

"Of course."

"It would help," I said, "if we knew exactly when these two guys were in Bangkok. Is there any way of figuring that out?"

Kawee said, "October fifteen."

"How do you know that?"

"I remember. One and five. It was day of unlucky sixes. The bad Americans come. My Aunt Sunthorn have birthday number sixty. She fall in cinema and break leg."

Pugh said, "Did the Americans arrive on October fifteenth or depart on that date?"

"They come Bangkok on fourteen, I think. They phone Mr. Gary. They come condo fifteen. They go way sixteen maybe."

Timmy looked at me and said, "Who needs computers?"

I said, "I'm pretty sure that the bulk of Griswold's funds are in Bangkok Bank Unless he's been moving his money around. Plus, he had all those ATM cards from multiple Thai banks."

Pugh got on his cell phone, speed-dialed a number, and carried on a rapid conversation in Thai. Then he repeated this conversation a second, third and fourth time with others he phoned. "This could take overnight," he said. "Nobody I know has access to bank records from home. But we may know what we need to know in the morning after folks arrive at their workplaces."

Now Miss Nongnat appeared from the house. She had taken time to make herself presentable, she said, after the bus ride from Bangkok. She was hungry and ready for some rice, she told us. She pulled up a chair and had a beer. She was dressed in a pretty blue skirt and a loose white slipover and had a monk amulet dangling from her neck similar to Kawee's. In her makeup, Miss Nongnat looked like a beauty pageant contestant, and I recalled how one evening during my first visit to Thailand I had come upon a cheering crowd at an outdoor plaza. Lovely young Thai women were parading across a stage in traditional Siamese costumes as the audience clapped and yelled enthusiastically. I stopped to watch and soon became aware that the beauty queens were not in fact lovely young Thai women but were lovely young Thai men. It was one of my earliest indications that the Siamese were in a number of ways far ahead of the rest of us.

Miss Nongnat told Kawee that if he wanted to do his toenails, she had his color of polish up in her luggage. Kawee hoisted a foot up, and we all — even Pugh — examined Kawee's pretty toes and spoke of them admiringly.

Miss Nongnat said she had to do her toenails almost daily these days. She had been dating a Korean who insisted that if she was going to paint her toenails, the polish had to be edible, and edible polishes just didn't last.

I caught Timmy's quick glance at me that said, "We're a long way from the Archdiocese of Albany now."

Soon Pugh's wife and three children arrived. The kids were all happy to be having an unexpected visit to the seashore. Pugh was about to accompany them up to the second guesthouse when his cell phone rang.

Pugh conversed briefly and then rang off. "That was Egg. He has located Khun Gary. He is unconscious in Hua Hin hospital. We should go there, I think, and make sure that Mr. Gary is not injured any more than has already been the unhappy case."

CHAPTER TWENTY-SIX

Griswold had been speeding down a road near Jack and Jackie's summer palace when a drunk in an old Nissan came barreling out of a side street with his lights off and knocked Griswold and his stolen bike into a banyan tree. Griswold had not been wearing a helmet and may have suffered a slight concussion, Egg had learned. He had been identified by the ATM cards in his bag, and one of Pugh's Hua Hin police sources had alerted Egg.

Pugh himself drove Timmy and me into town. The small hospital was an entirely modern facility, spick-and-span, with young female greeters in pale lavender uniforms who smiled like angels at visitors and exuded solicitude like a delicate perfume.

Timmy said, "Take note, Senate Republican caucus."

"They're otherworldly. Can you imagine this kind of treatment at Albany Medical Center? Or any US hospital?"

"And they're as lovely to look at as Miss Nongnat. I wonder if they have dicks."

Ek, Egg and Nitrate were positioned outside Griswold's room. Ek said he learned from a doctor that Griswold had no broken bones but had been badly scraped and bruised. He had been slipping in and out of consciousness and, when awake, had been muttering to the nurses incoherently. The doctor had said this mental fog was from both the painkillers Griswold was on and the concussion.

Pugh and Ek had an exchange in Thai, and then Pugh told me, "Mr. Gary has been intermittently gaga. He has been babbling about falling."

"That sounds rational enough. After what happened to Geoff Pringle and to soothsayer Khunathip — and almost to Timmy and to Kawee — a fear of falling sounds sensible. Also, Griswold himself was hurt falling off his bike — twice, in fact. And his parents died in a plane that went down."

"Khun Gary also, Ek says, has been going on confusedly about rounding or surrounding or something like that. It's hard to make out. Ek wasn't even sure it was English. But it didn't seem to be Thai either. And Mr. Gary said it repeatedly in a distressed tone of voice. *Rounding.* What's that about?"

A nurse came out of Griswold's room and said that he was more alert now than he had been earlier, and if we wished to greet him and wish him well we could enter the room two at a time.

Pugh and I went in first. Griswold was bandaged on his left arm and shoulder and had a bad scrape on his left cheek. He had another bandage across his nose and a blackened left eye. A large bandage was wrapped around his head. He was on an IV drip of what I guessed were painkillers and antibiotics.

Griswold immediately recognized Pugh and me and moaned, "Oh no, you guys," and squeezed his eyes shut.

"Khun Gary, we were so sorry to learn of your unfortunate accident. Mr. Donald and I are here to extend our heartfelt sympathies and our many good wishes for a speedy recovery."

"You can both go fuck yourselves."

"Not just yet."

I said, "Griswold, you are totally out of control and it's getting the best of you. At this point, all we are trying to do is keep you alive until April twenty-seventh. Then you're on your own. You and your latest astrologer-of-the-moment can take it from there."

He looked at me balefully out of his battered face. "I was handling this myself until you showed up, Strachey. You are the reason I'm lying in this bed with a headache to end all headaches. You and my clueless ex-wife and my evil brother. Everything was proceeding more or less smoothly until you were air-dropped into Thailand like some kind of sheriff's SWAT team with the wrong address."

"What would the right address be?"

Ignoring that, Griswold said, "All I need at this point is to be left alone to oversee a series of financial transactions that are of the utmost urgency. I need a computer and a phone, and above all I need *privacy*. And now here I am stuck in this medical Grand Central Station with even less opportunity to concentrate and control what I need to control than I had back when I was hiding out in Bangkok. I can only begin to tell you just how much you two are fucking up my project and...and...*my entire life!*"

I said, "Griswold, you and a group of Thai investors are trying to take over Algonquin Steel. Why is that?"

Griswold was hooked up to a machine monitoring his pulse, brain waves, and who knew what else, and when I said this the machine practically projectile vomited. It began to flash and beep something awful, though Griswold himself just stared at me with a small round O formed by his lips. He apparently wanted to say something, but his vocal apparatus had gone numb.

I said, "Several years ago, you wanted out of the steel business, and you got out, and you had a nice art gallery in Key West. Then you came over to Thailand presumably without giving steel fabricating and the home- and building-supply business a backward glance. Now you not only want to get back into the family business in a big way, but you want to force your brother out of it and replace him with yourself and a group of Thai investors that perhaps includes former finance minister Anant na Ayudhaya. Griswold, what's going on?"

Now the machine wasn't beeping and flashing so much, and the drooping line on one of its electronic graphs looked like the Dow Jones was having a bad day. Still Griswold said nothing.

I said, "It looks like you're taking over Algonquin Steel to finance the Sayadaw U project. Algonquin's earnings will make a nice endowment for the Buddhism center. If this is the case, why not just say so? It's no skin off my nose."

After a moment, Griswold croaked out, "Who told you this crazy shit?"

"Nobody, but it makes sense. I heard from Albany that there's a hostile takeover of Algonquin Steel under way."

"And people in Albany think I'm behind it?"

"Not as far as I know. My source — who is not one of your family members — just alerted me to the takeover but said nothing about opinions in Albany on who the buyers might be."

"Do you have any idea if my brother thinks that's what I'm doing — grabbing the company out from under him?"

"I don't know. Should I feel him out? I could talk to your ex-wife and see what she and Bill know or don't know. I'm working for you now, not them. I think."

Griswold shook his head and then grimaced from the pain of moving it. "What a goddamn screwup. And it's *your* fault. Though why am I surprised? You may not be aware of it, Strachey, but I had trouble with you in Thailand once before."

"You were here in the seventies? I don't remember you. What were you? Army? State Department? Viet Cong?"

"No, it was the eighteen fifties. Apparently you have not taken the trouble to examine your past lives. But I have examined mine and I remember you distinctly. You came from London ostensibly on a trade mission but basically you wanted to get your hands on a number of Siamese antiquities, including an emerald Buddha you were planning on grabbing for a private collector in East Kent."

Pugh was just inside my peripheral vision and I thought I picked up his suppressing a smile.

I said, "Well, Griswold, this is your second concussion from flying off a bicycle and whacking your head. But apparently this concussion did not reverse the effects of the last one."

Now Pugh actually chuckled. Griswold just looked at me hard and said, "I don't know what the hell you're talking about."

I said, "I heard that one of your aims with the Sayadaw U project is to atone for a great sin that was committed by one of your family members. It must have been a pretty spectacular sin if it's going to take a project costing tens of millions of dollars to set things right in your family, karma-wise. Would you like to shed some light on all that? I'm a skeptic on these matters, but Khun Rufus is likely to be impressed."

Pugh said, "Well put. I'm all ears."

"No," Griswold said and shut his eyes again.

"No, what?"

"No, I will not shed some light on something there is no need for you to know about, and if you did know you would just go charging around standing in the way of justice."

"Charging around and standing. Weird."

"I have a headache. Please go away."

"What do you mean by justice? Karmic? Legal?"

"Karmic and Hebrew. They are sometimes similar. It would be hard to say, in fact, which one can be the more interestingly lurid."

"You referred to your brother Bill as evil. How come?"

Griswold looked at me directly. "Don't mess with my brother. Believe me, you'll regret it. You aren't planning to tell him any of this, are you?"

"No," I said. "I'm not. Were the two seedy Americans who visited you six months ago your brother's pals or representatives? The bleach blonde and the other guy who were staying at the Malaysia Hotel and then moved to the Grand Hyatt? Did they come to Thailand with some kind of information or threat from Bill?"

Griswold's machine got excited again — *bleep bleep bleep bleep* — and his Dow Jones graph jumped around some more.

"April twenty-seventh," Griswold said. "That's all you need to know. Now please let me rest. I am so, so exhausted." He closed his eyes and turned his head away.

Out in the corridor, I described the encounter to Timmy. He said, "You've nailed it. Jeez, Don, you've figured it out."

"Maybe. But even if I have, what is it that I've figured out?"

Pugh said, "Khun Don, perhaps it would all be clearer if you understood the dynamics of your last troubled encounter with Mr. Gary. Back in the court of King Mongkut."

"I'll work on that. I may have to fly back to Key West and talk to a woman named Sandy. Though I suppose you have people here in Thailand, Rufus, who could help me out in that regard."

Pugh laughed. "Mr. Don, I do believe that you think all of us Thais have fallen off our bicycles and landed on our heads."

"Not at all. Buddhism is in your DNA, Rufus. It's not in Griswold's."

"How can you be so sure? In our belief system, a man can as easily return to earth as an Upstate New York American steel magnate as a Thai rice farmer or a rat in the sewers of Vientiane. It all depends on the man's karma, which is dictated by his behavior in present or past lives. A man could even return to earth as a silly farang dilettante dabbling in Buddhism in a shallow way that's embarrassing both to true Buddhists and to skeptics such as yourself. Which is the case with Mr. Gary? I am undecided about that.

"I must say," Pugh went on, "that it is unusual for Thais such as former Minister Anant to accept unquestioningly the Buddhism of any foreigner. Most Thais are skeptical themselves of the genuineness of farang Buddhism beyond the proven benefits of meditation and of course the adoption of decent ethical practices. And many traditional Thais are skeptical of — even hostile to — grandiose semicommercial schemes such as the one Mr. Gary is planning out by the new airport. I'm a bit surprised, actually, that Khun Anant, an old-fashioned man in many ways, is up to his eyebrows with a foreigner in this supposedly deeply spiritual project. It has occurred to me, in fact, that somehow Khun Anant is not out to assist Mr. Gary but perhaps to fleece him."

Ek had been on his cell phone, and now he interrupted Pugh and me and spoke in an urgent tone to Pugh in Thai.

Pugh said to me, "We have to get Mr. Gary out of here. Fast."

CHAPTER TWENTY-SEVEN

One of Ek's cop friends had tipped him off that a Hua Hin senior officer with personal loyalties to General Yodying had noted Griswold's name on the police blotter and had been asking questions about him. It was reasonable to assume that this officer had heard that Yodying was searching for Griswold — and for us — and that word would soon come crackling back from Bangkok to have us all rounded up.

Pugh had a doctor friend who ran a private clinic off the main southern road only a mile or so from Monkey Mountain. Griswold could be treated and well cared for there. The trick was going to be insinuating Griswold out of the hospital and into the back of one of Pugh's vans without further injuring Griswold or spooking the hospital staff into calling the police.

Pugh found the supervising physician and talked to him for a few minutes in Thai, and then told Timmy and me, "It's cool. They're going to load Khun Gary into the van in a few minutes. They'll even provide a mattress and sheets."

"What did you tell the doctor?"

"That Nitrate is a seer who did Mr. Gary's chart and discovered that if he is to recover from his injuries expeditiously he must do so in Bangkok. It's best that everyone here believe that that is where we are heading. Also, I mentioned to the doc that the *phee* of a man who has it in for Mr. Gary was spotted at the site of tonight's car–bicycle accident, and he was also observed outside this hospital a little while ago. So we must move the patient for his own protection."

"And the doctor believed that story?"

"Not necessarily. But he thinks I believe it, and he is acquiescing in my wishes."

"But won't he ask Griswold what he wants to do?"

"Ek is at this moment informing Mr. Gary that General Yodying is hot on his trail. And if he wants to complete his project instead of being flung into an abyss, he must come along with us and recover from his injuries elsewhere. Ek is also telling him that he will be provided with the phone and computer he wishes to have, and the privacy."

"Rufus, this is getting dicey. Are we going to make it to April twenty-seventh? I have a bad feeling that guys on motorcycles wielding Chinese revolvers are going to turn up well before then."

"That, Khun Don, is why it may become necessary quite soon to go on the offensive."

"And how do we do that?"

"Your guess is as good as mine."

§ § § §

The clinic was a small but well-appointed place the size of an American branch bank with a couple of tile-roofed bungalows out back surrounded by flowers and fruit trees. Pugh explained that Thailand had a two-tiered health care system, one public and one private, and as in the US, private was better, though the public system wasn't bad either.

It was after midnight when we got Griswold into his bungalow. The hospital staff had doped him up for the ride. So he was only half conscious when we laid him in his bed and Pugh's doctor pal, a woman named Nual Winarungruang, went over Griswold's charts, checked him out, put him on an IV drip, and hooked him up to her own monitors. A nurse had been called in to keep an eye on Griswold through the night. It did not appear that we had been followed by anyone from outside the hospital, so Pugh left Nitrate and the two part-time Dream Boys to watch over Griswold while the rest of us rode back to the guesthouses.

Everyone had gone to bed except Kawee, Mango and Miss Nongnat, who were still out by the pool drinking beer. Mango was giving Miss Nongnat a massage on the chaise. For the sake of efficiency, Pugh spoke to them in Thai and explained that Griswold was recovering from his injuries, which were not severe, and he had been deposited in a safe house outside the hospital.

We were all hot and worn-out, and Pugh said there were extra bathing suits in the pool house if we wanted to have a swim. We did want to, and we floated around under the stars for an hour or so. Pugh excused himself and said he wanted to pop in where Furnace and Miss Aroon were staying up the road and would be back soon.

After Pugh left, Miss Nongnat asked Timmy and me if either of us would like a smoke.

I wasn't sure if she meant cigarettes or weed. Anyway, I said no thanks, that I had quit years ago. Timmy mentioned that he had never smoked at all, and Nongnat, Mango and Kawee all had a good laugh over that.

Miss Nongnat said to Timmy, "No, honey, a smoke is a blowjob."

Timmy and I politely demurred, saying we had already had a full day. Though after we excused ourselves and were heading inside, we glanced back to see the three Thais strip off their bathing attire and slide naked into the pool together in a kind of eroticized NFL-style huddle.

Up in our room, Timmy and I talked it over and concluded that it was possible before we left Thailand we might join in one of those friendly huddles. But for the moment we just wanted very much to be next to each other, relieved to be reunited, and happy to be alive.

CHAPTER TWENTY-EIGHT

The unexpected flight from Hua Hin began just after dawn. Pugh banged on our door and said we were leaving town immediately. Police roadblocks had been set up on all the main routes, and we would be departing Hua Hin by boat in twenty minutes. His police sources had confirmed that General Yodying had learned that we — and Griswold — were in Hua Hin, so there was no way we could safely move about. And anyway the general might dig up information on who Pugh's friends and acquaintances were in Hua Hin and launch a raid on the compound. Pugh's wife and children were moving into a beach hotel under assumed names, and Miss Aroon and Furnace would drive the two vans back to Bangkok.

Griswold was already at the compound, accompanied by Dr. Nual and a nurse. He would be carried down to the nearby beach on a stretcher, and we would have to get him into a small boat and then out to a waiting cabin cruiser.

The skies had clouded over during the night, and just as we began the hike down a sandy track to the beach, the clouds broke loose and rain came crashing down in drops the size of melon balls. Ever efficient, Pugh had anticipated the bad weather and two of his crew had gotten hold of broad-brimmed straw hats that they passed out to each of us. There were a number of extra hats, and the Dream Boys wore those stacked up on their heads one atop another. Occasionally a gust of wind blew the extra hats off and all the Thais went chasing after them, joshing one another and laughing. We were all soaked in under a minute, although the air was so warm that nobody was all that distracted or uncomfortable. Thunder rumbled and I asked Pugh if people were ever struck by lightning on or near this beach. He said sometimes but that on this day he was feeling lucky.

A local guy Pugh knew had dragged his small boat with its outboard motor up onto the beach. The surf was light, even in the rainstorm. Griswold was wide-awake and complaining about being pummeled and shoved this way and that, and who could blame him? He still had a headache, he said, and he was sore all over. He agreed, though, that Yodying and his agents were to be avoided at all costs, and it would actually be easier to hide in Bangkok than in Hua Hin, now that Yodying had their number locally.

Kawee, Mango and Miss Nongnat were hungover and not happy about being yanked out of bed to go to sea in a rainstorm, but once they were on the beach, they began to play in the waves. The rest of Pugh's crew were helpful and attentive, but not without a lot of kidding around in between tasks.

The forty- or fifty-foot cabin cruiser Pugh had arranged for was anchored a hundred yards or more out in the surf, and we were ferried out to it four at a time. There were twelve of us altogether, and it took close to half an hour to get everybody on board. This included Griswold and his nurse, a young woman named Lemon. Dr. Nual said she was no longer needed — another physician would meet the boat in Bangkok — and she walked back up the trail. Meanwhile, the rain had let up and we could see bright blue sky to the north, the direction we were heading.

By the time we had passed the northernmost reaches of Hua Hin, the sun was streaming down and all the men took off their shirts and laid them out to dry. The two-man crew of the cruiser served us tea, pineapple and sticky rice with sliced mango in coconut milk.

Griswold lay on a chaise on the front deck and gradually his headache lessened and his mood improved. He tried to place a call on Pugh's cell phone, but by then we were too far from shore. And the ship-to-shore radio was not acceptable, he said, because he required privacy. When Griswold returned Pugh's cell phone to him, Pugh went belowdecks and I followed him. We both wanted to see what number Griswold had dialed. Pugh did not recognize the number, but he said it was in Bangkok. He wrote it down.

Pugh had said the journey to Bangkok would take about six hours. Back on deck, Timmy and I stretched out in the sun. Mango, Kawee and Miss Nongnat lay on mats in the shade of a canopy and snoozed as we plowed over the friendly swells of the gulf.

We overtook a Thai Royal Navy patrol boat and watched it a little anxiously as we passed. But its crew showed no interest in us. A garland of marigolds had been draped over the Navy boat's gun turret. Similarly protected against bad spirits was our boat, which had a sizable Buddha figure on a shelf in the wheelhouse just above us. Fresh jasmine hung nearby next to a wooden carving of an erect penis, which I remembered from my first visit to Thailand was a good-luck charm. Betty Friedan might have had something to say about that practice, but we were a long way from her aura.

Everybody on board gathered for lunch around noon. We had rice, tom yam kung and spicy pig colon salad, plus bottled water, fruit juices, and bird-spit drink for anybody who cared for some.

As we neared Bangkok, cell phone service came back and Pugh made some calls. He told Timmy and me after he hung up that it might be a good idea if we delayed our arrival in Bangkok until after dark. He had no reason to think that Yodying knew where we were, but that the general was definitely in a major snit, according to one of Pugh's cop friends, and precautions were called for. Pugh spoke with the captain of our boat, an elderly Isaan man with a formal manner and a high smooth forehead and tattoos all over his face that looked like a bead curtain in a Berkeley bar in 1968. The boat soon slowed and headed east as we began to cruise around near the mouth of the Chao Phraya for the rest of the afternoon.

Pugh summoned me belowdecks again and said, "The number Mr. Gary attempted to call in Bangkok was that of Seer Pongsak Sutiwipakorn. I am going to go out on a short limb and predict that Seer Pongsak has replaced the late Khun Khunathip as the soothsayer for former Minister Anant and for the Sayadaw U project. This is good. It may open up opportunities for us."

"Isn't that the seer who predicted a coup by the end of April?"

"That is he. Khun Pongsak failed to predict the last coup, the one that sent Prime Minister Thaksin fleeing with his billions of baht to the UK. But now the wizard is wielding his zodiacal instrument like a cudgel or perhaps a threat or possibly a warning. Or, maybe he is just a vain, oafish fellow who likes to get his name in the papers. I don't know which it is. In any case, maybe he would like to make a splash again by moving his prediction up a week. From April twenty-seventh to April eighteenth, another lucky number. The advantage of the earlier date is, it's the day after tomorrow. And if these momentous events could be accelerated, we would have a better chance of staring into the abyss and not having the abyss stare back for a very long eleven days."

"How would we get him to do that? Griswold is wedded to April twenty-seventh. The date plainly has magical properties for him. It's even when the Algonquin Steel annual meeting will happen."

"Ah, but these events are far larger than any mere corporation and its machinations."

"Tell Griswold that."

Pugh said, "I have obtained additional information that is likely to be helpful, though I am not yet certain exactly how. I found out that Griswold carried out a very large money transfer from the Commercial Bank of Siam to an account in Albany, New York last October fifteenth."

"One and five. That unlucky day when the two Americans showed up in Bangkok and made Griswold angry and sad."

"Yes."

"Do you have the name of the account holder?"

"I do. It is Mr. Duane Hubbard."

"No shit?"

"Who is Duane Hubbard?"

"He is the former personal trainer of Ellen Griswold, Mr. Gary's ex-wife and current sister-in-law."

"What is his connection to Khun Gary?"

"Good question. What's interesting about Hubbard is, he and his boyfriend, a sometime-criminal goon named Matthew Mertz, were present on a Caribbean cruise ship fourteen years ago when Bill Griswold's first wife, Sheila, disappeared at sea. Sheila Griswold was a huge pain in the neck and a financial drain on Bill. There were people in Albany who believed at the time that Bill — or even Bill and Ellen — paid Hubbard and Mertz to toss the endlessly annoying ex-Mrs. Griswold into the sea. There was no evidence, and nothing ever came of it. And Ellen turns indignant over any insinuation that Sheila's apparent drowning was anything but a stupid accident caused perhaps by Sheila's tippling habits."

Pugh said, "Rounding."

"What's that?"

"When Khun Gary was moaning in his semi-delirium, he kept going on about rounding, Ek said. But perhaps Mr. Gary was experiencing nightmares not about rounding but about drowning."

"Drowning doesn't have two *D*s in it."

"I know that. I attended college in New Jersey, just like you. But the guy was slurring his words, and Ek may have been slurring his hearing. Not having gone to Rutgers."

I said, "This is fascinating stuff, but my mind is a little dizzy over what it might actually mean."

"Well, Khun Don, hang on to your hat. Would you like to know how much money Khun Gary had transferred into Duane Hubbard's Albany account on October fifteenth?"

"How much?"

"Two million US dollars."

CHAPTER TWENTY-NINE

The first thing Timmy said was, "It sounds like the family member who committed the terrible sin that had to be atoned for was Gary Griswold himself."

"You mean Gary had his former sister-in-law murdered?"

"Possibly. And then maybe he paid off these two lowlifes to keep them from talking? The original fee was insufficient and they were broke, and they knew just where go for an infusion of cash."

"Why would Griswold do that?" I said. "He says he's interested in justice. Karmic and Old Testament."

"There is that. And he does seem sincere. Also, why would he want to get rid of his brother's ex-wife in the first place? He didn't even like Bill Griswold. He and Ellen remained friends, but Bill was just some annoying Bushophile Gary put up with for business and peace-in-the-family reasons."

"Plus," I said, "the appeal of Buddhism for Griswold is its adherence to nonviolence. He hates militarism and talks up peaceful solutions. Is that a guy who arranges to have his former sister-in-law fed to the sharks?"

"It's not a particularly Buddhist type of offering."

We were approaching Khlong Toei, the Bangkok waterfront area with its docks and warehouses and light industry. The sun was setting and the light was splashing flame all over everything: ships, fishing boats, docks, cranes, us. Everyone was on deck now and alert. Pugh had arranged for us to be picked up in three cars and driven to a house not far from Griswold's condo owned by a sometime client of Pugh's in Sathorn. Timmy and I were about to come full circle in our five-day Gulf of Thailand odyssey.

Griswold was feeling better now, and he was sitting on a bamboo mat under a canopy with Mango, Egg and Nitrate watching Khlong Toei glide by. Griswold didn't seem to be mad at Mango anymore, maybe because these days he had so much else on his mind.

Pugh and I had decided not to confront Griswold with the Duane Hubbard revelation until we had him safely locked away. In case my knowing more about them could turn out to be useful, I had phoned Bob Chicarelli in Albany — it was six a.m. there — and left a message asking him to track down Duane Hubbard and Matthew Mertz, who presumably were living in the Albany area. Or at least had been living there six months earlier when Griswold wired two million dollars to Hubbard's Albany account. I asked Bob not to spook the two in any way but to find out what they were up to lately, and did they appear to be living off the fat of the land? I was beginning to wonder, in fact, if bozos such as these two might not be acting as agents for someone else, and Hubbard's bank account was merely a conduit.

Pugh had been on the phone up in the wheelhouse, and when we pulled up to a dock just as the last flecks of gold faded from the soot black Bangkok night, he said, "Mr. Don, we're going to dine this evening with a celebrity. Do you have a streak of star-fuckery in you, or will you be unimpressed if I tell you that soothsayer Pongsak has agreed to grant us an audience?"

"Audience? I thought these Bangkok seer guys were humble Buddhists."

Pugh laughed. "Sure. Like Jimmy Swaggart was a humble Christian."

The three cars carrying our group of renegades each took different routes to Sathorn. I rode with Pugh, Egg, Ek, Griswold and a physician, a woman named Sukchaiboworn, who had examined Griswold on the boat when we landed and pronounced him fit enough not to be rehospitalized. Griswold said, in fact, that his headache was gone and he was eager to get to a phone and a computer to work on his business transaction — i.e., the takeover of Algonquin Steel.

The safe house Pugh had arranged for was on Soi Nantha, not far from Griswold's condo and only a few hundred yards from Paradisio. The place had a high wall around it draped with pink bougainvillea and a lighted pool in the back. We got Griswold inside the house and locked into an upstairs room with Ek on the small balcony outside it and Egg guarding the door. Griswold had his computer and phones now, and he at least feigned being satisfied. He promised us he would not try to bolt.

Miss Nongnat went to her room to redo her toenails, while Kawee and Mango decided to drop in at Paradisio and relax there for a few hours. Mango said there was a Bulgarian diplomat who often showed up on Wednesdays, and he hoped to run into him and perhaps add to the Chonburi house fund.

Two of Pugh's crew had gone out to bring food back for the household, and while they were gone, Pugh and I went up to Griswold's room to lay out a plan we had come up with during a confab out by the pool.

Pugh was seated at a teak desk with a PC in the middle of it, and he had phones on either side of him. A Buddha figure rested on a nearby shelf, and Griswold had lit nine candles just below it.

"Khun Gary," Pugh said to him, "we are attempting to sketch out a program for keeping you alive until General Yodying has been relieved of his duties or even his present life — we're not sure what your associates have in mind for him. At the rate events are hurtling forward, however, we fear we might not be able to last another eleven days, short of getting you out of Thailand. Maybe to Sihanoukville or even darkest Rangoon. Would you be able to conduct your business from either of those two locations?"

"Of course not. I absolutely must be on top of things here."

"Why is that? You can operate by computer or phone from just about anywhere nowadays."

"I must have access to funds. Not all of my funds are in banks."

"Oh?"

Griswold shrugged. "I have twelve million dollars in sacks under the spirit house platform in my condo. There are people I am dealing with who — for reasons that will be obvious to any Thai — will conduct transactions only in cash. Former Prime Minister Thaksin is believed to have left the country with tens of millions of dollars and euros stuffed into a dozen pieces of luggage. I appreciate that all the untaxed money floating around Thailand represents an economic injustice for the ordinary Thai. But as I have pointed out, there are larger and more profound issues involved here."

I said, "Griswold, you are so full of it."

"Am I? That's a rather sweeping statement about a situation that is financially, socially and morally quite complex."

"You're in bed with crooks. There's nothing overly complicated about that."

"Oh, is former Finance Minister Anant na Ayudhaya a crook?"

Pugh said, "Khun Gary, being a crook is in the finance minister's job description in Thailand. For goodness' sake, haven't you read it?"

Griswold sighed and said, "Look, I have already admitted that this deal is morally complicated."

"Anyway," I said, "if this guy Anant is dealing in cash, how do you know you can trust him? If he's the chief Thai backer for the Sayadaw U Buddhism center, what makes you think he won't pocket your cash for the project and have it shipped to Singapore? Or to his old pal Thaksin in the UK?"

This got Griswold's attention. "I can't imagine that a genuine Buddhist would do such a thing."

Pugh looked at him sadly and said, "Oh, Mr. Gary."

"Here's the test," I said. "You get Anant to speed up preparations for the coup or whatever it is that's supposed to happen on April twenty-seventh. Instead of the end of the month, they do it the day after tomorrow, the eighteenth, another auspicious date. And you tell Anant, too, that the money for the project — and the controlling shares in Algonquin Steel — will be turned over to his group only after General Yodying is out of commission *and* all the transactions go through the Bangkok Bank, with you as one of two signatories on any disbursements on the Sayadaw U project."

Griswold shook his head. "No chance. Khun Anant would never agree to any of that. He is a proud man, I can assure you. And a bit of an egomaniac, I think."

Pugh said, "What if Khun Anant's very own soothsayer, Khun Pongsak, read Khun Anant's chart and discovered that it is essential that events transpire in the manner Khun Don and I have just described? Wouldn't that make a difference?"

"Of course it would. But Seer Pongsak would never do such a thing. He is a man of integrity."

"What if you paid him half a million dollars to do it? You could write it off as overhead."

"Bribe a seer? Has that ever been done in Thailand?"

Pugh said, "Uh-huh."

Griswold screwed up his banged-up face and said after a moment, "I'll have to think about that."

"Think fast," Pugh said. "Khun Pongsak will be here in twenty minutes."

§ § § §

The great seer arrived in a gold Mercedes with two young monks in tow. He was a slight, bony fellow with gold-rimmed specs who wore a formal black dinner jacket over a Brooks Brothers button-down striped shirt. He had on a Burmese sarong instead of pants and on his feet he wore dollar-store flip-flops. His fingers bore a number of gold rings. Around his neck hung a gold amulet with a picture of a wizened monk on it. The seer's overall presentation of himself was that of a dubious character who had gotten away with some casual shoplifting at Harry Winston's.

The Thais all wai-ed the soothsayer. Timmy and I picked up on the cue and performed a show of respect, too. Griswold shook his hand, and the two had a brief, chatty back-and-forth like a couple of old Cornell alums. Pugh informed Khun Pongsak that rice was on the way, and we adjourned to the spacious living room for some small talk next to an enormous stone Buddha figure before which candles had been lined up. Each of us lit one.

Khun Pongsak said to Timmy and me, "So, how do you like Thailand?"

I told him that we had not had much time to enjoy its many pleasures but we hoped to do so as soon as our work was completed.

The seer did not ask about the nature of our work, but he did ask, "Have you ever been to the Trump Tower?"

Timmy and I both said we had walked by it.

"I hope one day to see the Trump Tower with my own eyes."

Pugh said, "You should go there, Khun Pongsak. You will be amazed. The Trump Tower is made of solid gold."

"So I have heard."

There were some more pleasantries exchanged and then the food arrived. We sat around a teak table while Pugh's crew served up rice, fish red curry and morning glory vines in a spicy sauce. Pugh and I had a beer, and the seer requested green tea. Griswold asked if any chardonnay was available, and somehow a chilled bottle was soon produced.

Pugh's staff and the seer's monk posse were then asked to step outside the room, and Pugh got to the point.

"Khun Pongsak," Pugh said, "as security agents for Mr. Gary, we wish to make a request of you. General Yodying, as you may know, wants Mr. Gary taught a lesson following the unfortunate currency speculation scheme that went amiss when Mr. Gary pulled out of it. General Yodying passionately desires that Mr. Gary be thrown down from a high place and smashed to pieces. And the general's wishes for us, Mr. Gary's protectors, are now, we have every reason to believe, nearly identical. Mr. Gary needs to remain alive, however, because for one, he so much enjoys living and breathing, and secondly, to complete the Sayadaw U project that you yourself have invested in and which we all believe has earned the blessings of the spirit of the Enlightened One."

"Ah," said the seer.

"Now, we have been led to understand that General Yodying is scheduled for early retirement, so to speak, following a government shake-up which perusal of the heavens has determined should take place on April twenty-seventh. But sooner than April twenty-seventh would be so much safer and more convenient for Mr. Gary and for all of us. What if a reconsideration of the comings and goings of the planets and stars were to reveal that April eighteenth is the more auspicious date?"

We all watched the soothsayer, who was peering over at Pugh with fierce concentration.

"It is not just the charts that must be taken into consideration," the soothsayer said finally. "It is practical considerations also."

"But surely," Pugh said, "if these events are fated to occur on April eighteenth, how could reality not fail to keep up? Would the army — or whoever it is that's prepared to move — dare to defy the karma of the occasion as it has been revealed in your latest examinations of the heavens?"

Khun Pongsak continued to stare at Pugh, and we could all but hear the whirring sounds of his brain cells attempting to rearrange themselves lucratively.

It was Griswold who spoke up. He said, "How much do you want?"

"Oh, dear me." the seer said. "I can reveal but I cannot control what is fated."

"Let's say a hundred thousand US."

"No, a million. You are asking me to alter history."

"Two hundred thousand. That's final."

"I don't think that's final at all. You are over a barrel."

"Two fifty."

"Eight hundred thousand."

"You're mad."

"No deal."

"Half a million. Cash."

"All right. Five hundred thousand. Half of it in advance. Tonight."

Griswold said, "Well, it is all for the spirit of the Buddha, isn't it? And for the memory of Sayadaw U."

"This moment will live in Thai history," Pugh said. "I congratulate each and every one of you." He raised his bottle of Singha beer in a toast, and the soothsayer solemnly lifted his cup of green tea.

CHAPTER THIRTY

Everything began to unravel when Ellen Griswold woke me up in the middle of the night. Griswold had been successfully spirited over to his condo and back, and half a million dollars extracted from a vault that had been constructed under his spirit house. Seer Pongsak had been paid off and been driven away in his gold car. Fate had been nudged into moving our way. But then my cell phone rang at two forty-eight a.m.

"Strachey?"

"Ellen?"

"What the hell are you trying to pull?"

"I'm not sure I should explain to you what I'm doing. You fired me, and I'm working for your brother-in-law now. It's a question of professional ethics. I think I can't talk to you. Also, I'm half asleep."

"What I am about to say will wake you up fast. Listen to me. Gary is trying to take over Algonquin Steel, and I think you not only know all about it but you are a party to the conspiracy. As is Bob Chicarelli. Who probably sent me to you so that you could spy on me and keep Gary up to speed on what I know about this monstrous betrayal and what I don't know. What you are doing is so professionally beyond the pale that I am certain I can get you disbarred. Would you like to comment on that?"

Timmy was now stirring next to me.

I said, "I'm not an attorney who can be disbarred, but there is a licensing commission for private investigators. Just Google New York State PI licenses to file a complaint. But here's the thing, Ellen. You've got things really bollixed up. Where did you come up with this wild-eyed theory anyway?"

"And the other thing is," she went on, as if I had never spoken, "you are dragging Duane Hubbard and Matthew Mertz into this, and I am so mad — and so insulted and so offended — that I am just...beside myself with anger! Is Gary himself now retailing the absurd story that Bill, or Bill and I, paid Duane and Matthew to shove Sheila off the cruise ship? Is this part of his grand plan to discredit Bill and take control of the company and come back to Albany and make us pay for something that is a pure figment of his and other people's imaginations?"

"I don't know if that's what Gary has in mind. I think, however, that I had better ask him. Timmy and I have been batting around a somewhat different version of what you have just outlined."

"I think you're lying, Strachey. I think you know exactly what Gary has in mind. Bill found out that the people in the Caymans trying to take over the company and drive us all into the poorhouse are fronting for a Thai group. Did Gary really believe that we wouldn't realize that he was behind this cruel and misbegotten betrayal of the memory of Max and Bertha Griswold? Or was he planning to tell us when it was all a fait accompli and then gloat over his ghastly trick and laugh at our pain?"

"The latter, I think."

"Also, Bob Chicarelli has been asking around Albany about Duane and Matthew. I demand to know why."

"Oh, has he? And what has he learned about them?"

"I am not in touch with them and I am not in touch with Bob. I heard about his obnoxious snooping through a reliable third party. But there is something you should know about Duane and Matthew. It will explain a lot."

"Okay. I'm listening."

"To bury those vile stories once and for all about Bill hiring Duane and Matthew to throw Sheila off her boat, I am going to fly over to Bangkok and show you something that will put everything into perspective and erase any doubt about who Sheila really was and about what became of her."

"You'll love Thailand, Ellen. It's exciting. But how about a sneak preview of your revelations? Events here are moving at too fast a clip for any leisurely explication on your part."

"I'll be there in under twenty-four hours. I'm at JFK now, and my Thai Airways nonstop boards in half an hour. And Bill is coming with me. He is going to try to talk some sense into Gary if it isn't too late. And to you." She gave me her flight information, and I told her that someone would meet her plane. One of Pugh's people would be at the airport holding up a sign that read ALBANY GROUP.

Timmy was awake now, and I repeated to him what Ellen Griswold had just told me.

Timmy said, "She's going to be awfully disappointed if she gets over here and her ex-husband tells her that *he* hired Hubbard and Mertz to kill Bill's ex-wife. And that now he's atoning for it by handing the family company over to a Buddhist study and retreat center."

"If that's what actually happened. But I don't think it did."

"I don't either."

"It's time for Griswold to fess up. I'm going to ask him to tell me the truth about Hubbard and Mertz. And if he refuses, I'll threaten to gum up the whole Buddhism center deal. Tell the seer that Trump Tower is made out of Cheez Whiz or something."

I got out of bed and into my pants. "You're going to ask Griswold now?" Timmy said. "He's on painkillers. How coherent is he going to be?"

"Not too coherent, but just enough, I hope."

§ § § §

One of the Dream Boys was on sentry duty on a chair outside Griswold's room squinting at a Thai soap opera on a TV set the size of a brick. I saw light under Griswold's door, and when I knocked lightly he murmured something and I opened the door. He was not only wide-awake but was seated in front of the computer in his underwear. He turned and actually smiled at me.

"The deal is done," he said. "On Friday, the eighteenth, our group will own the controlling shares of Algonquin Steel. This will coincide with a change of administration in Thailand that will rid us of the pesky General Yodying. We can proceed with the Sayadaw U center without having to worry about people like the general whose only motives are greed and self-aggrandizement. Having transferred most of my wealth into the project, I'll be close to penniless except for my condo and some cash reserves. But I will have helped establish an institution of great spiritual significance, and I will have helped atone for a great moral crime."

I sat down on the edge of Griswold's bed and said, "Was the great moral crime the murder of your former sister-in-law, Sheila Griswold?"

He flinched just once, then seemed to relax. "Yes. My brother and your former client — and my ex-wife — Ellen had Sheila killed. I'm going to confront them with the evidence of the atrocity they committed, and then I'm going to tell them that I have set the moral balance right and from now on it is only their consciences they need fear. And of course, the abject misery of their future lives."

Griswold actually looked peaceful. He had nine candles burning on his desk and a jasmine garland draped over the PC he was using.

I said, "So you didn't pay Duane Hubbard and Matthew Mertz to throw Sheila off the ship?"

He gave me a look. "Me? Don't be absurd. Why would I do that? God, Strachey, what kind of man do you think I am?"

"Then why did you pay Hubbard two million dollars six months ago?"

He registered mild surprise but was so into his reverie of moral satisfaction that he didn't seem unduly fazed by my knowledge of the two goons.

He said, "They blackmailed me. They came over to Thailand to tell me they had proof that Bill and Ellen had hired them to kill Sheila, and unless I paid them two million dollars, they would send an incriminating recording that they had to the police. They would then disappear, but Bill and Ellen would be prosecuted."

"Why were they blackmailing you? Why not blackmail Bill and Ellen? They could have saved a bundle on airfare."

"Because they had found out that I had cashed out my shares in the company and had access to large amounts of ready funds, and Bill and Ellen were merely stock rich. Duane and Matthew had some scheme they wanted to invest in — a chain of fitness-slash-fast-food centers called Bitchin' Burritos. The idea was, you'd spend half an hour on a treadmill sweating and then get a cheese and bean burrito as a reward, and with no net gain in calories for the visit. Have any of these places opened in Albany that you know of?"

"Not yet."

"I decided to pay those two criminals off for two reasons. One was, I really don't want Bill and Ellen to go to prison. There's no love lost between my brother and me, but I still have a soft spot in my heart for Ellen. She never gave me a really hard time when I came out, and she still really cares for me, I think."

"That's my impression."

"Also, there is a higher justice, and it is that higher justice I wanted badly for them to become acquainted with. It would mean that in their next lives they might choose to devote themselves to activities that could lead eventually to moral and spiritual redemption."

"How," I asked, "did Hubbard and Mertz find out that you had cashed out your shares in Algonquin Steel? Presumably they were not privy to company goings-on."

Griswold looked at me wearily and said, "I'll bet you can guess."

"Bill and Ellen told them?"

"When they approached Bill and threatened to turn him and Ellen in, he told them that company stock was down and he was unable to sell any shares, and he was cash poor. He told them I had a lot of cash, and he knew that I would do the right thing in order to protect the reputations and memories of our parents. And he was right about that. My parents were not understanding with me when I came out, and that hurt. But overall they were decent human beings who did their best in the world. And they never disinherited me either, and that has made the Sayadaw U project possible, and a lot of other meritorious works too. Not just concert halls in Rochester, but projects that will make the world a saner and more peaceful place for thousands of years to come."

"Did you listen to the so-called incriminating tape?"

"It was actually a video. A DVD, they said. I didn't want to see it and really didn't need to. Duane said they had showed it to Bill and Ellen, and that's when they were told to get in touch with me. Bill and Ellen, in fact, were given a copy of it. Of course, they probably destroyed it immediately."

"Did you tell them that Hubbard and Mertz had come here to blackmail you and that you had acceded to their demands?"

"No. My plan is to inform them after the takeover of the company by my Thai investment group and the transfer of the shares to the Sayadaw project. That would have been on the twenty-seventh, but now it'll be the eighteenth, which is even better. There's less chance that anything will go wrong if we wrap this up posthaste."

"There may be a hitch," I said.

Griswold stiffened. "What hitch?"

"Ellen and Bill know what you are up to. She called me. They are plenty upset about the company takeover. And they also know that you know about the Hubbard–Mertz connection. I seem to have indirectly and inadvertently tipped them off about that. Sorry. But it might actually be good that all the Griswolds are finding out what all the other Griswolds are thinking and what each of you is up to. And unless all of you lie through your teeth even when you are face-to-face, some useful clearing of the air might be about to break out. That's because Ellen and Bill are en route to Bangkok as we speak. They'll arrive later this afternoon."

Griswold went white. "Oh no. Do you realize what this could mean, Strachey?"

"What?"

"More sorrow and bloodshed."

Griswold sat looking over at me from between his bandages, his eyes full of desolation and fear. I wasn't sure if he was uncannily prescient or if he basically just needed to stay off bicycles.

CHAPTER THIRTY-ONE

Griswold would not agree to see his brother and sister-in-law until the day after their arrival late Thursday afternoon. He said this was for their own safety. On Friday, Griswold said, a change of government   would remove General Yodying from power, and he would no longer be a threat to any of us. Friday would also, of course, be too late for Bill and Ellen to talk Gary into holding on to the controlling shares of Algonquin Steel instead of turning them over to the Thai group running the Sayadaw U project. I asked Griswold about that, and he said, "Yep. Too bad."

Griswold was kept under close watch at the safe house through the day, and then while Nitrate picked up Bill and Ellen at Suvarnabhumi. They were coming in on the same flight from New York that Timmy and I had arrived on six days earlier. Kawee, Mango and Timmy splashed around in the swimming pool throughout the day. I had a brief swim too, and also managed to reach Bob Chicarelli in Albany just before he went to bed.

"Hey, Bob, somebody you were asking about Hubbard and Mertz blabbed to Bill and Ellen. They're spitting nickels. It isn't pretty."

"I know. Sorry, Strachey. They're trying to get me disbarred."

"Can they?"

"Nah. I'm not representing them in anything."

"Me either. I'm not sure I'm representing anybody. At this point, it's all for the Enlightened One."

"Don't forget to send him a bill."

"So, did you pick up anything on Hubbard and Mertz?"

"They're in Albany and not doing all that great. Hubbard is back working as a personal trainer, and Mertz is supposedly dealing crystal meth. They got hold of a lot of money somewhere last fall, but they lost it. Some guy from Miami conned them out of it with a scheme to open a Mexican fast-food chain where you could also work out. But then this dude disappeared with most of the dough. It was going to be called Taco Terrifico or something like that."

I told Chicarelli that Ellen and Bill Griswold were at that moment high above the Pacific en route to Thailand to confront Gary. "Gary thinks Ellen and Bill had Sheila Griswold killed by Hubbard and Mertz, and he's determined to ruin their lives. Their present lives anyway. Over here people make those distinctions. I'm not sure what Bill and Ellen know or think, but they absolutely deny any involvement in Sheila's death. The only really sure thing is, we've got quite a face-off in the works over here."

"It might interest you to know," Chicarelli said, "that Hubbard and Mertz used to dabble in gay porn. They're a little too mature for that by now. But a guy I know in the DA's office said there was a gay porn video production operation in Schenectady for a while in the nineties, and those two were involved in both production work and performing."

"So Schenectady was the Budapest of the Mohawk Valley? I never knew that."

"It didn't last, apparently."

I said, "Was it just gay? Or did they do bi stuff, too?"

"That I can't tell you."

"Well, good luck keeping your license, Bob"

"You too, Strachey."

§ § § §

The Oriental Hotel, where the Griswolds had chosen to stay despite their apparent precarious financial state, had retained its cachet but only a little of its former Victorian-era charm. The ghosts of Conrad and Maugham did not greet us as Pugh and I strode past the doorman toward the elevators. But even the rooms in the modern tower section of the hotel were spiffy and spacious and had a nice view of the hotel's riverside gardens and the dragon-tail boats on the Chao Phraya beyond.

The rooms also had TV sets with built-in DVD players, and that was useful for taking a gander at the video Pugh and I were about to watch along with Ellen and Bill.

"I'm really hurt," Ellen said to me, "that Gary would think I could kill another person. I thought he knew me better than that, and this really all just breaks my heart."

"Gary and I were never close," Bill said, "and I know he rejects many of my values. But same as Ellen, I'm really just terribly, terribly disappointed that my brother would see me as a person who would take a human life."

"Even Sheila's," Ellen added and threw me a look.

The Griswolds were not their freshest. Both had showered and changed clothes before Pugh and I arrived just after eight Thursday night. But the seventeen-hour slog across the Pacific and the twelve-hour time difference had beaten them down, and they looked as if they could have used a week on the beach at Phuket instead of a confrontation with a man bent on making them pay for committing a murder they denied having anything to do with.

Ellen had flopped onto an easy chair in her aubergine pantsuit and tangerine headband, and Bill was seated at the desk in fresh khakis and a white polo shirt. Here was the man I remembered from the Albany airport ten days earlier, a beefier version of Gary, with thinning hair and puffy dark eyes. He had popped a piece of Nicorette gum soon after Pugh and I arrived, and I felt for the guy. Having your wealth and your life's work crumbling while you were in nicotine withdrawal was a lot of people's idea of hell. I wondered if he would make it through the next few days without bolting down the street to pick up a pack of Marlboros, which in Thailand were required by law to display hideous pictures of rotting gums on the front of each package.

The Griswolds did not appear pleased to have Pugh in the room — their handshakes with him were brief and perfunctory

— but they apparently accepted my explanation that he was the man who would keep us all safe while these complex Griswold family matters got sorted out.

I laid out Gary Griswold's story that he had let himself be blackmailed by Hubbard and Mertz in order to keep Bill and Ellen from going to prison and to protect the memories of Bill and Gary's parents. They both shook their heads and threw up their hands.

"That's idiotic," Ellen said.

"Pure bullshit," said Bill.

"And what proof did Duane and Matthew offer of this heinous crime supposedly sponsored by Bill and me?"

"They said they had an incriminating recording and you had a copy of it too."

"Well, they *did* bring Ellen and me a DVD and try to extort money from us," Bill said. "But it was no proof of murder, for God's sake. It's the DVD you are about to see. They said we should pay up, or the family would be embarrassed by Sheila's history. Apparently they were bluffing with Gary about proof of a murder having been committed, and their outrageous bluff paid off. How much did Gary give them?"

"A lot. Two million dollars."

"Oh no!"

"He did it for you two supposedly. And for the future well-being of your souls."

"Oh, please," Ellen said.

Now Pugh spoke up. "Mr. Gary plans on building a Buddhist study and meditation center here in Bangkok, also with an aim of easing your way along the bumpy paths of time. It is a gesture of great magnanimity, and you will be among its primary beneficiaries. You may not wish to thank him in this life, but I am guessing that on down the road your gratitude and appreciation will be immense."

"Mr. Pugh," Ellen said, "when I die, I plan on staying dead. So if Gary wants to ease Bill's and my burdens, he might start by dropping this insane plan to rob us of the great company that Bill's father built out of literally nothing. And he might fucking apologize to Bill and me for going around calling us goddamn murderers!"

Pugh shrugged. "You two are of course free to aim your souls in any direction you wish, including anybody's idea of heaven, hell, purgatory or Venezuela. But it is your actions that will decide things, not your intentions."

The Griswolds shot each other a Who-is-this-guy? look. Ellen said, "Thanks for clearing that up. Now I can just close my eyes anytime I feel like it and drift toward the white light."

I said, "How did Hubbard and Mertz know that Gary was in Thailand with a lot of cash in the bank? They told Gary that you sent them his way."

Bill said, "They knew about Gary from another one of Duane's clients, a man Gary had dated when he was still in Albany and who had tried to contact Gary on a visit to Key West. Gary's friends there told this guy what Gary had done — left the company and moved to Thailand. Duane and Matthew told us if we didn't pay them — they wanted something laughable, like half a million dollars — they would go to Gary and show him the DVD and tell him what a slut Sheila was, and did he want this gross family stuff turning up at six and eleven on Channel Thirteen?"

"As if Gary would give a crap," Ellen said.

"As if *we* would," her husband added.

"Well," Ellen said. "Of course we would *care* if Bill's ex turned up on the news in the altogether with those two dorks, her face and tits all blurred out to save the Hudson Valley grannies and kiddies who were watching from wondering what *that* was all about. Yes, we would care. But not to the tune of half a million dollars. Or even half a million — what's the currency here?"

"Baht," Pugh said.

"Yes, or even half a million of those. Bill told Duane and Matthew to get lost. We never heard another word, and naturally it never occurred to us that they actually followed through and went after Gary for money. It all just seemed too preposterous."

Pugh said, "It is my duty to inform you that pornography is illegal in Thailand. That does not mean that it is not ubiquitous. Nonetheless you are breaking the law by possessing the DVD you have brought into the country, and I hope you do not end up in one of our notorious, squalid, soul-destroying prisons for eight or ten years. But anyway here we all are, so let's have a look."

The Sheila Griswold who soon appeared on the hotel room's TV screen was quite a specimen: rangy, taut, bright-eyed, nicely coiffed and made-up, and above all, eager and versatile. On the fifty-minute video — much of which Bill Griswold fast-forwarded through — the notorious JAP did everything but shop. Hubbard and Mertz were also physically well put together: muscular, fine skinned, with better-than-average endowments. And while equally busy, the two men seemed perceptibly more keen on each other's parts than on the ex-Mrs. Griswold's. Though they did do what the DVD's producers apparently had required of them, and at every opportunity Sheila Griswold was ready to help out.

Ellen had only just glanced at the video from time to time while Bill, Pugh, and I sat paying attention.

"Jesus," Ellen said when *The End* came on. "If any of you fellows need to go take a shower, feel free. Me, I could use a beer." She was seated near the minibar and got up and extracted a Singha.

I said, "So this is why Hubbard and Mertz were on the cruise ship with Sheila when she disappeared? What was it? They were blackmailing her too? Making her pay for their Caribbean vacations?"

Ellen laughed. "If only."

"Sheila was paying those two to travel with her and service her," Bill said evenly. "It was one of the expenses I was expected to pick up after the divorce."

"Too sad," Pugh said. "It sounds like a Thai soap opera. Except, in Thai soap operas of this kind, murder often *is* the result."

"What I still don't get," I said, "is why Gary ever believed that Hubbard and Mertz had proof of the murder accusation. This DVD certainly would not serve that purpose."

"In Thailand it might," Pugh said. "And Khun Gary had been living here and could conceivably have picked up some of the local attitudes."

"But he never even saw the DVD."

"Perhaps," Pugh said, "he wished to believe the worst of his brother. Is that a possibility, Mr. Bill?"

Again, Ellen and Bill glanced at each other. He nodded and said, "It could have happened that way."

"That may make it harder," Pugh said, "to talk your younger brother out of the transaction he is determined to conclude in a matter of hours — a transaction that will be detrimental not only to your financial well-being but to your reputation in the larger society. I know face is less important among farangs than among Thais. But may I please be the first to offer you my deepest sympathies for your coming out of all this with an awful lot of egg on your face."

It was then that Bill Griswold said he needed to have a look in the minibar too.

CHAPTER THIRTY-TWO

Pugh and I rode back to the safe house and went up to Griswold's room. We relayed to him Ellen and Bill's version of events.

Without hesitation, Griswold said, "They're conning you."

"Maybe. But we don't think so."

"Hubbard and Mertz didn't say a thing about a sex tape. That makes no sense. They told me their tape had evidence of a murder on it."

"It was a bluff, and you fell for it. That's what Ellen and your brother think."

Griswold's face drooped. "But if they didn't have Sheila killed — if she just got drunk and fell overboard — that would mean my whole exercise in atonement and trying to restore moral balance for me and my family has been — pointless."

"Making merit is never without its reasons," Pugh said. "And never without moral benefits for the merit-maker and for the human race."

I said, "I'd like to suggest that you at least see Bill and Ellen and hear them out before you take the final step. What's to lose? It might even make it easier for you. Tamp down doubts. Clear away any pangs of conscience. Maybe they'll even see how worthy a project the Buddhism center is and want to make a big contribution."

"But the deed is practically done," Griswold said. "I've already accumulated controlling shares in Algonquin Steel. They are in my name now, but unless I intervene the shares will pass over to Khun Anant and his group at noon tomorrow, and the consortium will begin work on the Sayadaw U project immediately."

Pugh said, "These valuable shares of stock are going through Khun Anant? Oh, Khun Gary, I don't know."

Now Griswold twitched. "But this is all for the propagation of the Four Noble Truths. How could Anant dare to interfere with such a worthy endeavor?"

Pugh shrugged. "Hypocrisy, as I believe I have mentioned previously, is not unknown among Buddhists. Do you really believe that Christians and Jews have a monopoly?"

Griswold looked at Pugh and then at me and then back at Pugh. Finally, he said, "I'll talk to Ellen and Gary first thing in the morning. Just to cover all the bases here. Can you set that up?"

"Of course," Pugh said. "Tomorrow is Friday, April eighteenth, an auspicious day by anyone's reckoning."

"But my plan is to go ahead with the project," Griswold said. "Whatever Ellen and Bill might have to tell me about Sheila and her death, it's really too late to back out of the Sayadaw U project. I'll explain it all to Bill and Sheila and try to make them understand. Anyway, they have been such staunch supporters of so much in America and the world that is greedy and destructive, they really do need to have their souls cleansed even if they have not committed murder directly. Which I am not yet convinced that they have not."

I said, "You're going to ruin their lives because they're Republicans, Griswold? That's harsh."

"Oh, I don't think so at all. No, unless Bill and Ellen can tell me something I don't already know about themselves and me and the lives all of us have led, I really see no reason to postpone the Sayadaw project at all. Also, I can't quite bring myself to believe that Khun Anant would attempt to cheat me. That strikes me as extremely unlikely. Khun Pongsak has vouched for him, after all."

I said, "You mean Pongsak, the soothsayer who you just bribed?"

Griswold nodded feebly, and you didn't have to believe in astral and planetary influences on human events to grasp that Friday was going to be memorable.

§ § § § §

The plan was for Nitrate to pick Ellen and Bill up at the Oriental at seven Friday morning before the morning traffic became too grisly. We would all have breakfast together by the pool, and then Bill, Ellen, and Gary would go sit under the banyan tree in the back of the garden and hash out their differences. Then Griswold would either proceed with his turning over Algonquin Steel to Anant na Ayudhaya at midday for the Sayadaw project, or he would do something else.

All that began to fall apart at six ten. That's when Nitrate drove back through the gate at the safe house ten minutes after he had departed. He told Pugh, who told Timmy and me, that roadblocks had been set up by the army — all over Bangkok, apparently — and nobody in the city was going anywhere. Public transportation didn't seem to be running either. Minutes later, Pugh's cell phone began to ring. Pugh's crew started monitoring Bangkok television and radio stations. No official word had yet come from anyone, including the king. But everyone in the city seemed to have concluded that a military takeover of Thailand's democratically elected government was under way.

Griswold came down from his room and looked almost cheerful. A nurse had been in to change his dressings and bandages, and he appeared less beat-up and bedraggled than he had a day earlier.

The air hadn't yet turned hot and soggy, so we all gathered by the pool for tea and fruit. Pugh had somebody walk over to the Topmost and come back with some rice and a bag of bacon.

I tried to phone Ellen and Bill at the Oriental to alert them that no one would be picking them up anytime soon. But by then the cell phone circuits were all jammed and I was unable to get through. The landline at the safe house wasn't working either. The hotel staff would no doubt cheerfully explain to Ellen and Bill about the coup, an occasional feature of the Land of Smiles.

Griswold beamed. "Khun Anant is as good as his word. General Yodying will be history by the end of the day, and we'll all be safe and free to resume our lives. Isn't that great?"

Timmy said, "What will become of Yodying? Will he be prosecuted for corruption?"

"Perhaps," Griswold said. "Or he may flee the country. That sort of thing happens."

Pugh said, "He might fly to Singapore and visit his money."

Kawee, Mango and Miss Nongnat came outside and joined us. They were all antiregime and were delighted to see the scoundrels getting heaved out.

Kawee said, "His Majesty the King, he save us one more time. I love my king!"

"Won't there be any resistance?" I asked. "The regime must have some support or they wouldn't have been elected."

"Pro-regime crowds will march around yelling and waving signs," Pugh said. "But they won't challenge the army. As soon as an official announcement comes from the palace endorsing the coup, people will go home and have some rice and burn incense and light candles and watch soap operas. Then in six months or so, new elections will produce another coalition of crooks to run the country in cooperation with the banks and the soothsayers and the tourism board. And the endless Thai cycle of political birth, death and rebirth will resume. It's all reassuring, if you really think about it. It works quite as well as the political setup in, say, New Jersey, is my impression."

"It works," Griswold said, "because Buddhists understand and accept that nothing is permanent. Change is the only reality, and Thais accept that truth and even embrace it. This attunement with life's deepest reality is why I love this country, and it is why this time I will never again make the mistake of leaving Thailand."

Pugh said, "Good luck, Mr. Gary. Just don't neglect to do your visa runs."

Griswold said, "I really am sorry I won't be able to speak with Ellen and Bill before the Algonquin Steel takeover and the commencement of the Sayadaw project. I think I might have been able to help them understand that it's best for all the Griswolds just to move on. Business isn't permanent. Family history isn't permanent. The only thing permanent is the spirit of the Enlightened One and his teachings and, of course, the *Sangha* that perpetuates his teachings."

Pugh said, "I share your sentiments, Khun Gary, and I am deeply disappointed that apparently I will not have the opportunity to observe, even from a distance, your explaining these matters to your older brother and your ex-wife. That would have been a sight to behold."

"Well," Griswold said, "those necessary explanations will have to take place in retrospect."

"It's bound to be dramatic either way."

§ § § §

By three in the afternoon, no official announcement had been made of a change of government. Speculation was rampant on the radio stations and television news channels as to what this might mean. Did the king change his mind? Was the aged king perhaps unwell, or worse? At three ten, Pugh's operatives, who had been out and about, began to filter back to the safe house. They all reported that the roadblocks were being removed and the military trucks and troop carriers were disappearing. Public transportation was soon up and running.

Radio and television began to report that the roadblocks and military operations were merely part of an "exercise" and that, contrary to widespread rumor, no coup had taken place.

Pugh said, "This is interesting."

Griswold said, "Oh fuck."

Pugh said, "That too."

Just after four, nine police vehicles pulled up in front of the safe house. Black-uniformed commandos quickly scaled the walls on four sides to prevent any of us from making a run for it.

A captain in a uniform that appeared freshly washed and pressed despite the heat had all of us gathered together in one place. He said calmly, "Please come with me. General Yodying wishes to speak with you."

CHAPTER THIRTY-THREE

At the police station, we were all placed inside the same holding cell. Four unwashed men with multiple tattoos were already in there, lying on the concrete floor, and they looked unhappy to see us. This was perhaps because now they would have to share the single pail being used for urination and defecation with the fifteen of us. The cell was unfurnished except for the reeking bucket, and somebody had forgotten to equip the room with air-conditioning.

"Surely they won't keep us here for long," Griswold said, and all the English-speaking Thais in the cell turned away from him and fixed their gazes instead on the cockroaches crawling up the walls.

Timmy said, "I was once in a cell like this in rural India. It takes me back."

"You deal drugs?" Mango asked.

"No, I had transported a village boy trampled by a bull to a hospital, and as a bureaucratic precaution, two policeman took me to jail, just in case it had been I who had crushed the boy's pelvis."

"How long you stay?" Kawee asked.

"Just overnight. The district poultry officer came and bribed somebody to release me."

Now everyone looked at Griswold again, Mister Moneybags.

Pugh said, "The general may let us marinate a bit. To clear our minds."

"I really don't see why he is doing this," Griswold said. "Obviously Yodying is in this with Anant. They have swindled me out of just about everything I own, including my family's company. What more can they possibly extract from me?"

"I am sure they are at this very moment compiling a list, Khun Gary. What else have you got?"

"My condo. What's left of the cash in the vault under my spirit house. Minus, of course, the two hundred fifty thousand I handed over to Seer Pongsak last night. Oh. I suppose he was also a party to the scam. And he knew where my cash reserves were kept. So I suppose he informed Anant and Yodying, who went over to the condo and helped themselves."

"You'll be lucky if they didn't lick the paint off the walls," Pugh said. "They are greedy."

"Maybe," Kawee said, "they water plants, make offerings."

"Let's hope so," Pugh said. "The general and the former finance minister are, after all, good Buddhists."

Griswold suddenly looked nauseated and hunkered down with his back against the filthy wall and lowered his head between his knees. "I think I'm going to throw up," he croaked.

Timmy, Mr. Peace Corps, was the one who picked up the bucket, carried it over, and set it down in front of Griswold.

Pugh said, "Let 'er rip, Khun Gary."

Griswold did.

The Thais all averted their eyes from the violently retching farang.

I said, "Timothy, at home you're so careful to turn up only in the most fastidiously kept surroundings. Maybe in one of your past lives you learned to adapt to conditions like these. Say, in the Crimean war."

Would he laugh? Nope. He glanced over at me noncommittally, but that was all.

After an hour or so, two guards returned. Were they going to release us? We had been on the cement floor, shifting about and trying to find comfortable positions without kicking one another in the face. The four men who were occupying the cell when we arrived, we had learned, were in on drug charges and facing long sentences or even death and had been inert in this cell for eight days. They hoped for a pretrial hearing within two or three months, they said. They knew better than to expect anything good from the guards when they came back, but the rest of us looked up expectantly.

The guards, however, were only delivering supper. One held an automatic weapon while the other unlocked the cell door, and two kitchen workers came with a cart and passed out to each of us plastic plates of rice and bowls of dun-colored soup.

"This food makes me ashamed to be Thai," Pugh said. "It must be Burmese."

The rest of us weren't crazy about it either. Most of us ate the rice but skipped the soup. The four tattooed drug dealers ate the rancid soup eagerly. They considered the extra food a treat.

Timmy said, "Is it really possible we'll be here overnight?"

Pugh shrugged.

I said, "But Rufus, nothing is permanent. All we have to do is wait for the transitory nature of all things to notice us here. Am I right?"

Pugh chuckled, and he translated my joke to the non–English-speaking Thais in the cell. Everyone laughed except the drug dealers.

At ten o'clock, the guards came back and handed in a bucket of water with a single plastic cup floating in it. All the Thais looked grateful, but I guessed that the three farangs — Timmy, Griswold, me — were all thinking the same thing: Bangkok tap water. No San Pellegrino was going to be provided.

§ § § §

Just after eleven, two new guards turned up. They opened the cell door, and one of them asked in English for Pugh, me, Timmy and Griswold to follow them.

The second-floor captain's office was more sanitary than our cell, but it also lacked the charm we had come to associate with Siamese furnishings and decor.

The captain himself, the man who had arrested us at the safe house, was present but he had little to offer us beyond a few pleasantries. He said General Yodying would be along shortly.

The captain apologized for Bangkok's steamy weather. Griswold asked if we would be permitted to phone the United States embassy. The captain said no, that we should just sit tight.

General Yodying ambled in around eleven thirty carrying a sheaf of papers. The captain and Pugh wai-ed the general. Griswold, Timmy and I followed their lead. The general wai-ed us back and there were friendly exchanges of sa-wa-dee-cap.

He was big for a Thai, light skinned, with a broad forehead and an immobile face. He was wearing a full dress uniform and looked as if he might have come from a formal occasion, possibly official. I doubted the general had dolled himself up for us. He seated himself at his raised desk, and we took seats across from and half a foot below him.

The general looked at Timmy and me and said, "It is a pity your visit to Thailand has been disrupted by the taint of your association with this bad man." He indicated Griswold with a curt nod. "And I certainly hope that neither of you shares Mr. Griswold's unfortunate tendencies. If so, I would advise you to leave Thailand and take up residence instead in Phnom Penh, Cambodia."

I could see just enough of Griswold with my peripheral vision to catch the flinch. He knew what was coming, and he knew what had happened to him, and he knew he was finished.

"And you, Khun Rufus. I am surprised and disappointed that you would allow yourself to be employed by such a depraved pervert. I know you well enough to know that your sexual appetites are entirely healthy. I suppose you are in it for the money — protecting a man like this — and I can appreciate that. We all have families to support and temples to which we must make appropriate offerings."

Pugh looked at the general evenly but said nothing.

Flipping open his packet, the general pulled out a wad of eight-by-ten color photos. He said, "Mr. Griswold, investigators under my command have compiled incontrovertible proof that you have been molesting helpless little boys in and around

Bangkok. People like you have been coming to Southeast Asia for years to prey on poor and vulnerable urchins like the ones in these photographs. But I have to tell you that those days are over. Finished. Monsters such as yourself now serve long prison terms for these despicable acts, and I want you to know that you will be prosecuted to the fullest extent of the law. Would you like to make a statement?"

Griswold was entirely calm. His months of meditation were paying off. He said, "I'll make a statement. Aren't you going to record it?"

"That won't be necessary."

"May I see the photos?"

"Of course."

The general spread them out on his desk facing us. They were bad. Boys no more than eight or ten grimacing and crying as they were being penetrated by a foreigner who plainly was not Griswold — although Griswold's face had been ineptly Photoshopped atop the face of the actual perpetrator.

Griswold said, "Where did you get these? That's not me, despite the crude attempts to make it look as if it is."

"These photos were on your computer."

Pugh said, "A mistake has obviously been made. I am in possession of Khun Gary's computer."

"Perhaps you have one of his computers," the general said. "But this one was found in a hidden vault beneath the spirit house in Mr. Griswold's condo here in Bangkok. And of course, the photos speak for themselves."

Griswold said, "How much do you want? I have very little left. Basically just what's left in the vault under the spirit house."

"No money was found in your vault, Mr. Griswold. Just your laptop with these despicable pictures of your despicable acts."

"So what do you want from me? What can I possibly offer you to secure my freedom, General?"

"You can offer me nothing, Mr. Griswold. However, I am a man of mercy. The only thing I require of you is your absence from Thailand. Your visa to remain in Thailand was revoked half an hour ago. Members of my department will personally escort you to the airport at nine tomorrow morning. You will be placed on a flight to Frankfurt and you will never be admitted to Thailand again. We don't want your ilk in our country. We simply will not stand for it."

Griswold said, "What about the Sayadaw U center? Will it be built?"

The general smiled. "Of course, of course it will be built. If that's what you're worried about, have no fear. Your name will not be associated with the shrine, however, now that you have the taint of moral corruption on you. And I should mention perhaps that the center will be completed on a scale somewhat reduced from what you had in mind. Your idea of it was far too grandiose for Thai tastes. We are a humble people."

Griswold sat quietly gazing at the general. After a moment, he said, "I still love Thailand."

"Oh, even though it has disappointed you! I am relieved to hear that, Mr. Griswold. You are in many ways a good man — despite your proclivities. You are a man of spiritual depth and perspective. Perhaps after your soul has been purified by chaste behavior and generous offerings over a series of lives, you will return to Thailand under another, better guise. I am certain our immigration department would have no objection to that."

Griswold said, "What about my friends here? They have done nothing wrong. Of course, neither have I. But it seems as if there is no point in discussing that."

"No. You are correct. There is no point in discussing that. But your friends will be released in the morning. Khun Rufus can resume his colorful career as Bangkok's Mickey Spillane. And Mr. Donald and Mr. Timothy will, I hope, enjoy some of the splendors of Siamese culture and civilization, and perhaps have a pleasant visit at one of our hundreds of excellent beaches. I don't want them to return to America with a poor impression of my country."

Timmy said, "I like your beaches, General. We've been to Hua Hin. But your criminal justice system leaves a lot to be desired."

Had Timmy fallen off his bicycle and landed on his head? I had been determined to keep my mouth shut and leave for the airport at the first opportunity. I thought, *My God, he's turning into me.*

But General Yodying nodded sympathetically. "I do apologize for detaining you, Mr. Timothy, and for doing so in our admittedly fetid accommodations. Do understand, however, that I could have left you all to rot over the weekend in that cell. But I did not. In fact, I drove over here following my own sixtieth birthday celebration at the Dusit Thani to deal with Khun Gary and to assure the rest of your group that in the morning I will be totally out of your hair. I could have gone straight home with my wife or to my delightful girlfriend's house. So don't complain too much."

Pugh said, "Today is your sixtieth birthday, general? Please let me offer my heartiest congratulations."

"My birthday is actually tomorrow, the nineteenth," the general said. "Ah, it's after midnight now. If I may say so, happy birthday to me!"

Pugh sang out, "How wonderful!"

Pugh's enthusiasm seemed weirdly misplaced, until we got back to our cell and he explained to me that the confluence of events he had just learned of was heavy with auspiciousness.

CHAPTER THIRTY-FOUR

True to his soiled word, the deeply corrupt General Yodying had Griswold escorted out of our cell at nine Saturday morning. Griswold's passport had been retrieved from his apartment in Sukhumvit, and the police had picked up clean clothes for him too. He was also handed ten twenty-dollar bills for his immediate expenses once he arrived in Frankfurt. After that, he was on his own. The general said he would not notify Interpol that Griswold was a notorious sex offender, so long as Griswold left Thailand forever and didn't raise a fuss about his having been bilked out of thirty-eight million dollars.

We all said good-bye to Griswold, and I told him how sorry I was that it had all turned out so badly for him. I asked him what I should tell Ellen and Bill.

He thought about this, and said, "Just tell them I said mai pen rai. And that I hope they enjoy the rest of their stay in Thailand. It's really a lovely country."

Griswold was led away, and we thought we would be leaving at the same time and stood ready to go. But a guard said, "You wait."

Around nine thirty, a whole squad of corrections officers arrived at our cell. The sergeant in charge told us to take off all our clothes and hand them out. What was this? Were we going to be deloused? Hosed down? Gang-raped?

Anxiously, we disrobed and handed out our garments, including — as we were ordered to do — our underwear. One of the guards then passed out large plastic garbage bags, one to each of us. Holes had been cut for our arms to protrude, and when instructed to do so, we donned the garbage bags. Our money, wallets and keys, confiscated the day before, were returned to us.

We were then led out to a convoy of police vans and driven to Wat Pho, the magnificent temple that housed the largest reclining Buddha in Thailand. Hundreds of tourists were queued up outside in the sunshine waiting their turn to enter the sacred shrine. They pointed and laughed as we were dropped off and the police vans drove away, and the tourists all got some great snapshots.

We had enough money among us to take taxis back to the safe house, where we had all left a few belongings. Timmy's and my plan was to return to the Topmost, clean up, and then track down Ellen and Bill Griswold and try to explain how and why they had lost control of the family company despite their not being murderers, and why Gary Griswold was en route, or soon to be en route, to Germany.

My cell phone was at the safe house, and it had one message, from Ellen: "Call me at the hotel *immediately*." I did call and when the Griswolds didn't answer the phone in their room, I left a message at the Oriental for them to try me again. Maybe, I thought, they were among the throngs at Wat Pho waiting for a glimpse of the giant reclining Buddha and they didn't recognize Pugh, Timmy and me dressed in garbage bags.

Pugh got on his own phone, made a call to people close to Seer Thammarak Visetchote, the soothsayer working with the younger, anticorruption army officers. Then he hung up and gave me thumbs-up. "Four nineteen!" he shouted and gave a little hop.

Kawee, Mango and Miss Nongnat shared a cab back to Sukhumvit, though Kawee said he wanted to drop by Griswold's condo on the way and water the plants and light some candles.

Just after noon, as Timmy and I were walking back to the Topmost, we noticed military vehicles moving in convoys up ahead on Rama IV Road. We walked on past the hotel and watched as the trucks soon pulled over on the main thoroughfare and soldiers poured out of the trucks across the road near the kickboxing arena and the night market. We could make out other groups of soldiers down the road toward the Silom metro station, as well as four tanks.

Timmy said, "Tanks. There's something we don't see on Central Avenue in Albany."

People were coming out of all the restaurants now, and the shops and 7-Elevens, and traffic was starting to clog up. Small groups were forming, and some of the people in them had radios and every few minutes a cheer went up. There were occasional bursts of laughter. We overheard somebody say in English that in just a few minutes His Majesty King Bhumibol would be making a statement to the nation about the change in government.

Timmy said, "It's a Land of Smiles coup d'état. It's the best kind, if you're going to have one."

Soon there were sirens, and traffic parted for an army convoy of SUVs with flashing lights coming from the north. In the mess of traffic, the convoy had to slow briefly to a crawl as it went by us, and we caught a glimpse of a big man in a police uniform inside the middle vehicle seated between two smaller army commandos. No other police were visible anywhere. The senior police officer in the SUV appeared to be in army custody, and Timmy said, "Could that be who I think it is?"

"It does appear to be who you think it is."

"It looks like he's under arrest."

"Yeah, unless this is yet another feint."

"The politics here do resemble Albany politics in the mid–twentieth century when the O'Connell machine ran it."

"But the O'Connells didn't smile so much."

"I guess we'd better wait and see how all this shakes out," Timmy said. "But have our bags packed just in case."

"You really like this place, don't you? And these sweet, formal, spiritual, humorous people."

"I do like Thailand. A lot. If we had come here under any other circumstances, I can imagine being totally smitten with the place."

"You predicted back home that we might get hurt by the culture's nasty underside. And we did. You especially. Will you ever forgive me for almost getting you tossed off a balcony?"

"I think I will. Not quite yet, Donald. But soon enough. Anyway, I've become much more philosophical about dying since I've been here. I can't say I'll ever believe in reincarnation, but being around people who do believe in it and who accept death as a natural part of being human has been good for my perspective. I feel more at peace here than anywhere I've ever been."

"And the undercurrent of violence and corruption doesn't just make you want to scream? Or run away?"

Timmy thought about this. Crowds were moving now toward the soldiers gathered in front of the kickboxing arena. From where we stood, we could make out people starting to throw things at the soldiers. At first it seemed as if something was wrong and we had misunderstood the situation, and perhaps violence would suddenly break out. Then we realized it was flowers that people were tossing through the air, and some of the soldiers had wrapped garlands of marigolds and jasmine around their helmets.

Timmy said, "I hate the corruption in Thailand. I really do. And I'm not prepared to mutter, 'It's Chinatown, Jake,' and just gloomily move on. If I were Thai, I would definitely be up to my receding hairline working with the good-government groups, just like I did in Albany in the eighties. But the corruption here isn't what's most profoundly Thai. What's most deeply Thai, I think, is Buddhist perspective and ethics and sane-heartedness."

"Don't forget sanuk."

"Maybe that especially."

"And of course, lying down in the early evening with some satiny-skinned butch lady-boy for a few kisses and a relaxing mutual wank before enjoying a splendid green curry under a full moon."

"Those are definitely among the most enchanting forms of Thai sanuk."

I said, "It's a shame about the Griswolds. Especially Gary — the guy's instincts were as pure as they could possibly be. He was oh so naive, but his heart was good. We have to track him down when we get home and see if we can be of any help. It's the least we can do, since I was hired to get the guy out of any scrape he was in and I didn't exactly succeed at that. Anyway, without Griswold, it's unlikely we would have come here and rediscovered — discovered for the first time in your case — this magical kingdom."

"I wonder," Timmy said, "what really happened with Sheila Griswold? It was her disappearance that set all this craziness in motion in the first place."

"Sometimes," I said, "'It's Chinatown, Jake' isn't about a strange and unknowable place. It's about a strange and unknowable family. The Griswolds may be one of those families."

Timmy said, "Do you think we'll ever know the truth about Sheila?"

"Maybe in our next lives," I said. "We'll just have to be more patient than we're used to."

But then people all around us began to shush one another, and us. For the king was about to speak.

Thailand was inexpensive enough for us to stay around for another eight days without breaking the bank. The coup discouraged new tourists from arriving, so it was never hard to get a table in a restaurant, and there were fewer buff Bavarians to compete with during our predinner visits to Paradisio.

Both General Yodying and Anant na Ayudhaya, choosing exile over jail, had flown to Singapore for extended stays, so it was unclear what would become of Gary Griswold's condo. Meanwhile, Kawee, Mango and Miss Nongnat moved into the apartment. All three had been hired by Pugh to work as operatives for him, so among them they could afford the maintenance on the condo.

A few months later, we heard from Pugh, the condo was sold for a good price. Pugh took a commission, but the bulk of the proceeds went to Griswold back in the US. He used the money to open up a Sayadaw U storefront Buddhist meditation and study center on Duvall Street in Key West. Somebody also established a Sayadaw U center in Bangkok, but it wasn't a thirty-eight-million-dollar operation. That money had flown away, into Algonquin Steel stock and elsewhere. The Bangkok center was just a stall in the lobby of the Grand Hyatt, and Griswold's request for a visa to attend the formal opening was denied. He never returned to Thailand, although he told us later that he had become involved with a Thai-American orthodontist in Miami who was into ballroom dancing and model railroading. Also, a friend in Massachusetts ran into the two men when they got married on a beach in Provincetown in a Buddhist ceremony.

Timmy and I were startled to read in the *Albany Times Union* a month or so after we returned from Thailand that two men had died when they somehow fell from the roof of the high-rise apartment building where they lived together on Central Avenue in Albany. The two were identified as Duane Hubbard, a local personal trainer, and Matthew Mertz, a businessman and sometime actor. Police said it looked like an accident — tests showed that the two men were high on crystal meth when they fell — although officials were not ruling out a double suicide. Friends said both men had been despondent after losing money in a business investment that had not worked out.

Bill Griswold was just barely able to wrest back control of Algonquin Steel. A sizable minority share of the company remained with a group whose base was in Singapore, although Griswold found out that this organization was almost certainly a front for unidentified Thais.

I learned about Algonquin Steel's fate when I ran into Ellen Griswold at the Subway shop down the street from my office in the early fall of that year. She was a morning-shift volunteer at the fund drive for the public radio station across from my building, and she had stopped in at Subway to pick up some eats to take home for her kids' lunch.

"Well," she said, "if it isn't the man who swindled me out of — how much was it?"

"I actually lost money on your case," I said. "Or broke even at best. And I didn't appreciate your trying to have my business-class plane ticket back to New York downgraded to coach. Somebody Rufus Pugh knows at Thai Airways tipped him off, and he told me what you were trying to pull."

"The airline basically told me to go fly a kite. I was just terrifically upset at that point. So was Bill."

"But he's still CEO at Algonquin, I see. So you two landed on your feet well enough, it looks like."

It was then that she told me about the legal machinations — as well as a sizable cash payment to the group in Singapore — that enabled the family to retain control of the company.

"So you must have some fairly bitter feelings about Thailand," I said. "Your experience with the place was less happy than mine was in the end."

"Yes, for a while that was true. But it's all worked out for the best between Bill and me and Thailand. Bill is opening three

Econo-Build stores in Bangkok next year and one in Chiang Mai. In fact, he's in Bangkok right now working on the financing. Three of the younger army generals are investing, as well as a few others. I'm actually looking forward to going along on Bill's next trip. Both of us have always loved travel, and we travel well together. It's one of the best things about our basically good marriage. Speaking of significant others, how is your partner Timothy? Has he fully recovered from his near-plunge-off-a-balcony ordeal?"

"Timmy came through all of that less traumatized than you might expect," I said. "In fact, he's so enthusiastic about Thailand that we'll probably take a winter vacation there."

"If we're there at the same time, maybe you could join us for dinner at the Oriental. You could pay. On second thought, that might not work. Bill still holds you responsible for siding with Gary in his absurd attempt to give away Algonquin Steel to a group of religious fanatics."

"I know you're not in touch with Gary," I said. "I've spoken to him a few times in Key West. He seems to be doing okay, but he did not speak well of either of you two."

"No, the misunderstandings between us were just too ugly and complicated to sort out. It's all just kind of sad and pathetic, is what it all is."

"Gary was especially disturbed to find out that the two men who extorted two million dollars from him, Duane Hubbard and Matthew Mertz, died in falls from a building half a dozen blocks from here not long after we all got back from Thailand. He thinks you and your husband had something to do with their deaths."

She sighed theatrically and slowly shook her head. "Here we *go again!*"

"I guess it is far-fetched," I said. "Unless, of course, the sex-movie DVD you showed Pugh and me in Bangkok wasn't the proof-of-murder recording those guys claimed to possess, and there was a second, very different CD somewhere that some of us have never seen. And Hubbard and Mertz tried to blackmail you and Bill a second time. And you had had just about enough of those two bozos, and you hired somebody else — is there a Thai community here in Albany? — to get those two pests out of your hair once and for all."

She looked at me evenly and said, "You know, Strachey, when I hired you, I have to admit I wasn't sure what my own motives were. I really did care what happened to Gary. I loved him once — for his moral seriousness and for his truly good heart. And I really did not want anything terrible to happen to him or to his money. But I confess I was also worried at the time about whether Duane and Matthew had turned up in Bangkok and maybe planted some screwy ideas in Gary's head. Idiotic ideas like the one you have just outlined. And lo and behold, it turned out that that's precisely what happened. I thought you might smoke all that out, and you did. So I guess I must be some kind of soothsayer myself, wouldn't you say?"

"I want you to know, Ellen," I said, "that Timothy and I live just over on Crow Street in a two-story townhouse. We don't plan on moving into a high-rise building in the foreseeable future. Or maybe even visiting one for a while."

She seemed to decide that I was joking, and let loose with a good-natured snort.

ABOUT THE AUTHOR

RICHARD STEVENSON is the pseudonym of Richard Lipez, the author of nine books, including the Don Strachey private eye series. He also co-wrote *Grand Scam* with Peter Stein, and contributed to *Crimes of the Scene: A Mystery Novel Guide for the International Traveler*. He is a mystery columnist for the *Washington Post* and a former editorial writer at the *Berkshire Eagle*. His reporting, reviews, and fiction have appeared in *Newsday*, the *Boston Globe*, *The Progressive*, *The Atlantic Monthly*, *Harpers*, and several other publications. He grew up in Pennsylvania, went to college there, and then served in the Peace Corps in Ethiopia from 1962 to 1964. The Don Strachey books are being filmed by here!, the first gay television network. The first in the series, *Third Man Out*, starring Chad Allen as Don Strachey, aired in September 2005, followed by *A Shock to the System* in 2006, and *On the Other Hand, Death* and *Ice Blues* in 2008. More film adaptations are planned.

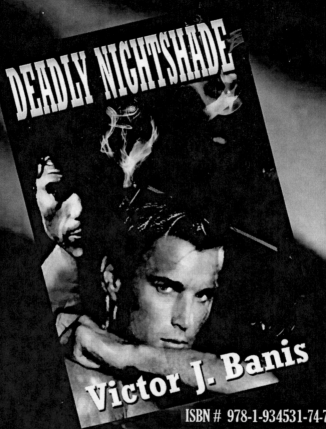